DESTINY
by
Choice

ISBN: 978-1-949648-94-2

Cover and text layout design: Kristi Yoder

Printed in the USA

TGS002004

Published by:
TGS International
P.O. Box 355
Berlin, Ohio 44610 USA
Phone: 330.893.4828
Fax: 330.893.2305
www.tgsinternational.com

DESTINY
by Choice

Stories of journeys through life's crossroads

LILY A. BEAR

Table of Contents

Preface vii

Author's Introduction ix

Roadside Assistance 17

Caught in the Current 25

Cry of a Seeking Heart 31

    Part One: Who Is God? 31

    Part Two: Entering the Storm 53

    Part Three: Shelter of Safety 63

Emergency Landing 85

Fear in the Jungle 95

Tempered Through Trials 101

    Part One: War Bonds and Questions (1939) 101

    Part Two: Hardships in Russia (1905–1924) 106

    Part Three: Hardships in Canada (1924–1933) 120

    Part Four: Standing for Truth (1939) 128

    Part Five: The Call to Service (1942) 135

Part Six: What Future? (1996) 152

Destiny by Choice 155

    Part One: Ellen 155

    Part Two: Todd 161

Who Will Be My Daddy? 167

Weighed in the Balance: *Stories of Three Lives* 177

    Part One: Galen 177

    Part Two: Kenneth 181

    Part Three: Lamar 185

Trust—Prayer—Praise 193

Living the Dream 199

The Verse on the Wall 217

Lesson From the Mango Seed 223

About the Author 239

Preface

What should I do? Which way is the right one? This is more than I can bear! I'm fearful! What will others think? Does no one care? Lord, why me? The choices were all different in these true stories, yet they all held long-lasting consequences. They all determined a destiny. In some of the stories, the characters placed their circumstances into God's hand. Others did not. Some searched for truth, and in their searching, they found God.

How did Karen respond when confronted with the name of Jesus? What did Richard do when he realized his landing gear had malfunctioned? What is Esther to make of her husband's rejection? Was it really God's will for Paul to be in Papua? Meet Mark, a commercial airline pilot, and Lamar, who was held at gunpoint in a deep ravine far from home.

In this book, I had the privilege of sharing a story from the life of my earthly father, Jacob. Though his childhood and teen years were filled with hardship and adversity, my father continues to bring glory to the heavenly Father through an inspirational story he left behind for his family, his friends, and all those who read it here. What a rich legacy!

Life is a continual journey, but short when compared to eternity. "We spend our years as a tale that is told," Psalm 90 informs us. What tale am I leaving for others to read? Am I following God's will and direction? Will the path I choose lead to the short-term happiness the world offers, or eternal peace and a refuge of safety?

My prayer is that you will experience a safe, rewarding journey, with the Father welcoming you home when you reach your eternal destiny.

—Lily A. Bear

Author's Introduction

"Attention! Flight 2245 has been canceled. Attention! Flight 2245 has been canceled due to mechanical problems. Your flight will depart tomorrow morning at 9:15. All passengers going to Eureka, please come to the counter where an agent will issue your new tickets, and you will receive a hotel and meal voucher. We are sorry for any inconvenience this causes you. We are here to assist you as best we can."

A groan rose from the waiting area as passengers quickly formed a line at the ticket counter. I had been sitting in the Sacramento airport for over two hours waiting for my already-delayed connecting flight to be called. My watch showed it was almost 6 p.m. on the West Coast, or 9 p.m. at home. No wonder I was tired! It had been a long day flying by myself. I walked over to claim my luggage, looking forward to a good night's sleep.

Once I got to my room I called my husband to let him know where I was, as well as my sister-in-law to inform her of my new arrival time. "Is this going to mess up your fitting schedule for tomorrow?" she asked.

"It shouldn't," I replied. "If I get to your place by 2:30, I will still have a couple of hours to get the two suits ready for the 5:30 fitting. I think we will be okay."

"We can always change the fitting time for after supper," she said. "I'm sure Pete and Steve won't mind."

My work, which included altering lapel suit coats into the traditional Mennonite ones, had brought me to California for six days. The delay would put me at least half a day behind. *But who orders our steps?* I asked myself, resting in the promise that God had a purpose.

Lord, I'm not sure why you planned this delay, but I'm thankful you are in control. I opened my Bible and read Psalm 46. "God is our refuge and strength. . ." I read the treasured Scripture. *Yes,* I mused as I turned out my light, *the Lord of hosts is with me and the God of Jacob is my refuge. What assurance! God is with me in this unfamiliar city and lonely hotel room.*

The next morning found me back at the airport waiting for my flight. A woman whom I had seen in our group as we went to the hotel the previous evening sat down beside me. "I do hope this flight leaves on time!" I now remarked, trying to make conversation.

"Will you be staying in Eureka?" she asked.

"No, I'll be going on to Fortuna where my brother lives," I answered.

"I wondered." She nodded knowingly. "What is your brother's name?"

Surprised by her interest, I explained why I was making the trip from Ohio. "We want to begin fitting suits yet this afternoon. That is why I am hoping this flight is on time."

"My name is Mary Carson. I know your brother Richard and his wife Arvilla quite well. They babysat my son for three years! When I saw you last evening, I wondered if there was a connection." We both found the coincidence remarkable.

Then the familiar disheartening announcement broke into our

conversation. "Flight 2245 to Eureka has been canceled." *Lord, what will I do? Will I even get there today?* My heart sank as I listened to the next part of the announcement.

"There will be no flight to Eureka today. We are sorry for this inconvenience. We will be busing all passengers to San Francisco. There is a flight to Eureka from San Francisco later today. You may be able to book a flight after you arrive in San Francisco. The bus trip will take five hours, but there will be plenty of time to make the late afternoon flight.

"All passengers, please come to the ticket counter if you are taking the bus to San Francisco. If you are going to rent a car, or plan to make other arrangements, please use the temporary desk on my right. An agent will assist those passengers with a $200 refund voucher. Again, we are sorry for this inconvenience, and thank you for choosing to fly United Airlines."

"Right!" someone groused behind me as I gathered my luggage and coat.

"Don't go to San Fran," Mary spoke up as soon as the intercom went silent. "I am renting a car, and you are welcome to go with me. I am on a business trip and the car will not cost me or you. I will gladly drop you off at your brother's place."

"Are you sure?" I stammered. "It won't be intruding on you?"

"Not at all. I go right by your brother's place to get to my house. Besides, the flight will be full—if it goes.

"Trust me," Mary continued. "I have been there and done that! It is a little airplane and it's always full. There is no way all these people will get on. You will be in San Fran until tomorrow and maybe longer, as there is only one flight a day to Eureka."

My mind churned with uncertainty, but her offer seemed the only way for me to get to my destination yet that day. *Did God schedule Mary on this flight for this purpose?*

"Thank you," I swiftly decided. "I will go with you. How many hours is it to Fortuna?" I asked, trying to calculate when we would get there.

"Seven," she replied as we got into line for the refund.

A little later she came back and said, "I have two other passengers wanting to go with me. One is a college student and the other is a former lawyer."

What now! Do I still go? I breathed a prayer for guidance. Nothing alarmed me except the thought of riding with three strangers for seven long hours! *Seven hours! What do you have planned, Lord?*

Soon our rental car was leaving Sacramento behind. Sitting beside me on the back seat, Jane, the college girl, took out her phone to call her mother. I heard Jane's mother go ballistic as she found out her daughter was in a car with strangers, and her distress moved me. She was worried for her daughter, but there was nothing she could do. *What a helpless feeling,* I thought as she continued to rant. I touched Jane's arm and whispered, "Tell your mother you are sitting by a Mennonite grandmother. Tell her not to worry, that everything is all right."

"Mom, I'm sitting by a Mennonite grandmother! The driver knows her brother!" As Jane relayed this information, I heard her mother's tone change, and in a calmer voice she asked about the man in the car. Jane looked at me with raised eyebrows, as though expecting me to supply the information. By now she knew I could hear their conversation as our seats were only inches apart.

"He was a lawyer," I mouthed, "and our driver's husband is a police officer." I gave her all the information I knew. Jane relayed those bits of assurance to her mother, and I heard her mother's voice return to a more normal key, her fears allayed in realizing Jane's fellow passengers were not psychopaths.

Conversation flowed between us as we shared personal interests. Derek, the former lawyer, had never met a Mennonite before. He asked me many questions. When he asked if I was married, I showed him a family picture.

Next, Derek wondered what I was doing so far from home, so I explained I had come to alter suit coats for some of the church men. That opened a door to explain why we believed in separation of dress.

Was this why my flight was canceled? I thought. *To leave a testimony for Christ?*

"I'm divorced," said Derek awkwardly during a lull in the conversation.

Mary promptly informed him, "A Mennonite would never divorce!"

"Why is that?" asked Derek, genuinely surprised. God was certainly opening doors for me to share my faith during this ride. Next Derek asked if I wore the white cap for a reason. I answered his questions the best I knew how. He was respectful and listened thoughtfully.

We stopped to eat at a small and crowded diner. I was the last one to order and hoped to find a quiet table where I could enjoy my food alone when Derek motioned for me to sit at the table where he and Mary sat eating. I wanted to pray but they kept talking, so I quietly said, "If you will excuse me, I would like to say a prayer of thanks to God before I eat."

"That's fine," Derek assured me.

I bowed my head and prayed audibly. "Thank you, Lord, for this food. Thank you for caring for me and providing transportation. Bless these new friends. Keep each one in your care. Amen."

"Amen," came the quiet response from the lawyer.

Traveling was subdued when we returned to our journey. "Do you mind listening to a little music?" wondered Mary. I had the impression the question was directed at me. "No, I don't mind," I answered.

But the two in the front had a hard time deciding on an appropriate CD. "Is it too loud?" Mary wondered not long after the car was filled with booming so-called music. She turned the speaker down before I had time to reply. The lyrics seemed to make them uncomfortable, and they soon turned the CD player off. *Thank you, Lord. Their style of music and mine are not the same!*

The seven hours did end eventually. "Thank you so much, Mary," I said as I retrieved my luggage from the trunk. "I will not forget your kindness!"

"Those three have probably never had such a quiet seven-hour drive!" I said later as Richard and Arvilla accompanied me up the steps to their front door. It was then I learned that Mary had never once asked any questions about their faith in the three years she had left her son with them.

"God definitely had a purpose in my delay. Mary didn't ask any questions, but she listened intently as the lawyer and I talked," I said. "I'm glad I had the opportunity to present the Gospel message of salvation and other Biblical truths to her.

"I used this experience to witness to Mary and the other two passengers. Who but God would send someone who knew my brother and would drive right past their place on her way home! The lawyer shook his head when I told them I was roughly three thousand miles from home, yet God knew the circumstances I would face and what I needed. God had someone waiting to fill my need before I even knew I had a need! I told Mary how I had prayed desperately when I realized no flights were going to Eureka today. I also told her how she was the answer to that prayer." We grew quiet as we contemplated the mighty works of God on my behalf.

"You gave a wonderful example of God's care and provision for His children," Arvilla broke the silence as we entered their home.

A busy yet profitable week ensued. Friday evening came and I began packing up to go home again. Then I received the news: a severe snowstorm was on its way east to Pennsylvania from Colorado. Despite a foreboding feeling, I hoped and prayed I would be able to get home before the storm disabled flights.

"I think we had better call the airport and see if your plane got in before the fog," Arvilla advised. "If the plane lands tonight, it will leave even if it is a foggy morning. We know from experience!

"If it doesn't come in tonight, you will almost certainly be departing late," she continued. "It is always foggy here in the mornings! And there's no point in going to the airport early if your plane isn't in tonight."

"I'll call," my brother offered, taking my flight information. A half hour later he informed me of his findings. "The plane is in, but they have no record of your reservation and they tell me all seats are full. An agent is working on the problem."

Not again! I thought in dismay. *I want to get home tomorrow!* An hour went by and still no word. "You go to bed and I'll take care of this," he graciously offered. So I did, setting the alarm for 4 a.m.

"Richard did get you a seat." Arvilla met me with the good news in the morning. Since all was in order, we headed for the small airport. Upon arriving, I gave the ticket agent my information and waited for my boarding pass.

"I don't understand this," she frowned as she continued typing. "Your name and reservation are in the system but we have no seat for you. Whoever issued this last night did so without giving you a seat. No seats are available until Monday morning. There is nothing I can do but book a new reservation for Monday morning."

Delayed again! At least I am with family! I gathered my belongings.

"This mistake should not have happened!" the agent said, and she handed me my new ticket. "I am sorry for the inconvenience. Here is a travel voucher, and thank you for choosing United Airlines."

Back in the car, I looked at the voucher. "Five hundred dollars!" I exclaimed. "That was what my ticket cost. And they gave me a two-hundred-dollar voucher in Sacramento!"

"Thank you for choosing United Airlines," my brother mimicked dryly, and we had a good laugh.

I didn't find out why God allowed the mix-up on my ticket until Monday morning. Many flights out of Denver, my second connecting city, had been canceled over the weekend due to the crippling snowstorm. Even the city of Dayton, my destination, had been closed because of bad weather.

When I arrived in Sacramento for my connecting flight east, I had my first glimpse of disgruntled humanity. The airport was chaotic.

Stranded passengers had been sitting since Saturday. Tempers were hot as people waited for boarding passes, but no seats were available. Seeing the mayhem as I passed through Sacramento, I was overwhelmed with gratitude at God's provision in sparing me from these terrible conditions. Denver was even worse. The airport was seething, in more ways than one. I felt almost guilty as I wove my way among the angry throngs to my gate. In my purse was a coveted boarding pass.

Thank you, Lord, for taking care of me. My heart could not stop praising my compassionate, caring God. My heavenly Father had saved me from being stranded in this mess. I hadn't experienced a delay at all! I had been living within God's perfect timing.

I thought of the verse in the Psalms, *God is our refuge and strength, a very present help in trouble.* God had given me refuge before I needed it. He had provided a place of safety and kept me from waiting at an airport over the weekend. God had provided more than I could have asked.

Roadside Assistance

*R*onald glanced over at his friend Dean who was expertly maneuvering their heavily loaded pickup truck through the maze of unfamiliar city traffic. *Glad it's him and not me. Give me the country any day.* Ronald shifted on his seat. He rolled down his window hoping for fresh air, but all he got was a blast of exhaust fumes.

How do people survive in this? he wondered as he viewed the endless stream of humanity and vehicles thronging the streets and sidewalks.

Souls with a destiny. The thought struck him with a jolt. As he contemplated the many souls living in this city, he was challenged with a question from a sermon their pastor Paul Mast had preached several Sundays earlier.

"How are you using your time? Each of us is accountable for what we do with it. Are you using your talents to do kingdom work? Or do you bury them by doing what you want to do?

"How often have you taken time to talk to a needy soul this past week, or month, or year?" Paul had asked.

Ronald shifted on the hard truck seat. He couldn't shake the questions, but was stumped at how and what he could do. *I've never had much contact with needy people,* he mused. *But the message has certainly kindled my desire.*

His eyes swept across the city. *How many souls are prepared to meet God? How many know God, or even want to know about Him? What should I be doing? Am I living selfishly when I'm glad to live in the country instead of a place like this?* The thought of lost souls burned on his mind. Its intensity obliterated all else, and they were well outside the city limits before Ronald realized they were no longer driving in bumper-to-bumper traffic.

"Dean, do you ever wish for more opportunities to witness?"

"I have thought of it," Dean answered honestly. "With our line of work we don't have a lot of contact with the public. How often do our remote farms bring us opportunity to share the Gospel? Sure, we occasionally meet our neighbors. They all respect us, and what conversation we do have with them is mostly friendly chitchat. Did that one Sunday message hit you too?" Dean exited onto another road.

"Yes, it did," said Ronald. "I have done so little witnessing. I prayed that God would give me an opportunity today. So far all we did was back up to the dock and pick up our order of fencing, and then we signed the papers and paid through a window. Not very conducive to starting a deep conversation!"

"True," his friend answered. "About living in a city, I'm sure our prospects would escalate, but I don't believe God is asking you or me to leave our parents and siblings and move to the city for the sake of witnessing. I feel I am where God wants me, don't you?" Without waiting for an answer, Dean continued. "It would require a real sacrifice to live in the midst of a city. All that traffic, rubbing shoulders with people all the time, everyone in a big hurry—I don't think I could handle it!"

"Well, you handled the traffic like a pro today!" said Ronald with a smile. Silence settled over the cab as both young men contemplated the question further. Both loved the wide-open countryside surrounding their family farms. Both had over ten miles to town and it was a three-hour drive to the city. In fact, today was the first time they had come to the city without their parents. What chances did they have to increase their talents?

"Maybe we need to pray for opportunities." Dean glanced over at his traveling companion as traffic thinned and the road narrowed to two lanes.

"I have," Ronald confided. "Since Paul's sermon, I've had a real burden and desire to do something for Christ. I'm only nineteen, but in the four years I have been a Christian I don't believe I have ever shared the plan of salvation with an unbeliever. It hit me today when we were in the city."

The next half hour passed in a blur as the two friends discussed their dreams and goals. They were comfortable with each other, and both relished the rare opportunity of traveling together.

"Looks like someone has car trouble," Ronald said as he pointed out the parked vehicle ahead with its raised hood. "Want to stop?"

"Let's!" Dean agreed.

"Can we help you?" Ronald asked, as he opened his door to meet the middle-aged man hurrying toward them.

"My—" was the only intelligible word he caught before the stranger spewed out a string of profanity. It was hard to understand what the man was saying as his foul words far exceeded his good ones. Ronald held up his hand to stop him.

"Sir, I'm having a hard time understanding you. I don't use swear words. Could you refrain from using them too? We would like to help you if we can." The man's mouth dropped open. His eyebrows shot up and he swallowed and opened his mouth to say something but no words came. He shook his head in confusion.

"We are going to Landings," Dean came to his rescue as he joined Ronald. "Would that direction be of help to you?"

"Landings?" The stranger's eyes lit up, "Yes!" More curse words slipped out before he caught himself. He shook his head. "Sorry," he muttered. "I need to be close to Landings by five. My son's getting married tomorrow and there's a big party tonight. Can't miss it. By the way, my name is Scott."

A silent message passed between Dean and Ronald as they nodded to each other, agreeing to offer this stranger a ride. "You are welcome to ride with us to the next town or to Landings, whichever would help you the most," Dean offered.

"Better go with you. Time's short. I'll go get my stuff." Scott swore profusely as he returned to his car.

"You feel we are doing the right thing?" Dean questioned. "Such foul language!"

"I've never done anything like this," Ronald admitted. "But yes, I feel it is the right thing to do. I'm praying for wisdom to say the right words. It will be a long drive unless God controls his tongue."

The two friends soon learned that where their passenger wanted to go was not too many miles out of their way. Plans were made to go directly to his son's place so he would not miss the party.

"Stop at the next town and I'll buy you each a beer. Even two or three if you want!" Scott waved his hand generously. What nineteen-year-olds wouldn't jump at the chance to have someone of legal age buy drinks for them? "You can take it home and have a party yourselves!" He slapped his knee, laughing uproariously at what he considered a good joke.

"We appreciate you wanting to return the favor," Dean answered carefully. "But we actually don't drink. You see, both of us are followers of Christ and we don't use alcohol."

"What! You don't drink?" Scott nearly rose off the truck seat. "I don't believe you! Are you serious?"

The cab became quiet as the boys prayed for wisdom. They didn't want to offend their passenger but they wanted to defend Christ. Was this the first encounter he had with someone trying to live a Christ-centered life?

"No, neither of us have ever tasted an alcoholic drink, and by God's grace I hope we never do." Ronald broke the silence with a half-smile.

"I've never heard anything so, so . . ." Both boys tried to shut out the vile language erupting from the man's mouth. This time an uncomfortable stillness pervaded the interior as Scott realized his speech was not welcome.

"Scott," Ronald began hesitantly, but was cut off when their passenger interrupted.

"You boys caught me by surprise. I'm sixty-two years old and I have *never* met young men like you before." He shook his head to emphasize his disbelief.

"Okay, Scott," Ronald went on amiably, "may I ask you a question?"

"Sure," came the quick response.

"Do you know who Jesus Christ is?" Ronald was shocked to see Scott shaking his head.

"Are you saying you have never read the Bible or been taught from it?" Ronald asked.

"Nope," came the short reply.

"Let me explain. Jesus is the Son of God who left heaven to come to earth. He died on the cross for our sins. My sins and your sins. The sins of all men. He came to bring salvation, or in other words, to redeem us from sin.

"When I asked God to forgive my sins, I confessed them. Then I was reborn, or given a new nature by Jesus Christ. I now want to live a life that pleases Him."

"Never heard anything like it," said Scott. "You lost me. I'm not one for religion." He gave a short laugh. "I'm an oil rigger. Been on the oil crew since my twenties. Nope, never raised on religion like you boys have been. Never had a Bible. Never heard one read. Never had time or interest for church."

In plain, simple words the boys explained the plan of salvation and the need for each person to confess his sinfulness to Jesus Christ. "Faith is a real part of our lives," Dean spoke now. "A person must believe Christ can and will forgive us our sins. We must believe and understand that nothing we do earns salvation. It is a gift from Jesus. He loves all men and is willing that all come to repentance.

"I'm no better than you or anyone else. I am just as sinful. I am saved only because of the grace and mercy of Jesus."

Ronald took a deep breath. *Lord,* his heart cried out. *Give Dean and me the right words to say. Help Scott to see you.*

"You may be wondering why salvation is so important, or why we are telling you all this." Ronald chose his words carefully. "Well, the best way I can explain it is to say that having a person's sins forgiven is the most important decision you can ever make. The Bible says we will all face eternal judgment when we die. I want to be ready to meet God whenever that time comes for me."

Scott dropped his head into his hands while Ronald was talking. His elbows rested on his knees. He looked confused and utterly dejected. Dean was thankful he could drive and pray at the same time. He marveled at God's faithfulness in answering their hearts' cry to be a witness. How quickly God had answered!

Let these seeds of truth take root and bring Scott to the understanding of salvation, he prayed.

A subdued trio rode toward Landings. Scott continued to be lost in thought, and neither of the young men felt led to say more. In due time they arrived at his son's place. As they turned into the long lane, Scott opened up.

"My son is divorced and this will be his third marriage. You wouldn't approve of that either, would you?"

"God wouldn't approve," Ronald corrected. "That is what is important.

It is not what we think is right but what God says in His Word, the Bible." Dean parked the pickup and all three got out as Scott's son strode toward them. His language sounded just as his father's had when they first stopped to help him. Scott put up his hand and silenced his son with a scowl. His son hesitated, confusion spreading over his face.

"Thanks, boys," Scott said as he faced them. "You're good boys." Emotion played across his face and his voice grew husky. He gripped Ronald's hand in a firm handshake. Turning to Dean, he said again, "You boys are good. Don't change." Three times he shook their hands, reluctant to let them go.

"I would encourage you to get a Bible and read it," Dean said softly. "It contains the words of life, and provides wisdom for our problems."

"I am glad we could help you," Ronald added sincerely. His smile rose from the depths of his heart, conveying the love of Christ and the yearning of his soul for this man's salvation.

"Don't put off seeking God," he encouraged. "The Bible says, 'Behold, today is the day of salvation.' Scott, I want you to experience the same peace and rest we have found in Jesus Christ."

Scott nodded but made no comment. Instead, he raised his hand, gave a short wave, then turned and followed his son toward the house. He walked like an old man with the weight of the world on his shoulders.

"He is carrying a great weight, the weight of sin," Dean said quietly as he backed his truck out the lane. "I think God had a reason for him to have car trouble and for us to stop. I pray the truth he heard today will never leave him."

Ronald nodded, emotions flooding him as he watched the retreating figure enter his son's house. Tonight would be party night. Would Scott remember the afternoon's conversation, or would it leave his mind forever? There was no way to tell. Yet Ronald had peace in his heart, knowing he had heard from God and followed His leading. It was now up to Scott to determine his own destiny.

Caught in the Current

"*T*alk about flooding!" Aaron whistled under his breath as the three men stood viewing the immense area of backwater spilling over the river-bottom flats. "It must be a quarter of a mile across the water to where the cattle are marooned," he estimated.

"Looks like it," his father, Jerry, agreed. "A good quarter of a mile at the least. I hate sending you over in this cold water. The last thing your wife needs is a sick man along with a three-day-old baby to care for."

"I'll be fine," Aaron assured him. "Unless neighbor Jackson here is up to doing the fording for me. He has more experience than I do."

"Better not, better not." Their neighbor shook his head. "Age isn't as kind to me as it was fifty years ago. You might have another rescue on your hands if I went." Jackson shook his head again as he studied the cattle huddled together on the small island in the midst of rushing floodwaters. "I've never seen that island so small, or the river this high.

If the cows weren't ready to calve I would suggest you leave them there until this water goes down. But you know how cold September nights can get. Much too cold for newborn calves to survive."

The three men stood at the water's edge watching the churning river sweep by when Aaron ventured, "Do you think it would keep me from drifting downstream if I cross a quarter of a mile farther up? That current seems plenty swift."

"A good idea. A very good idea," the older men agreed.

"Take your time," Jerry advised. "Give yourself ample distance as you cross. This river is noted for its hidden currents. With this much water you never know what you will encounter." Under his breath he muttered, "I don't like this at all."

Finally he nodded to his son again. "You get going and we will move on downstream where the river narrows. Let's plan to meet the cattle at the spur." Jackson waved as he and Aaron's father turned their horses in the opposite direction.

What a flood! I've never seen the river like this! There's so much water everywhere, I'm not even sure where the channel is. Whistling to himself as his horse followed the floodwaters, Aaron remembered other times he had forded this very river to bring in stranded cattle after a flash flood. But never had it come close to this width. *And to think I'm going out in it and can barely swim! I wish now that Mom had allowed us boys to swim in the river. I would feel better in starting across.*

"No, it's too dangerous to learn how to swim in a river," his mother had always stated firmly. "Rivers are death traps with hidden currents. I just can't let you boys take that chance." So, the only swimming the boys did was in the cattle tank, where keeping your head above water wasn't even a challenge. How they had envied Dad when he told stories of his swimming days as a boy. But Dad's swimming had been in a lake, not a river, and that made all the difference to his parents.

At least Dad gave us boys good verbal swimming lessons. Aaron found himself thinking of his father's instructions for what to do to keep from drowning. *As a boy I always wanted a chance to try those lessons, but now I hope I don't have to*, he chuckled.

Aaron turned Chestnut into the floodwaters, and horse and man headed for the stranded cattle. As soon as they hit deeper water, Chestnut started swimming. Aaron slipped off her bare back, hanging onto her mane while paddling up against her left side. The horse's powerful swimming rhythm gave him a sense of comfortable security while in the rushing water. He loved the weightless feeling and the way the swift current fought against him.

Suddenly, without warning, Chestnut hit an underwater snag. She reared straight up out of the water before flipping over backward. In stupefied fright, Aaron clung to the horse's mane and found himself being dragged down, down, into the water. Thrashing hoofs caught him in the stomach, knocking the wind out of him. Gasping in pain, he lost his grip on Chestnut's mane and found himself alone in the cold, swirling water.

When he resurfaced, his horse was just ahead, her tail inches away. Desperately he lunged for Chestnut's tail, but missed. Once again, he found himself beneath murky, rolling water. Without really thinking about it, he stopped fighting the water. As he relaxed, he rose to the surface and paddled. *Keep paddling. Keep your nose above water. Breathe easy. Keep paddling.* From somewhere deep inside him, his father's verbal swimming instructions hammered through his brain. The current was far swifter than it had appeared from shore, and he felt completely helpless. He could do nothing but try to stay afloat. Land seemed far away. Despairing thoughts of drowning threatened him.

Twila, Twila. My dear wife! his heart cried as he struggled on. A wash of water swept over him, submerging his head as he envisioned her grief-stricken face when Dad and Jackson carried his lifeless body home.

Oh, God, save me! He fought to breathe above the suffocating water. *My children! Three-year-old Donald, sweet little two-year-old Amanda. What will happen to them? My children! Oh, God, save me! And baby Lorna! Will she never know a father? Save me, God! Save me!* He struggled to paddle, to keep his nose above the churning water. A crosscurrent grabbed his legs, spinning him around and around in a hidden whirlpool. Briefly his eyes caught sight of the bank. He took great gulps of air and gained courage as he saw his father and Jackson running along the bank. Round and round he whirled in the whirlpool. He caught glimpses of the men stripping off their jackets and gum boots as they ran. *Strength, God! Give me strength to fight this awful suction.*

He was totally helpless in the whirlpool's unyielding grip. Suddenly, one of the spins tossed him from the whirlpool, the raging current shooting him downstream. River sounds thundered in his ears. His senses were on high alert as the endless throbbing from the swirling waters pulsed loudly around him. He felt the current weaken. As it babbled in softer tones, his hopes rose. *Is this my chance to make it to shore?* But before he made any headway, another crosscurrent swept him into its death grip of rushing momentum.

Strength, Lord—just give me strength and another chance, he pleaded. Everyone who knew Aaron would have agreed that he was ready to meet God. His prayer for rescue was for another reason. *I have a wife and three little children! I want to stay alive for them, but I can't fight against this current. It drags me wherever it wills. I'm completely helpless. Oh God, I am so helpless!*

Weariness plagued every effort he employed in keeping his head above water. He felt himself weakening. He felt his senses getting sluggish. *Is this how it feels to die?* Suddenly, shouting penetrated his brain.

"Aaron! Head for the land spur! Head for the land spur!" His father's shouts roused him, sending renewed energy through his arms and legs. He caught a glimpse of land, a thin finger jutting out into the water. His father and Jackson were wading out to rescue him!

Strength, Lord! Strength! He felt his trembling limbs moving. He paddled furiously to meet the men. The current was swinging him toward the spur in a curve. At the curve his father was waiting, waist deep in water, with his hand outstretched. Jackson was hanging onto his father, giving him stability in the rushing water.

Destiny *by* Choice

"Now!" both men yelled. Aaron poured all his energy into one last, desperate lunge. His body broke the current's grip and his fingers caught his father's life-saving hand.

Relief and overwhelming joy surged through him as he collapsed into the strong arms of safety. *Thank you, Lord, thank you! I will see my dear wife and children again!* Gratitude pulsed through him with every ragged breath he drew.

That night he lay in bed, unable to sleep. He marveled at the miracle of life God had extended to him, and his mind was drawn to spiritual parallels. *Those currents were like the kingdom of darkness. We don't understand how dangerous its grip is. We think we can leave the world's fast flowing river whenever we want, but we don't see the hidden snags, the crosscurrents, the whirlpools, until it is too late.*

Aloud he whispered, "Thank you, Father in heaven, for helping me escape the river's grip. Thank you that I can reach out and grasp your outstretched hand of mercy when I flounder in the world's currents. You gave me only one opportunity to clasp my father's hand. If I had not reached out my hand when Dad and Jackson yelled, my chance would have been gone.

"Lord God, thank you for not only physical salvation, but also the salvation of my soul. Keep me from getting swept into a death current that destroys my soul."

Aaron crept out of bed to check on each of his sleeping children. He needed to see them, to hear them breathe. They were doubly precious now. "Lord," he prayed as he knelt by the bedside of his oldest son, "help me to be a strong arm of safety for these children you have blessed us with. I want them to know the only safety they have in this world is through you and the saving blood of Jesus Christ.

"I come to you in humble thanksgiving. Lord, don't let me forget the feeling of helplessness I had while in the water. May it always remind me to avoid the grip of the world's currents."

Though Aaron returned to bed in the darkness of night, God's divine light illuminated his soul.

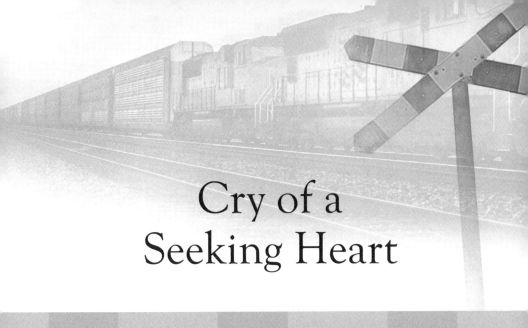

Cry of a
Seeking Heart

Part One
Who Is God?

"**D**addy, when is Kelly coming home?" Karen Henderson's innocent question about her twin sister hurtled across the tile floor of the library, vibrating louder and louder within Chad Henderson's heart. He drummed his fingers unthinkingly against the mahogany desk, unmindful of the bright mid-morning sunlight filtering through the royal palms outside his windows. Dancing sunrays highlighted the rich tones of Chad's masculine domain, but all he saw was his daughter standing alone in the elegant, arched entry.

"Come, Karen," said Chad, keeping his voice soft. "I know you are lonely for Kelly and your mom, but I am here with you." Pushing back his chair, he held out his arms to the daughter who held his greatest affection. He considered the pain of losing Karen, each heartbeat feeling like a cannon prepped to explode. He couldn't give her up! He wouldn't. He would give her everything. She would never question his love!

"When will I see Mom?" his daughter asked as he tilted her chin upward and tucked a wisp of short, sandy hair behind her ear. He hated the pain clouding her eyes. Ever since the divorce, he had been worried about her quietness. Pulling her onto his lap, he breathed in the scent of her freshly shampooed hair. He could feel the rapid rise and fall of her little heart and vowed he would do all he could to give her a perfect childhood despite the divorce.

At least he and Tanya had stayed friends. Chad was thankful that they had been able to agree on visitation hours. They both saw the value of keeping the children's interests and limiting their hurt. Fortunately for Karen, Tanya and Kelly lived only five blocks away and going back and forth was not too difficult.

But despite feeling good about how he and Tanya had handled their divorce, frustration clouded his mind. Resentment ate at him. Why had their relationship soured? Why was it easier to run a business than a marriage? As all their friends could testify, he had always let Tanya have what she wanted. Why then was there so much dissension between them? Why couldn't his bank account, their social standing, and the estate on Pelican Point be enough for his ex-wife? Where had he gone wrong?

Marriage? Never again! Two failed marriages were enough. He had definitely learned his lesson. But his children! He agonized over them.

He acknowledged that Kelly did better with Tanya. After all, they had the same interests. But it was comforting to know that Karen loved being with him. He determined again to do everything in his power to make her happy and make sure she would have everything she could possibly need. It was a relief that she and Lea, the well-loved nanny and housekeeper, got along so well. He personally would see to it that Karen's life went well. He would bring the sparkle back into his young daughter's eyes!

"You know you can see your mom anytime you wish," Chad Henderson answered his daughter's question now, trying to strike a lighter mood. "You do whatever makes you happy, Karen. Don't let other people run over you. Remember, what Karen wants *is* important."

He tapped her on the chest, and she giggled.

"Remember, when you are happy, Daddy's happy." He gave her a hug and set her down.

"Yes, Daddy, I'll remember," came her careful reply. Then she flashed him a bright smile. Reaching up, she hugged him around his neck. It made him feel like a good dad again.

The divorce did not seem so big in Karen's eyes after her daddy talked to her. Though she did not understand why Mom and Dad had to live in different houses, she had friends who lived the same way, and did not question it. She loved her parents and they loved her. They were good to her. She saw her sister at school and her big brother Ken, now living by himself, came to visit Dad occasionally.

The Henderson children lived luxuriously. Wealth brought acceptance and fulfillment, frequent vacations, world travel, and almost anything else the children wanted. Chad worked hard to provide them with every advantage they needed to succeed.

As Karen spent more time with her father, their relationship grew. Meanwhile, over on Elm Street, her twin sister's relationship with their mother also grew. The separate households did not seem to have major impact on the girls' carefree childhood. Karen worked hard at her studies, at sports, at friendships—and at skirting conflicts.

Her passion for gymnastics brought her father's approval, since athleticism was highly prized in the Henderson households. Each girl chose the sport of her choice. Each was expected to discipline herself above her peers and excel just as her parents had. Much to her father's disappointment, Kelly chose horseback riding. Since this was Tanya's favorite sport, it meant Kelly would be spending even more time with her mother instead of him. He desired the undivided attention of both of his daughters.

By choosing different sports, Karen and Kelly also ended up in different high schools, and although they still considered each other friends, they spent little time together. Both parents gave their affection and approval, but it was to her daddy that Karen came home. It was to her daddy that Karen eagerly shared her new practice routines or upcoming competitions. It was her daddy who came to the gym to cheer her on. Pride filled Chad as he watched his daughter perform, thrilled that she was becoming what he considered to be a perfect young lady.

Karen thrived under her father's care. Though she could do no wrong in his eyes, she strove to please both him and her mother. She wanted to make them as proud of her as they were of her brother Ken. Being at the top was number one priority in the Henderson households. How you achieved it didn't matter.

God was not part of Karen's life. She had no fear of God, and she never thought twice about indulging in illicit pleasure, envy, hate, selfishness, or academic and athletic obsessions. She never gave thanks to God for anything, nor did she seek Him in any way. She had no needs. Chad Henderson saw to it that every need or wish of his daughters was met.

Their father came to them with an announcement. "I want you girls to attend Saint Mary's High School this fall. It is an excellent school! Ken attended there on a scholarship earned through his hard work at football." Pride glowed from both his words and face.

"Where is Saint Mary's?" Karen asked. "Who is Saint Mary?"

"The name refers to the school's Catholic heritage," her father explained. "They are well known for their academic and athletic prestige. By attending this school, both you and Kelly will have better opportunities in life. Just wait, someday you'll thank me for it."

A Catholic school? She pondered the news. *It has to do with religion, but what does Catholic mean?*

Kelly preferred a school closer to the stables so she could continue horseback riding. In the end Karen entered the new high school without her sister.

Definitely religious! Karen observed as she reached her classroom and immediately spotted the front wall display of a cross with a wounded man hanging from it. His arms were outstretched and a wreath of thorns circled his drooping head. *What does it mean?* Her brow wrinkled as she studied the display. The face appeared to be in great agony. Karen suddenly felt uncomfortable, like a fish out of water.

Transition into the new school became a breeze, though, when the student body discovered Ken was her brother. His athletic popularity gave her instant status. Older students sought her out to talk of Ken's brilliant accomplishments. *Will I fare just as well?* she wondered, determined to do her best.

Before the week was over, Mrs. Egbert, her English teacher, approached her. "Miss Karen, I can see that you are an athlete. Tell me what sports you play."

Pride filled Karen as she smiled and replied, "Gymnastics."

"Well, it looks to me as though you would make an excellent runner too," said Mrs. Egbert. "I coach the boys and girls cross-country team here. Would you consider coming out to our practices and joining the team? We want to be the best in the state! Maybe your participation will help us achieve our goal!"

Wow! I am being accepted! Karen thought. *I am following in Ken's footsteps!* Wanting the social approval, Karen changed her sport to cross-country. Her new friends were all on the team and she loved the rigorous exercise, the laughter and gossip, the competition between team members, and the shopping they did together as they looked for designer clothes that matched the season. High school was proving to be quite fun.

One day at practice she was brought face to face with her ignorance of anything related to religion. "Seven laps!" her coach's voice rang out as he gave the warmup instructions.

"Seven laps," Troy muttered under his breath. "What is he trying to do? Bring down the walls of Jericho?"

Her classmates erupted in laughter while Karen listened in confusion. *Whatever did Troy mean?* She figured it had a religious meaning but was too embarrassed to ask. *Just like my religion class,* she moaned.

Everyone else has been to church and thinks I should know what they are talking about, and I haven't a clue.

Why do they think religion is so important? Does it teach them to be better people? Is that why they have curfews and avoid certain places? Does that mean I am a bad person if I'm out of the loop? This religious thing was confusing. Furthermore, Karen could not see that it made a difference in the students' everyday actions. Only one girl stood out in the whole class, and she wasn't even Catholic—she was Muslim!

Clarissa was a modest, devout girl who wore a hijab as a symbol of her dedication to Islam. Karen admired her courage to stand for her profession of faith. Though Clarissa's actions and sweetness far surpassed any of the other classmates, she was not accepted among them. *How does one know how to choose a religion? Why is one religion considered superior to another?*

Karen tried to convince herself she did not have time to waste on something as unimportant as religion. Yet she found herself uncomfortable when her classmates in religion class talked about stories they read in the Bible. *Why do they talk of this Jesus as though He is someone important? Why do they say they had nothing to worry about after they went to mass? Should I do what they do?* These thoughts lasted but a moment before she brushed them aside. She needed to excel in the courses that would prepare her for college. She didn't need to worry about religion; her life was great as it was!

One day she arrived home to find her father waiting at the front door, wearing a huge smile. "You got a letter today, Missy!"

"A letter!" Karen squealed. She kissed her father's cheek as he handed it to her. Ripping it open, she blurted, "Dad! Listen! 'Congratulations! It is our pleasure to announce your acceptance to the 2001 summer term at the University of North Carolina.'"

"Dad, I can't believe I get to attend such a prestigious college! Are there palm trees and fountains on campus?" She was so excited she could not stand still. She had been accepted into the top school of their state and received an academic scholarship! Dad had said the Catholic school would change her life. Not only had she received a better education, but she also saw endless opportunities in her future.

Karen entered summer semester without any of her former friends. They had chosen other schools, leaving her to navigate the new halls by herself. *It will work out, I'm sure*, she reminded herself as she walked up to Turlington Residence Hall to sign in. The receptionist led the way to her assigned room on the third floor.

Karen found herself staring at a dark-complexioned girl sitting on the floor sorting through a pile of clothes. She jumped up and smiled brightly. "Hi! My name is Chantelle and you can probably tell by my accent that I am Jamaican!"

Karen took a deep breath and timidly replied, "Hi, I'm Karen." She walked around the clothing pile and plopped her luggage onto the empty bed. Slowly she started pulling out her things, not knowing what else to do. Her heart hammered. *Just what am I getting into!* Her new roommate was not in the least perturbed with her silence, and she burst out with a stream of questions. Karen grew alarmed at her spirited friendliness. *I just met her. Her style of clothes is so different. I don't need to be best friends immediately.* She wanted to grab her suitcases and escape, but her father's expectations meant too much.

But as the summer went on, Karen grew to appreciate her roommate. She decided Chantelle was an upbeat and gracious person, but just a little over-zealous about her faith. *It's the way she was brought up and I can't fault her. But I wasn't brought up to believe I need God to be a good person; my head tells me I don't need to change anything!* She dismissed the difference between them, and simply enjoyed rooming with Chantelle, nonetheless feeling a measure of relief that they would not be sharing a room at the end of summer.

But God had other plans. Before leaving summer semester, both Karen and Chantelle had received notice that they had been assigned rooms at Betty's Square for the fall semester, but they were not assigned their room numbers. That September Karen followed the now-familiar procedure of signing in at her new dorm. Upon entering her dorm room, she stopped, surprised. Chantelle! *Out of over 10,000 students living on campus. I didn't know they reassign us the same partners.*

"Karen, this is so exciting!" Chantelle jumped with joy and gave Karen a bear hug. "We get to spend the whole year together!" Her roommate's bubbly personality was spilling over when a third girl walked in.

"Hi! My name is Natasha and it looks like I will be living here too."

Karen could not understand. The room was barely large enough to hold two people and certainly not three! There had to be some mistake.

"I . . . know the room is small," Natasha stammered at their perplexed expressions. "But they told me they overbooked students and have to triple up to accommodate everyone."

Karen sighed inwardly. This was not the best of circumstances! Suddenly she heard the other two girls jabbering about Jesus and hugging each other. Fear flooded her. *Am I to room with not one Christian, but two? This was* not *how I envisioned college!* Tears threatened and she excused herself and hurried to the receptionist's desk.

"I'm sorry, but there are no other options for you." The receptionist's response sent her hopes plummeting. "Maybe later, but don't count on it."

Karen held back her tears. *This is awful. I want to be free this year. I want to be part of the college scene. Now everything I dreamed of is wiped out. Everything! Why, this is even worse than when Mom and Dad split!* She choked out her thanks and walked numbly from the office. Her whole year seemed ruined. Her roommates would constantly talk about God. There would be no fun or social life whatsoever as long as she was in her dorm.

Karen cried her tears in private and treated her roommates as she wanted to be treated—free of conflict. It didn't take long for Chantelle and Natasha to change her perception of the meaning of *Christian.*

They were delighted to room with her and freely extended friendship. In time, Karen found herself captivated as her roommates read and discussed God's Word. Had she perhaps overreacted to staying with them?

Karen soon detected a stark contrast between her life and the life Chantelle and Natasha strove to live. She was shocked to find she actually liked being with these Christian girls more than any of the girlfriends she had grown up with. None of her old friends attended this college, so she was free to embrace her roommates' friendship without embarrassment. Something about them drew her, yet unsettled her.

Her roommates attended a Pentecostal church off campus. Karen heard them read their Bibles to each other. She watched them pray together, observing the way their inner joy bubbled over and spilled out to her and other campus youth.

She was baffled when they talked of confessing the name of Jesus, or used terms like "salvation" and "work of grace." It is important, they said, to experience inward transformation, not just an outer one. *What do they mean? Who is Jesus? Why does talking of their faith fill them with excitement? What do these Christian girls have that I am missing?*

Karen used a week of her vacation to fly to England and visit Kelly, who was taking college classes there. After exploring London, the sisters made plans to go to Amsterdam and enjoy the Dutch city with some of Kelly's college friends. To save money, the girls chose to stay at an economical Christian hostel while reveling in the pleasures the city offered. *Why did we stay here?* Karen wailed to herself when they sat down to eat yet another meal, and their host prayed.

"Bless not only our food, but bless and protect the girls in their stay here. Help us to be shining lights for Jesus," was the sincere prayer given.

Each day they stayed at the hostel, Karen felt more condemned. *We are not in Amsterdam for the right reasons. Our hosts treat us so well, and all we do is join the party scene and pursue shallow activities.* Staying with Chantelle and Natasha these past months had opened Karen's eyes to the differences between Christian and non-Christian youth activities. But she pushed her troubling thoughts away. She did not want to think of her Christian friends in America; she was in another country and wanted to experience night life in Amsterdam.

Seeing the unashamed lewdness as they strolled the downtown streets brought mixed feelings to her heart. *I can't believe this is happening right in the middle of the city!* Uneasiness crept in. The girls stopped at a coffee shop to socialize. Marijuana-laced brownies—it caught Karen's attention as she scanned the menu. *Why not?* she thought and sampled one.

Heading back to the hostel late that night, Karen started feeling dizzy. Her vision blurred, and just before they arrived at their room, she passed out. She awoke to find herself being carried to bed by her sister and some of the staff.

"Are you okay? Do you know why you fainted?" the staff asked. Thoroughly ashamed, Karen stayed quiet. She did not want the Christian staff to know what she had done. Chantelle and Natasha would not have approved of the outing either, she knew. *But is partying really wrong? If it is, why do so many people enjoy doing it?* Karen flew home with these unanswered questions, determined to leave Amsterdam and its perplexing emotions behind.

"What an incredible year! I am so glad we could live together," said Chantelle, closing a zipper on her duffel bag.

"Me too!" Natasha agreed. "God surely directed our living arrangements!"

Karen smiled at her roommates. She doubted God had anything to do with putting them in the same room, but she wanted to approve of her friends and show them love. "I will miss you two, and look forward to seeing you next term," she said. She caught herself, realizing she meant every word. Bidding them goodbye, she left for her summer adventure.

Several weeks later Karen found herself inside the bustling Charlotte International Airport, hurrying toward her gate and the jetway, bound for Asunción, Paraguay. Another dream was coming true: Karen was going to be an independent lady. Even though it was only for the summer months, and only as a nanny, she was still off on her own! Her dad had let her plan and pay for the trip all by herself. Well, he did so because he wanted her to learn to handle money, but that did not dampen Karen's excitement.

The plane had barely left the ground when she reached for her backpack and extracted *Idiot's Guide to the Bible,* her most recent purchase at Barnes and Noble.

Maybe she was an idiot when it came to the Bible, but she did not want to be completely out of the loop when Chantelle and Natasha talked about the Bible next year. How could they know so much more about what they believe than what she had learned at Saint Mary's? Not even her most diehard Catholic friends knew as much about their religion as her roommates did. Maybe they were all too absorbed in schooling and sports. It takes hours of studying to make the honor roll and hours of commitment to be on the sports team. Opening her book, she began reading.

Karen thought the Bible itself too intimidating to touch, and she hoped her "Idiot's Guide" would make some things clear. Who was Abraham? What made Jesus so important anyway? And why did Chantelle and Natasha both keep talking and hoping for the "baptism of the Spirit," as they called it? Reading her book, she expected to get pat answers to her many questions.

Two months later when Karen returned to America, she felt better equipped to understand her friends' Bible knowledge. Her dog-eared book gave testimony that it had been read, studied, memorized, and puzzled over at length.

All three Henderson youth were now attending the University of North Carolina. To save his daughters the expense of renting a house, Chad Henderson bought a house for them. Each girl was free to invite a friend to share in the living arrangements. Unfortunately, the situation soon proved to be less than ideal. The young people's self-centered attitudes and different backgrounds caused strained relationships. Instead of the pleasant conversations Karen had enjoyed in the dormitories, she came home to parties, loud music, and jeering voices.

Karen was surprised to find herself wishing to go back to living with her old roommates. But since that was not possible, she was glad they had at least maintained their relationship with her. She was thankful that at least Kelly and her roommates did not pressure her to join them in their activities.

Karen found herself spending as much time as she could with Chantelle and Natasha, opening up to them more than she had the previous year. They in turn encouraged her to stick to her studies and make wise personal choices despite her difficult surroundings. They invited her to church, and though Karen never found time to attend, she learned to trust them, and she did ask questions about their faith and hope. Little did she realize what heartache she was being spared by choosing them as her friends.

Another Saturday rolled around. As Karen made her way to the library to study, her friends approached her. "Come to church with us tomorrow." Natasha's entreating eyes radiated the lovely, gentle spirit within her.

Karen hesitated. "I can't, Natasha. I'm sorry, but I just don't have time! This semester will soon be over and I'm not nearly ready." Karen felt bad for continually refusing her dear friends' request to attend church, but if she wanted to survive medical school, she could not afford to let up on her studies. Driven to excel, she had become enslaved to her academics. She had exchanged her love of sports for textbooks. Even time with her father faded as she pursued her dream.

It was not unusual to see students participate in Campus Crusades Ministry, an event in which students walked the campus passing out pamphlets with short Scripture portions. One day, two smiling girls came up to Karen where she was eating her usual power lunch, a peanut butter bagel and veggies.

"We are part of the campus organization Crusades for Christ, and we are doing a religious survey. Would you mind answering a few questions?"

"Not at all. Sit down!" They had caught her by surprise, but Karen really was interested. "I had two Christian roommates last year who talked about their faith, but I never understood it. If you would sit down and explain it to me, I am all ears!"

"We would be delighted!" the girls answered almost in unison. They sat together on the bustling college campus. Even after Karen's foray into the *Idiot's Guide to the Bible*, she felt the need for more teaching.

They told her of her need to be born again and about having a daily relationship with God the Father. The taller girl handed her a pamphlet with a picture of a deep chasm and the statement, "Sin separates man from God." The girls read through the tract with Karen, but her mind could not grasp the message. The girls seemed to realize this, and they suggested ending the discussion with a short prayer.

"God, help Karen's soul find you. Amen." Though the teaching went over her head, more seeds of truth had been planted in her heart.

During her second year at the University of North Carolina, Karen had various stark reminders of Christianity. "Knowing Jesus means the world to me!" was how Marie Tobin, a young lady from biology class, put it. But Karen chose not to give the subject much thought. She admired her friends' courage to stand for what they believed, but she had no desire to change her beliefs or lifestyle. She was happy and she was not doing anything bad, so why feel guilty?

One night Karen was studying late at the library when a woman approached her. "I don't know you, but I think God is telling me to talk to you about Him," began the petite, middle-aged woman.

Karen was stunned. Someone she had never met interrupted her studying because she heard God tell her to? The stranger's honesty impressed her and she listened with an open heart. "It is such a joy to have a personal relationship with God," the woman told her. "It's quite simple. Just believe in Jesus! God has a plan for you. He is real and wants to know you." After the short conversation, the woman walked away, leaving Karen shaken by the encounter.

Karen was bewildered. How could a person know God? Maybe, just maybe, God did want a relationship with her!

Near the end of the second year, her friends told her of an upcoming spiritual weekend retreat. "You would have so much fun! Everyone loves it!" they said. Karen decided to go. She felt distressed with life, and her pursuit of academic excellence was enslaving her. She longed to know what the Christians meant when they said, "We have a relationship with God. We don't have to worry. We trust in God."

The retreat was pivotal for Karen. When she left after the weekend, she still felt that she was in shock. Not only had she made a confession to follow Christ, but she had also received baptism! It was, the pastor had said, a public confession of her commitment to follow God.

"Wow!" she said as her friends hugged her. Even though she could not fully explain Christianity, she knew she had changed in the core of her being. She had taken a big step toward a God who was alive, eternal, and all-powerful. She was serious about her decision to find out more.

Now my family will think I am weird. They will not understand at all! Karen drove her blue Toyota toward home. *But one thing I am going to do from now on is let God be in my life!*

And from that day onward, Karen did just that. Each morning she opened her heart, expectantly praying this simple but profound prayer, "God, I want to give you my life. I want to know you, and I want you to order and direct my steps."

God seemed to be answering that prayer. Karen bought a Bible and started attending the large Pentecostal church where her friends attended. There, she learned of their summer Disciple Internship Program. Excitement filled her at the thought of being under intense godly influence, and she decided to sign up for it.

"You? A serious Christian?" the devil mocked. *"You just made a profession of faith! How can you be part of this group? You won't know as much as the others."* With such negative thoughts bombarding her, Karen feared she would be denied. Still, she was determined to try. "God, I want to know you," she prayed. She felt a deep peace with her decision to pursue it.

"Pastor John," Karen approached the pastor of the Pentecostal church. "I know I don't qualify as a serious Christian because I only recently committed my life to God. But I am asking if you would allow me to join the Disciple Internship Program?"

Pastor John looked into the fresh, eager face. Rich brown eyes glowed with enthusiasm. He sensed inner peace and a passion for God radiating from Karen who stood calmly, yet expectantly, as if she already knew his answer.

"We would be happy for you to join our group," he assured her, sensing she was a rare individual whose heart was tuned to God. He was certain she had given her all to Christ, even though she was like a young child in her level of understanding. The pastor gladly welcomed her, joyfully anticipating the role he might play in molding Karen for the work of God's kingdom.

It was time, Karen knew, to tell her parents of her intentions. They did not even know she was a Christian, though they knew she had recently attended church. When she explained the recent developments, they were taken aback. Why did their daughter want to go to church? What was she looking for that they weren't giving her?

"What does this internship entail?" Chad asked.

"It is a summer internship," said Karen. "The program will put me in church six days a week, for at least ten hours a day, for the next two

months. I will get to learn more about the Bible and church stuff."
She hesitated. "Could you support me doing this?" she asked finally.

While her parents investigated her request, Karen waited, refusing
to worry. Instead, she prayed for them, knowing her life was in God's
hands. She loved her parents and she was determined to honor their
decision, especially her father's.

Praise God! Her heart sang when they did not object, but gave her
their blessing. Her parents worried she was becoming a religious
fanatic by joining the summer course, but they were also aware how
weary their daughter was and thought it might be just the break Karen
needed to rejuvenate.

Those months, spent among a dozen zealous college students,
changed her life. The purpose of the internship was to draw closer
to God. Everyone had a different background and a different story to
tell, but this they all had in common: their desire to experience God
more fully. Every morning they met for a minimum of two hours of
prayer. The remainder of the day was spent in fellowship, Bible study,
volunteer work, and evangelism.

Karen loved the passion the group had. God used these golden
months to draw her to Himself by developing in her a strong love for
reading Scripture, praying, and fellowshipping with the saints. Though
Karen had stepped forward and received baptism, she had not understood all the concepts concerning salvation. She still hadn't come to
see that she was a sinner, separated from God. Yet despite her ignorance, she surrendered all to God, and in God's perfect timing, each
of her needs was met and each blind spot illuminated.

She kept asking questions. "Why is God so important? Why do you
make such a big deal about Jesus? Why did people make Jesus equal
with God? What is sin? Is everyone a sinner? Why did Jesus die on the
cross? Is Jesus the only way to heaven?"

One by one, her questions were answered. Her new friends at the
internship did not give her pat answers, but pointed her to prayer and

reading of the Scriptures. The book of John became Karen's grounds for understanding the Gospel and salvation. She spent hours reading and studying. God in His great mercy and love had revealed to her the answers she was seeking. She claimed the message of Matthew 7:7. "Ask, and it shall be given you; seek, and ye shall find; knock, and it shall be opened unto you."

Pastor John proved to be a gifted, inspiring leader with whom the young people felt kinship, and his zeal for evangelism soon became contagious. His passion for personal Bible reading and prayer provided an example for Karen as she sought a deeper relationship with God.

Pastor John was convinced of the power of the Holy Spirit in a new believer's life. Over and over he challenged the youth, saying, "If you fall in love with the Scriptures and prayer, you will receive all God has in store for you! All faith, all knowledge, all love, all hope; all these will be given to you to allow completeness in Christ."

Karen had a tender heart before God. She longed to know God as her friends seemed to know Him. By spending time in prayer, times she treasured highly, she began to grasp what Chantelle and Natasha meant when they had talked of a personal relationship with God.

Coming to the understanding that everyone was a sinner was especially hard to accept, but Karen determined to believe the message. God sent His Son into the world to save sinners. *What gross sins do I have in my life?* she puzzled. *I think I've been a pretty good person. If I'm a sinner, I need to become aware of the sins I did so I can stop doing them.*

Fear came over her one evening as she read a story in Luke's Gospel. "Wherefore I say unto thee, Her sins, which are many, are forgiven; for she loved much: but to whom little is forgiven, the same loveth little."[1] Karen read and reread the story with a sinking heart.

"God, does this mean I will never be able to love you as this woman did?" Karen wept in agony. "Will I never be as close to you as someone

---

[1] Luke 7:47

who committed a lot of sins?" Tears ran down her face. "I thought I loved you so much already! Is there anything more I can do?" Academics no longer held her captive. All she wanted now was to know God and be filled with the power of His Spirit.

Excitement filled her one day when she found a cross bracelet. She picked it up and held it reverently. "Now I can show my relationship with Christ through jewelry! Everyone I meet will know I love Jesus," she gushed, feeling as though she had found a great treasure.

Door-to-door evangelism in a low-income neighborhood opened her eyes to the spiritual needs of mankind. Rows of tenant buildings greeted Karen and her companion. Here there were no spacious, landscaped lawns; only cracked, dirty concrete with a few scraggly blades of grass poking though. No cool shade trees diffused the hot mid-morning sun baking the street. Loud, harsh music blared from open doors and windows and clashed with the noise from adjoining apartments. Karen had never been in such close proximity to sounds and smells as these. Feeling conspicuous and vulnerable in her spotless designer clothes, Karen followed her companion to the long open porches where men, women, and children languished. It seemed as if they had landed on a foreign planet.

I'm sure glad I'm paired with Pete. She edged closer to her hefty six-foot-one partner. She wanted to leave this squalid area. Her heart raced, and she was sure everyone watching could see her fear. Suddenly, she remembered the woman who had loved Jesus so much because of how many of her sins were forgiven. She willed herself to focus on that truth. *Look how much opportunity these people have to love God! More than I ever will.* The thought stabbed her. She felt a mixture of love for the unlovely and wistfulness at how much these needy people could be forgiven.

But several weeks later, just before fall classes resumed, God began opening Karen's eyes. With long-suffering patience, He slowly yet surely revealed sin in her life—sins of pride and lusts of the flesh that she had committed unashamedly all her life; her conduct, her speech, and the places she frequented. Conviction came upon her as she thought of the impurity and immorality of her past habits. As she realized her need of a Savior, she sought God in repentance. For the first time she did not feel she was lacking in intimacy with God.

Karen fell in love with her church, her family in Christ. She cherished the rich fellowship, feeling sometimes as though she was suspended between heaven and earth. All the searching had paid off. Finally she felt her thirst for truth being quenched.

Reality hit hard when school began. Karen was no longer immersed in Bible study and prayer for ten hours a day, six days a week. She chafed at how academic studies ate up the hours in a day. Sundays seemed like paradise, and she attended morning, afternoon, and evening services, and even volunteered as the Sunday school teacher for the fourth grade children. In time she learned to handle her school schedule better. Putting God first was possible, even amid almost constant studying.

Attending Campus Fellowship with Chantelle and Natasha gave her opportunity to lead the ladies' Bible study on Tuesdays. Pastor Rick and his wife Kathy provided leadership for Campus Fellowship, and Karen soon came to appreciate them. Both of them had also become born again Christians while in college. They held prayer services on Wednesday evenings, along with Fellowship Ministry on Friday nights. But even with four evenings of church involvement, Karen did not feel satisfied with the amount of time she was investing for God. But what was she to do? No other events were available, so she used every available opportunity to evangelize. "God is so good! A relationship with Him is the most wonderful thing that can happen in your life!" Karen spoke to anyone who listened.

Her life belonged to God. She was determined that others would find the same joy she had. God, in His great mercy, allowed His child to grow and feed on His Word, giving her a year of calm before the storm building on the horizon unleashed its fury.

"Natasha, why are you wearing that pink scarf over your hair?" she asked her friend. It seemed odd. For several days, Natasha had been wearing different scarves, her hair tucked neatly underneath. Was she doing it to make a fashion statement? That was so unlike Natasha. Besides, it did not look stylish at all!

"It's a veil," smiled Natasha. "I am covering my hair because it is taught in the Bible. Go read chapter eleven of 1 Corinthians and tell me what you find," she challenged.

Intrigued about finding something new in the Bible, Karen looked it up that very evening. "Wow!" she exclaimed to her empty room. "That is so obvious! Why hasn't Pastor John addressed this passage? Why isn't every Christian woman wearing a veil?" Then she sobered at the mental picture of hundreds of women sitting in church looking like Natasha. *Ugh! Surely God doesn't expect us to do something that drastic!* She thought of all the compliments she received on her hair. *My hair is the most beautiful thing I have! Would God actually expect me to cover it?*

Taking a scarf, she tied it around her head and peered in the mirror. She made a face at her reflection. *I look like I have cancer.*

But as the days went by, Karen could not forget what she had read in the Bible. She felt in her heart that Natasha was doing what God commanded, but she wasn't convinced it was for her. Well-schooled in Protestant theology, Karen tried to convince herself that salvation was only an internal matter and therefore needed no outward expression to validate it. *Salvation is a work of grace. God accepts people from all cultures. God does not want people to think they have to look religious to love Jesus. It is nonsense to think Natasha deserves more of God's love because of some outward adorning.*

Confusion continued, but conviction increased. The more Karen studied 1 Corinthians 11 and the subject of women wearing a veil, the

Destiny *by* Choice

more she was convinced it was something she should be doing. *I will look so awkwardly religious,* she argued. *So different. So, so unattractive and ugly! And my family—they would never accept it.*

Daily she struggled with what she should do. She noticed a handful of other students now wrapped their hair in veils as they went about the campus. Karen wept and prayed. She felt powerless and hopeless, like God had distanced Himself. One day her eyes lingered over 1 John 5:3, "For this is the love of God, that we keep his commandments: and his commandments are not grievous." *Not grievous? Ever since I was confronted with this teaching on the veil, I have had nothing but grief!* her heart cried in near despair.

"For this is the love of God, that we keep his commandments," she repeated the words late one night as she combed John's epistles for further spiritual insight. Suddenly she sat bolt upright, shocked but thrilled by the simplicity of it. *What joy! I can't believe it is so clear.*

Why did she struggle so long when the context plainly showed obedience to be a test of love? *This is the love of God, that we keep his commandments.* Keep. Keep His commandments. The words leaped off the page, soothing her turmoil with its divine message.

Hurriedly flipping pages to 1 Corinthians, she read aloud the passage that had held her captive in previous readings. *But every woman that prayeth or prophesieth with her head uncovered dishonoureth her head.* Her eyes scanned the page. *For if a woman be not covered, let her also be shorn.* Nine long months had elapsed since Natasha had begun wearing a veil. Nine months of unrest. Now Karen was taking her stand too. "God's Word stands alone. All of God's Word is solid," she spoke in awe. Her confusion melted, and the way became plain.

Deciding to wear a veil was one thing; putting her decision into practice was quite another matter. *Lord God, I'm afraid I will disappoint my family and they will suffer. Every time they see me, it will remind them that I have changed. I'm afraid of what Daddy will do. He has done so much for me, and now I do this?*

Tears streamed down her reddened face. She imagined herself standing at the edge of a vast ocean. Behind her, like a smooth, sandy beach, lay the life she was familiar with. It was lined with fun, alluring pleasures, and luxurious condominiums. A spirit of ease governed her thoughts and actions there. Before her lay the vast expanse of uncharted water full of hidden dangers. What about the riptides? Did she have the stamina to endure if it cost her connection with her family?

Entering the Storm

God, are you asking me if I love you more than my family? The question tore at her heart.

If ye love me, keep my commandments.[1] God's clear, Scriptural instructions resounded in Karen's soul. *Wherefore come out from among them, and be ye separate, saith the Lord.*[2] Leaving her house, she went to find Natasha. She was ready to join her in wearing a veil.

Taking her large brown scarf, she draped it over the top of her hair, tying a knot at the back of her hairline. She went to find a mirror. Gazing intently at her new person, Karen did not feel one bit beautiful. "I am doing it to please God, not Karen Henderson!" she reminded herself.

Suddenly, her dark eyes flew open. Immodesty glared back at her, mocking the veil covering her hair. She had never given thought to how God perceived the rest of her clothing. Now the words penetrated her subconscious mind: *"You must cover your body too."*

That very afternoon, Karen went shopping for modest clothing. Cardigans were easy to find, but dresses were non-existent. Finally, she found several outdated long skirts at a thrift shop. By layering her

---

[1] John 14:15
[2] 2 Corinthians 6:17

clothing, she felt she had achieved modesty. This time, as she looked in the mirror she felt no shame. "But I look so odd!" she murmured in dismay. "My clothes don't match. I have no sense of fashion." A long sigh filled the room. She gazed at the strange person staring back at her.

After deciding to wear more modest clothing, she also bought modest, delicate jewelry as accessories. A flame kindled in her heart. She felt an urgency to serve God and the church, to bring spiritual enlightenment to her friends and fellow students. Finishing college lost its appeal. *I will find a job on campus so I can bring more people to Christ,* she decided, impulsively throwing away her plans for medical school.

"*What* are you wearing?" Her mother's loud, harsh demand sent Karen's heart plummeting. It was a Saturday afternoon, and she was visiting her mother the first time in her new attire.

"It's a scarf," she replied innocently, alarmed by her mother's reaction.

"You don't plan to keep wearing that, do you?"

"I think I do," Karen replied, disheartened and sober by the disgust so plainly expressed.

"What am I going to do with you? When are you going to get over this religious thing? Honestly, it looks terrible on you! Karen, you look ugly! No man will ever be attracted to you." Then her mother's voice softened. "Oh, honey," she said, "God gave you such beautiful hair. He doesn't want you to hide it at all. God loves you the way you are. Do you really think God is pleased at how ugly you look?" Her face and tone had changed completely. "I love seeing you with your beautiful hair flowing about your shoulders."

Discouragement settled over Karen. She thought of how she had looked earlier. Her mother was right—she did look ugly and odd now. But wasn't it more important to do what the Bible says than to please her mother? She couldn't understand, why didn't all Christian women do this? It would make it far easier for those who do. The Scriptures are so clear!

Her mother wasn't the only one angry at her. "Why the tiny pieces of jewelry?" her father scorned. Karen was shocked he had even noticed.

Shopping became extremely frustrating. Karen wished she could dress in a way more pleasing to her family, but modest clothing was not in fashion. So she did the best she could, often wearing layers of clothing to look more modest.

Chad Henderson was disgusted. How could his daughter wear that frumpy-looking thing on her head? *To show submission,* she had said. How could she! It galled him when he thought of how she was so dismissive of a college education and exciting career opportunities, and now . . . now this. To think she even wanted to throw her career away! Sitting with the family inside a fine restaurant one evening, he gave his daughter a hard look. "Karen, have you looked in the mirror? Do you know how you look?"

Kelly snickered, and Karen's heart bled. She tried to hold back the tears.

I won't let her get away with this, Chad seethed, hurt and angry inside. It was as if she was taking after those Mennonite neighbors he had years ago. Chad had hated the subservience he thought he saw in those women. Oh, they were nice enough people, but it was disgusting how the women stayed at home. They didn't value education, and they never held leadership positions in the workplace. Sure, there was value in the way they dressed and acted. He had seen the evidence. But his own daughter doing the same?

My daughter is not some doormat. She is sophisticated and educated! She doesn't need to hide behind walls! Besides, she has no husband; she needs to work. She is too young and immature to understand how her decisions affect her. He wouldn't let her quit college. She was beginning her senior year, and if he had anything to do with her decisions, she would be back on track before graduation.

What hurt Chad even more deeply was the rift between him and his daughter. Karen was his pride and joy. They had always been close. She had never opposed him before. Hadn't he loved her enough? Hadn't he given her everything in his power to make her happy? Acute pain thrust through him like a knife. What had he done wrong to make her embrace something so bizarre? He couldn't understand. Money had always bought her happiness before. What had changed?

In the restaurant, Karen couldn't meet her father's eyes. She did not want to hurt him and felt ashamed that she was doing that very thing. Finally she raised her head and spoke in a whisper, "I'm sorry, Dad. I am really trying."

"Karen, you have been given a good upbringing, a good education, and good opportunities for the future. I'm afraid you are throwing it all away in your religious zeal! People in the workplace won't understand why you wear that thing. When you apply for a job, they will think you look weak and uneducated. Mark my words." He paused a little before shaking his head in disgust. "To think my own daughter would be like this!"

He recalled Karen's decision to stop drinking alcohol as well as her refusal to be the designated driver for Kelly and her friends. It infuriated him. *Does she think we are all a bunch of sinners? Will she cut family ties because we don't embrace what she thinks she believes? There are no grounds for her decisions!*

Chad wanted to scream. Instead, he left the restaurant and headed for the golf course where he pounded out his frustrations with each swing of the club.

Karen honored her father's wishes to finish college, but changed her degree from medical to dietary. Though the whole ordeal was painful, Karen was not surprised at her father's opposition to her obedience to the New Testament teaching of wearing the veil and modest clothing.

She was not prepared, however, for the opposition that came hurtling at her from another place. Two weeks after Karen began wearing a veil, the pastor in charge of the college campus scheduled a meeting with her, along with his wife.

"Karen, we and others have noticed you wearing a scarf these past weeks. I know you are doing it in response to 1 Corinthians 11, but your interpretation of the passage is wrong. The heart and meaning of this passage is submission. My wife shows submission, and she doesn't need to put anything on her head to do that.

"What you are doing is causing other people to question me. I do not believe the veiled head is for today. We don't practice things from the Bible that were strictly cultural. We don't show submission through dead external practices like the veiling. Furthermore, you are not showing submission to me. It is not a practice I stand for, and with your being in leadership, you will need to come under my authority and guidelines.

"You have two choices. You will show submission to me, take off the veiling, and continue to lead the women's Bible study, or you will no longer serve our campus fellowship."

The stern ultimatum paralyzed Karen's tender heart, shattering her trust and confidence in the man she had respected and looked up to. This man had encouraged, taught, and inspired her in the Christian faith, and she looked to him for spiritual authority.

Shock, disbelief, and pain washed over her as she sat in stunned silence. As her pastor watched her face, he was reminded of her zeal to know God, and her selfless giving as leader of the weekly ladies' Bible study. Here was a gifted lady who was willing to be used in kingdom work. Indeed, she had been used ever since confessing Christ. *Why did she have to get caught up in believing external works were needed for salvation?* In a gentler tone, he tried again to convince her that she was in error.

"Wearing what you do on your head will hinder people from seeking God. We want to point them only to Jesus. My burning desire is to bring souls to Christ, not hinder them!

"What you are doing brings confusion to someone seeking Christ. You are not even being submissive. You are wearing something external and breaking the very principle within. You can't *earn* merit with God. By faith we are saved, not by works. The heart is what matters. I haven't asked you to wear this, and in fact I am asking you now to take it off. Please, consider my plea and submit to me."

Karen sobbed in anguish when she returned to her home. "Lord God, I can't go back on what you command me to do. Oh God, I do not wear the veil to sow discord. I love my church and my pastors. I love their passion for evangelizing. What do I do now? Because I am obeying you, they are challenging me." The pain was almost more than she could bear.

"I was despised and rejected of man." Jesus' prophetic words brought a measure of comfort to her wounded heart. Karen spent many hours praying, seeking comfort in the Scriptures, and weeping at Jesus' feet until she felt ready to face whatever lay ahead. She would continue to obey God's authority and wear the veil.

During this period of trial she was accused of dressing to set herself apart. Her dress, she was told, was offensive to other church members. More pain, more rejection—this time from the church she loved. But Karen kept wearing the veil. Though she stepped down from leadership, she wanted to show support to the campus fellowship and attended the usual Friday evening meeting. As soon as she entered the room, it became obvious she wasn't wanted. Eyes avoided her. Tension surrounded her. Though their rejection broke her heart, she loved the college ministry and went again the following Friday. Once more she knew she was not wanted. But since it was such an important part of her life, she went again the following week for a third time. Only then did it become clear to her: she could not be a part of the college ministries if she wore a veil.

Though Campus Fellowship soured, she continued to enjoy the First

Assembly of God church near the campus. The church was quite popular and thousands attended it every Wednesday and Sunday. Pastor John greeted Karen when he could, and did not seem perturbed by her veiling. At any bus stop Karen used, and in many of her college classes, she seemed to find someone attending the church and they would start talking about God. She was comforted to find she could wear her veil and dress to church without offending anyone. Her close circle of friends were not offended by it and most of her male friends didn't mind it at all.

Most of the resistance, it seemed, came from the leaders. Next it happened in her work as a teacher in the children's ministry. Tiffany, a co-teacher in the ministry, struggled to overcome a certain sin. She sought out Karen and confided she could not get victory over it. "I feel so guilty. I don't know what to do," she confessed.

Karen was pained for her co-worker. "Tiffany, surrender your life to Christ. It is only then that the Spirit of God can fill you with holiness and give you victory," she assured the troubled girl.

But Tiffany continued to struggle, and Karen was bothered with her co-teacher's permissive lifestyle. Not knowing how to handle the situation, she took the problem to Rick, one of the pastors at the church.

"Karen, we know Tiffany has serious struggles, but she is a Christian!" Rick affirmed strongly. "Let me read you something from Romans 10.10. 'With the heart man believeth unto righteousness: and with the mouth confession is made unto salvation.' Do you believe that Scripture, Karen?

"I cannot have differing views in leadership. I have spoken to Tiffany, and I want you to apologize for your actions. I wish to be clear; Tiffany is saved. She has told us she is not sure if she is a Christian, and it was you who put those thoughts into her mind! Tiffany needs confidence. She will continue in leadership." Rick paused to adjust his glasses. "I want you to affirm her security in Christ. Confirm she is a child of God. If you don't, you can no longer work with the children under me. I have a serious issue with what you told her."

Karen sat dumbfounded by his accusation. This was a complete turning of the tables. Never had she expected a rebuke when she came to him about Tiffany's enslavement. She had wanted to help her co-worker find victory, not to look down on her as Rick seemed to accuse her of doing.

She was speechless, devastated by his theory. *I'm not big on doctrine, but surely someone who has been cleansed and washed in the blood of Jesus would live as Jesus lived.*

"Karen." Her pastor leaned forward in his chair and looked squarely into her face. "When someone makes a confession of Jesus, we are never to question that confession. Salvation is simple, and we dare not complicate it. When people make a confession of Jesus, you are never to question that confession, because they *are* God's children. It is that plain and simple!

"Furthermore, I want to warn you of the direction you are headed. Be careful. Read the book of Galatians carefully. It gives serious warning to Christians who started well and have fallen into a works mentality. I am afraid you have fallen from grace and are trying to earn your salvation by works. Wearing those," he waved his hand over her veil and clothes, "is doing works. Do you understand, Karen? You need to submit to my leadership and repent for questioning Tiffany's salvation."

At a loss for words, Karen finally managed to say she would pray about it and, shaking Rick's hand, she left the meeting. Questions stormed her. *Have I been attending a church where the leaders are not following the Bible? Something is terribly wrong here.*

Karen did pray, asking God to show her if she was wrong. That evening she spent hours searching her Bible, considering various angles of the issue. It was becoming clear: she could not submit to her pastor, but she was saddened for him. She wrote a short letter to him, expressing her appreciation for Tiffany, and her own desire to walk the Christian way. She closed her letter by writing, "I cannot affirm Tiffany as a child of God at this point. Though I make mistakes, I always cared for her the best I could and I do not feel I have something to repent of in my relationship with her." With a heavy heart, Karen sealed the letter. She understood why her pastors felt as they did, but she could not agree with them. What about other Scriptures, such as the one where Jesus said to keep His commandments if we love Him? *Where do I go now?* she cried out in anguish. The answers seemed too far away to reach.

Almost two years had passed since she became a Christian. Loneliness now replaced her initial joy and excitement. Trust had been broken. She felt as if she had no church, no authority figure, or parents who knew what was happening in her life—or even wanted to know.

"Lord God," she wept and prayed. "I need confirmation. I don't want to be deceived, and I need your protection. My heart's desire hasn't changed. I gave you my life two years ago. I give you my life now. I thank you that I do know you. I need you to order and direct my steps. Show me, Lord God, what you would have me to do."

God did hear the cry of her heart. None of this had taken Him by surprise. He had allowed the storm clouds to break, to unleash their fury, to pound, to sift and refine, to bring Karen out of partial truth so the light of the glorious Gospel of Christ would fill her life in *all* truth.

"Karen, meet my friend Bruce. He believes as we do." Karen looked up at the tall, blond young man. "Bruce studies the Scriptures deeply," Natasha assured her. "He too wants to obey Jesus with his whole heart. He agrees that women should wear a veil, and he supports the teaching against divorce and remarriage. He won't treat us like the pastors from church, and he has consented to teach us things we don't understand.

"Karen, Bruce has offered to hold some open Bible studies at Starbucks!" Natasha rushed on. "We are to invite anyone we think is interested!"

Wow! thought Karen. *I don't know him, but he believes in the veiling so he must be on the right track.* Aloud, she said, "I'm ready!"

"Bruce is like us—he wants to know God more fully." Natasha beamed up in confidence at her male companion.

Their small nucleus, made up mostly of girls wearing veils, spent many hours studying and discussing the Bible with Bruce. Karen embraced their friendship, thrilled at the love of God prevalent in the group. Rarely did a mean-spirited argument surface among the friends.

These meetings were but a step in the plan God had for Karen. As of yet, she didn't know about a meeting with a woman in a store, a meeting that would change her life forever.

Part Three
Shelter of Safety

Karen was at Walmart with her family, perusing some books while she waited for Kelly to finish some purchases. Her father was grabbing a few things in the dairy aisle.

Looking up from a book, Karen noticed an unusual woman. Wearing an old-fashioned dress, she reminded Karen of the quaint woman in a children's book she had growing up. A serene expression graced the woman's face. And what was that on her head? Excitement surged through Karen. Intuitively, she knew the woman was wearing it because of religious conviction, and not fashion.

I can't believe she is here. I'm positive she is a Christian. I'm sure she knows why she is wearing that head covering and will give me an answer from the Bible! Quickly, before her courage fled, she left her family and hurried over to the woman. In breathless wonder she pointed to the woman's head and exclaimed, "Hi! I wanted to meet you!"

Karen's smile and voice radiated her own love for God. Though somewhat startled, the stranger graciously took time to talk. "I knew you were a Christian as soon as I saw your veiled head," Karen rushed on. "I have never met a Christian dressed like you, and I am both intrigued and curious. It is exciting to see another person obeying 1 Corinthians 11." Time seemed to stand still as the two women exchanged names, and Karen recounted her story to Gloria, her new acquaintance.

"I would love to have you come visit our church," Gloria invited. Karen eagerly accepted the contact information, not knowing what would, or could, come of it.

"Could I bring my friends along?" she asked. Suddenly, she heard her father's voice behind her and hastened to wrap up the conversation.

"Do bring your college friends. We will welcome you," Gloria assured her as they parted.

"Who were you so eager to talk to?" Kelly asked in disdain.

Karen told her sister of the comfort and security she had received from conversing with a total stranger. *We are strangers, yet we are able to go to the same passage of Scripture and agree it is God's truth!* She marveled at the divine meeting and the welcoming spirit she sensed in Gloria.

God knew Karen's heart. He knew she was at a crossroads, and He understood her struggle. That's why He planned for her to meet Gloria. God would never allow a temptation for which there was no way of escape, the Bible said. More than once, Karen had clung to that promise, and God had provided a way for her once again.

"We'll go with you," her friends answered when she told them of her encounter with Gloria and her plans to attend the Mennonite church that Sunday. "But," Natasha added, "we need to ask Bruce for his opinion. He seems like such a godly leader." Karen was surprised. She hadn't thought about asking, but it seemed appropriate. In some ways, Bruce was taking the place of a pastor.

"I know the Mennonite people. They believe the Bible." Bruce encouraged them to attend, suggesting he would go also.

Sunday found the college friends driving north to the Mennonite church. Karen was shocked to walk into the simple, unadorned structure and find all the women seated on one side of the church, and all of them wearing white veils. For some reason she had expected only Gloria to wear one, not all the women!

Once they were ushered to a seat on the women's side of the church, Karen realized that not only did the women all wear veils, but they all dressed in the same pattern of dress. Her heart desired to know more of these intriguing people.

She looked over to the other side of the church and saw the men and boys sitting in straight rows, dressed in dark suits and light shirts without ties. The men looked so similar it was hard to tell one apart from the other. *How unusual!* Her mind flew to the big college church with its array of fashions in dress and hairstyle. *I may not dress exactly like these ladies, but I fit in more here than there!* She shook her head, a look of delight on her face.

One of the men walked to the front and announced a song. The ladies opened their hymnbooks. Karen tried to follow their example, though she had never seen a hymnbook before. No choir, no words on a screen; the leader simply sounded the pitch on a little gadget and the whole congregation burst into singing. Beautiful, worshipful, four-part music filled the humble sanctuary. It was heavenly music that stirred Karen's emotions to a deeper reverence for God.

Karen listened with an open heart, enjoying the verses read in Sunday school, and hearing the godly men lead out. Listening to the sermon was even more exciting. Never before had she heard so much Scripture read from the pulpit. The congregation listened reverently. She had never seen a whole congregation kneel to pray. It was all so new, so refreshing, so right. Many verses passed through her mind, verses she had read and known but had never applied like this before. The whole service seemed geared toward seeking and obeying God. It felt as if she must be sitting at Jesus' feet.

After the service she noticed the discreet handshake and kiss on the cheek as women shared the practice with women and men with men. Instantly, she knew they were practicing the Bible command which she had recently read in Peter's epistles, "Greet ye one another with a kiss of charity" (1 Peter 5:14). *Beautiful,* she breathed to herself, though she was puzzled when only a handshake was extended to her and her friends.

"The whole service was an astounding experience," Karen told her group of friends as they returned to college. "I can't believe there is actually a church where they try to live out all of Jesus' teachings! This has been an incredible day! Will you go back with me?" she asked.

"I suppose I will," one of her friends answered with reluctance. She noticed Karen's surprise at her lack of enthusiasm. "Oh, I enjoyed it. I just have some questions."

"It was certainly different!" declared another. Karen was glad they too appreciated the service, but she sensed they were not as impacted as she had been, so she kept her feelings to herself. In fact, she wasn't sure she would want her friends to know just how impressed she was.

However, her friends accompanied her to the Mennonite church again over the next few weeks. After hearing more sermons preached from the Bible and learning what the group believed and practiced, Karen was still amazed at how seriously they took the New Testament's teachings. Women wore the veiling at all times; divorce and remarriage were sin and not permitted; and non-resistance was taught and practiced.

For some time Karen had felt that war was wrong. Yet taking part in war was so prevalent among the Christians in her church that she had started to second-guess herself. She listened and longed to open her heart to those who did not share her views on war, but she was afraid. On both occasions when she had done so, she had been dreadfully hurt. The Mennonite practice, on the other hand, impressed Karen and she wished to follow it.

"Don't you think they carry things a little too far?" Natasha asked after observing the communion service, offended that they had not been asked to take part.

"What do you mean?" Karen asked. To her, the service had been inspiring, uplifting, and extremely sobering. Like the rest of the congregation, she had examined her heart and life as the minister had challenged them to do. For the first time Karen felt she understood the importance of living each day in tune with the Holy Spirit. Her heart wept at the remembrance of what Christ had suffered for her. *What am I doing for Him? Am I giving Christ my all?*

"For one, they all look exactly the same," Natasha answered. "Do any of the women ever have a conviction to wear longer sleeves? What about their transparent coverings? Ours are opaque. And their dress. It looks like the 1700s! Is there something sinful about looking modern? Or within the twenty-first century? To me, it doesn't seem Spirit-led, but formal and legalistic."

"I agree," Chantelle nodded. "None of us sews. Where would we get our clothes if we would join their church?"

"I think they believe their separate lifestyle saves them," Natasha commented. "When we are invited to their homes for a meal, they talk about common things, the things of the world. Why don't they talk about the Bible and spirituality?"

Bruce made no comment, but the expression on his face showed that he agreed with Natasha and Chantelle.

"They seem rather superficial," Natasha continued, "I noticed that not many talk about spiritual things when the service is over."

The conversation hurt Karen. She was carrying all her distrust, skepticism, and hurt from her previous church, and she simply did not have the energy to address what the girls were saying. She had come to the Mennonite church longing to connect with God's people on a spiritual level. In her experience so far, their commonality was Christ, and the love of God was shed abroad in each of their hearts.

Karen considered the Mennonite church's guidelines, or standards as they were called. "We try to base our standards on the Bible," Gloria had said. Karen struggled with fresh questions. *Are the members obeying them out of cultural or peer pressure? Are they just submitting to church authority? Or are they doing so out of personal conviction?*

Were her friends merely judging these people wrongly because none of them had been raised in this kind of setting?

Though Karen struggled with these conflicting thoughts, she kept attending. She grew to love Gloria and the other ladies in the church. Esther, a widowed grandmother from her new church, taught her to sew a dress like the Mennonite women wore, and she fell in love with it. "I never dreamed I would be sewing my own clothes!" she confided to Esther. "This is so much easier than spending hours in a store, mixing, matching, and layering everything. That was always such a battle."

One day Karen came across *A Godly Woman*, a pamphlet about modesty and submission. These were both principles Karen agreed with. The first part talked about women covering their heads. *Yes, I'm doing that*, she checked in satisfaction. She read on, and stopped short. The hair was not to be cut. *Never cut my hair? What interpretation is this? My hair is long! It is simply good hygiene.* Her defenses were rising. *Doesn't a person's hair continue to grow if it is never cut? Do Mennonites think it is a sin to cut your hair? God, must I change everything I do?*

The next page held another surprise. "Are you willing to give up your jewelry (ornaments) for Christ?" She looked at her cross bracelet, her tangible symbol that told others she had a relationship with Christ. *How could this be wrong?* Mystified, she kept reading.

True beauty, the author explained, does not come from outward decoration but from the inward beauty of character. God commands us to wear one ornament, the ornament of a meek and quiet spirit. Man tends to despise humility but in the sight of God it is of great price.

Karen was confused, even hurt. She looked at her jewelry. Did it truly mock the One she wanted to obey? "God," she cried, "I didn't realize this was inappropriate. If that is what you want, I am fine with giving up my jewelry, and I won't cut my hair again." It was another step in learning complete obedience to the truth in God's Word.

She felt the rift between her and her friends widen as she realized they did not accept the Mennonites' understanding of the Bible's teachings as she did. Her college friends had come from varied backgrounds, which created some strong opinions. They found it difficult not to criticize when they thought a passage from the Bible was interpreted incorrectly.

Graduation came. She received her diploma with honors—and mixed feelings. Chad Henderson insisted his daughter continue her education in another state. A few weeks later, a letter arrived in the mail with Karen's name on it. "We are glad to let you know you have been accepted at the University of Tennessee Physical Therapy Internship Program."

Her father, excited about the news, insisted that she follow through with it. But Karen dreaded moving to a new community. Would she ever see Mennonites again? She did not protest, however, as she wanted to honor her father's wishes.

Hurt ran deep as she relived her father's fury upon seeing her wearing a cape dress. She longed for his approval, and her heart ached at the widening chasm she found between her and her family. "God, I want to live my life for your approval. Help me bear my family's anger and rejection. Help me to be submissive and honor my dad.

"God, please help. Every time I find a place of fulfillment, it is taken away!" She wept in agony as the words fell from her lips. Continuing in prayer, she felt her fear of the unknown being replaced with rest—a rest that came from knowing God would be with her wherever she went.

Karen knew her friends were dissatisfied with the Mennonite church, and though she wanted to see their perspective, she could not agree that the church was legalistic and spiritually dead. But since she would be moving out of state anyway, she did not feel it necessary to encourage them to keep attending. Besides this, Bruce had become a bigger authority figure in their lives than when they first knew him, and he was pressuring the girls to sever ties with the Mennonite church.

Karen often disagreed with him, and this added fuel to her friends' dissension.

As Karen made plans to move, Bruce reinforced his leadership, insisting that the small group of students continue fellowshipping. "God's people are few; we need to value each other's friendship if we are to remain faithful to God and the brotherhood. Since a number of us are moving to different localities we need to start a weekly phone contact so we can discuss Bible questions and help each other come to Scriptural conclusions." His reasoning was convincing and the group was willing. Before Karen left, they scheduled Sunday afternoons for a 2:00 conference call.

Karen completed her move, finding the small country town to be a startling contrast to bustling city life. The town's hospital was small, its accommodations were limited but adequate, and its shopping facilities were minimal. No stately manors graced the countryside, only hard-working families who lived in cute, homey houses with neat fenced yards and simple flowerbeds.

Businesses closed early, and many shops were also closed on Sunday. She noticed more women wearing skirts. People waved as they passed. Though not highly-educated or well-traveled, the locals were friendly. The community seemed to love staying at home, and she enjoyed hearing children play outside her apartment. She drank in the charming sights and sounds of a small town.

Not long after moving, Karen discovered a Mennonite church close by, similar to the one she had been associating with. "Lord God, my cup of joy is full and running over!" she rejoiced. "My dad thought I was going to be far away from these people, but it seems you have used him to put me even closer to them! I praise you for these Mennonite people who have welcomed me and made me feel at home. Lead me and use me to share the Gospel of salvation with all who are lost in sin."

Not all was easy in her transition. Though the Mennonite church graciously befriended her, Karen had many questions, and several times misunderstandings happened. But she opened her heart and life to the church, and she found godly counsel there.

One Sunday Karen returned to her apartment with the morning's sermon burning in her heart. Thomas Yoder, the minister, had chosen John 17 as his text, and it had gripped her: "Jesus lifted up his eyes to heaven and prayed, 'Father, the hour is come.' "

Thomas had explained, "When Jesus prayed, 'the hour is come,' He was showing His submission to the will of God. Likewise, our desires must reflect the heart of God. Our prayers must glorify God. We must all search our hearts. Do I know God? Am I growing in my relationship with God? Am I glorifying Him?"

In the quiet of her living room, Karen raised her face heavenward as she communed with the Father. No one could see her inner peace or the desire reflected on her countenance. No one heard her lips spilling praise to her Maker and Redeemer as she whispered in devotion, "God, I do want my whole life to glorify you." But God heard and saw, and He touched His daughter with His presence and blessing.

Karen continued to associate with the Mennonite church. She focused on developing friendships, wondering when she would see anger and selfishness among her new friends. Instead she witnessed continued peace and willingness to reach out and help others. She was inspired by their consistent testimony of living a Christian life. It thrilled her to discover they were always ready to stop what they were doing to pray with her or discuss the Scriptures.

Interacting with the ministers took her back to Pastor John and his compassion to reach the lost, and she wondered if she would experience disappointment with these church leaders too. But her fears were unfounded. Bishop James Miller and his wife Ruth completely accepted Karen when she visited their home. As time went on, she became more confident that she would not have to fear any more unpleasant surprises from those she attended church with. Ruth especially seemed like a safe, motherly person. She took Karen under her wing and invited her to eat countless meals with the family.

Ruth had a heart for prayer. Many times Karen sought refuge in the Miller home, with "Mother Ruth" dropping whatever she was doing to listen. "Come, let's bring our need before God," she would say, and the two would pour out their hearts to God.

James and Ruth prayed daily for Karen. They loved and accepted her as one of their own, a child of God placed in their lives for His purpose.

Another couple, Paul and Leah Miller, also opened their home to her. Their friendship proved instrumental in helping Karen rebuild trust. One day Karen arrived at the Millers' door sorely agitated. "Leah, I want to live in this area after I graduate," she burst out, "but my dad said I am not allowed to!" Karen's eyes filled with tears as she thought about how hopeless she felt. "I've been so worried about where I will go when my internship is up. I hoped I could get a job here, but Dad says I have to get a job in another state! I don't understand, because he was the one who made the decision for me to come here in the first place. Why is life so hard?" she wailed.

"Karen," Leah replied gently, searching for words, "I will help you pray. Let's rest in God. Remember, God's plans for us are perfect, even when we don't understand."

"Thanks, Leah," Karen said as she wiped her tears, feeling a measure calmer. "I guess I was not feeling very submissive to God before coming here. I was caught off guard by Dad's obstinacy, and—and it seems I just came here, and now I have to face moving again." A sad smile was on her face.

"It seems that everything I think God wants me to do, my parents are against. Everything my parents think I should be doing, I can't do and remain true to God. I want to honor Dad whenever I can. But I want to stay here so badly!" Tears began again in earnest, and Leah touched her arm compassionately.

"Let's commit this to the Lord. Meanwhile, I don't think it is wrong

Destiny *by* Choice

for you to see what jobs are available in this area. This is where you are living now. We will both trust God and pray for His leading."

Several weeks later Leah invited Karen to her house. She met Karen at the door with a huge smile. "Has something happened?" Karen inquired immediately. "You seem bubbling with something to say!"

Leah's eyes sparkled. "I found out there is a job opening at Taylorsville Rehabilitation Hospital for a physical therapist position. Isn't that what you are?" she chuckled.

Karen's mouth dropped open. "A job opening in the country, and right at the time of my graduation!" She scanned the notice. "But I haven't graduated yet. Will they accept my application?"

"It couldn't hurt to apply," said Leah.

A job opening right here with my friends! The description sounded perfect. But she had to remind Leah, "You know Dad said I can't stay here."

"I know he did, but we have been praying," Leah encouraged. "Maybe he has changed his mind."

Karen did apply. She was interviewed and offered the position, all before graduation. *Is this God's way of telling me to stay?*

She called her father. "Dad, I have a job offer here, and if you are willing for me to stay I would like to accept. It is a good opportunity, and I'm not sure if I could find one as good, or as soon, if I moved someplace else." Karen held her breath. *Will he agree? He has to. Surely this is God's plan!*

"I don't care what job you have been offered." Chad's answer exploded like a thunderclap. "I don't want you living there!"

She thought back to a confrontation that took place last Christmas when her father had booked a flight for her to come home to be with the family. Even now, she wilted as she thought of the hurt she had caused her family. It was Saturday, and they were talking and playing games around the table, enjoying each other's company, when she received a phone call.

Bruce and the girls were on the line, wanting to have another short conference. "I heard from the girls you are at home with your family," said Bruce. "It is fine to be home, but I want you to know you can't go out to eat with them. Most restaurants are pagan-filled and you shouldn't be in that environment."

Taken aback, Karen started to protest.

"This is not to be discussed," he interrupted. "You need to obey if you want to walk the narrow way."

Karen hung up, not at all in agreement, and greatly confused. She wanted to go out with her family that evening, but Bruce had strictly forbidden her. She still felt that he was one of her spiritual leaders, and she found it difficult to go against him. She knew staying at home would cause conflict within her family, but she felt trapped and helpless.

"Why?" Chad asked in bewilderment when she said she was unable to go out to eat with them. Karen had no answer but tears.

After her family returned, Ken sought her out. "Karen, who is influencing you? You are not the same! You don't interact much with us anymore. I know you are a Christian, but it seems you have taken things too far! Why are you distancing yourself? We want to work things out! We want to accept you and we are concerned about you." Karen sighed brokenly, feeling unable to explain to her brother all the conflicting thoughts in her heart.

"We need you back," her father added, clearly agitated.

"Okay, Dad," she answered quietly, hoping to pacify his anger. Thankfully, someone changed the conversation to something positive, and they soon told each other goodbye.

Now, with the new job offer, the conflict had been reopened. "God," she prayed, "you understand my desire to take the new job. You can arrange things so I can stay. You can work through my dad. I know he cares about me, and I know you are in control of his life too." Karen's heart broke, but she submitted it all to Christ.

When she told Leah what had transpired, Karen was surprised but encouraged at her friend's response. "We need to pray that God will change your dad's mind if it is His will for you to stay here. We will share this with the church family. The book of James says the prayers of the righteous are very effective."

Exactly one week after her chat with Leah, Karen's father called. "I've been thinking about your job offer and changed my mind," he said. Karen's jaw dropped silently, and she was nearly unable to believe the words that sounded like music to her ear. *Thank you, Lord God*, her heart whispered.

Chad went on. "I think it would be a good idea for you to start out where you are and see how it goes. You can always seek another job placement later. Taking this job will give you background employment when you move to another place," her father finished.

"Wow, Dad says I can stay! I have a job!" she sang for joy. *Could this mean . . . ? Dare I think of being a part of the church here? Is that in God's will too?* Contemplating these questions, she called her college friends in North Carolina to tell them she was not coming back. Since Karen had been so hesitant to leave, they found this hard to reconcile.

"Are you still having contact with the Mennonites?" they asked suspiciously, and Karen finally informed them of her new church. Learning she had been in contact with Mennonites the entire nine months upset her friends.

"Where are your loyalties?" Bruce's voice was sharp and threatening. "The Mennonites are not Scriptural! I have been laying out repeated warnings for you, Karen. I'm afraid for you. Your association with them hasn't been good. You are being deceived. If you choose them, you will be apostate and go to hell. We are the only ones who truly care for you. We are concerned for you."

I thought I was experiencing a closeness with God and the Mennonite people!

I love Ruth and Leah, and the other women. How can I be dying spiritually? She wept in agony after the phone call with her college friends.

Phone calls from her friends intensified, and with each one Karen's guilt increased and her peace diminished. She stopped her regular attendance at the Mennonite church, but they did not stop praying for her, having her over for meals, and offering friendship. They were grieved as they watched her struggle and slip back into confusion, hurt, and distrust. James and Ruth knew of Karen's contact with the group of friends from home, but they did not know the group was trying to wield control with an iron grip.

At first, Karen chose silence as a way to pacify her friends, but merely agreeing not to disagree brought sharp contention. Bruce challenged her about various controversial doctrinal viewpoints. Also, as time went on, it seemed to Karen that the group was making their own church rules an issue of salvation. They even made some new rules. Karen did not feel these new standards were based on Scripture or essential to living for God.

Karen spent many hours in tears as Bruce continued to warn her that she would lose her salvation if she continued interacting with the Mennonites. The web of deceit was tightening. She was being grievously deceived by partial truth, but the prayers of God's people on her behalf rose like incense as they ascended to God's throne.

Karen wept and prayed. "I don't even want to live anymore!" she wailed. "It is like I'm being smothered." The thick cloak of despondency held her in its grip. "I don't want to lose my relationship with you, God! I don't want to live in spiritual darkness again! Am I really becoming complacent and falling away in a dead religious faith, as Bruce says? Am I actually being deceived, unequally yoked with unbelievers, being turned away from the truth of the Gospel by the Mennonites? Do I have an evil heart?"

"Lord God," she pleaded. "I have experienced many hardships and been betrayed by so many people. But I know in my heart I have always desired to obey Jesus Christ. Search my heart, Lord God. I give you my life. Lead me."

In brokenness and sincerity she sought God. How long she knelt in prayer she did not know, but when she rose from her knees she felt a calmness and renewed sense of purpose. Karen felt an urge to talk to Ruth. The relationship she had with Ruth and James gave her confidence to open up and share the struggles she was facing with her college friends.

"Karen, I know you have been friends with the group for a long time," said Ruth. "They did initially help you, but that friendship has changed. Your friends are not a church, and Bruce is not a minister. Do you think he should tell you to submit when he himself doesn't submit to anyone? It is scary when a man goes off on his own. People involved in such a situation can quickly find themselves in a dangerous cult. The Bible should be interpreted by a group of mature believers, not by one individual."

Suddenly Karen picked up Ruth's Bible lying on the end table. "Thinking of all the restrictions in fellowship my friends were putting on me reminds me of what John wrote in his third epistle. Here, let me read it.

" 'I wrote unto the church: but Diotrephes, who loveth to have the preeminence among them, receiveth us not. Wherefore, if I come, I will remember his deeds which he doeth, prating against us with malicious words: and not content therewith, neither doth he himself receive the brethren, and forbiddeth them that would, and casteth them out of the church. Beloved, follow not that which is evil, but that which is good. He that doeth good is of God: but he that doeth evil hath not seen God' (3 John 9-11).

"Oh, Ruth and James," she said brokenheartedly. "How could I have been so blind? The fellowship in Bruce's group was so narrow, and I almost couldn't hear any outside voices anymore. They were extremely critical and distrusting of the Mennonites. I still need a lot of help, but

I praise God for His patience in leading me back to His truth." She paused. "And for giving me sound, Scriptural friends like you.

"I don't trust myself anymore. Twice I gave my whole life to what I thought was pleasing God, and each time was a huge disappointment." Karen allowed the tears to escape as she opened her heart.

Ruth quietly brought a glass of water, setting it on the stand beside Karen. *Why has she had to suffer so much for you?* she wanted to ask God. But a verse came into her mind: "Whom the Lord loveth he chasteneth" (Hebrews 12:6).

Once Karen had calmed down, she continued to share what was on her heart. "Headship is important to me. I can't ask to be part of a church now, but I trust you, James. Would you and the leaders allow me to submit to you? Can I have guidance even though I am not a member?" she asked. Ruth opened her arms to the young woman.

"The leadership here would be glad to give you direction, Karen," James told her. "Furthermore, Ruth and I have talked. God has already laid it on our hearts to offer that we can be like a mom and dad to you."

Tears ran down Karen's face. She felt so loved, so accepted. She had been hurt so many times, yet these two dear people loved her just as she was.

"This means so much to me." Karen released a sigh. "More than you can possibly know. I feel like I have been handed tremendous freedom." Peace and the love of God filled her heart. For the first time she felt she was perfectly in God's will. She went on, "I feel so unworthy! I have doubted, been caught in deception, not trusted in God as I should, yet He loved me enough to show me His truth, and now has given me such godly adoptive parents.

"Mother Ruth, when I am with you it feels like I have entered a shelter of safety," Karen finished.

"My dear girl." Ruth gave her a hug as tears sprang to her eyes. "That is a beautiful thing to say. My constant prayer is to be someone God can use to bring glory to Him. God bless you and continue to lead you in your walk with Him."

"Praise God!" said James. "As Romans 5:8 says, God loves all of us, and He even loved us while we were still sinners." The verse gave her assurance that this godly man could be trusted. Karen felt a different spirit than what she felt around Bruce. *James and Ruth want me to succeed. Bruce wanted to control me.*

"If we are dealing with a cult, I want you to be aware of the power and darkness of Satan," said James. "His power is greater than our human strength. We are helpless to withstand him unless we put on the whole armor of God. One of Christ's commands is to separate ourselves from the works of darkness.

"To be completely free from the influence of the group likely means you will need to sever all ties. I know it will feel as though you're betraying them, but it will be okay to stop having phone conferences with them." Karen looked stricken when she thought of how hurt her friends would be. She touched her veiled head, remembering how Natasha was the first one to show her this Scriptural teaching. But they no longer held the same convictions.

She bowed her head. The words James had just spoken penetrated her mind. *We are to separate ourselves from the works of darkness.* Her clouded vision cleared. If she wanted to continue walking with God, she needed to heed James' instruction. James and Ruth, faithful and obedient to God and His Word, were here to show her the patterns of goodness. "You are right," she spoke quietly but firmly.

Later that day, Karen wrote the fateful letter:

> Dear Bruce, Natasha, and Chantelle,
> It appears necessary to write that we are no longer in agreement on Scriptural issues. I need freedom to exercise my conscience as God calls me to do. I need to live according to His commandments so I can have peace within my heart.

I am choosing to stand in fellowship with the Mennonites and have asked the ministers here to let me reside under their authority. I am not ashamed of loving and befriending them, as they are truly following Christ in accordance to all Bible doctrine. I know this decision ends our friendship.

She finished her letter, saddened it had come to this, yet glad to be free from the deception.

A response letter came to her, stating how they mourned her decision to lose out on true faith. Karen put the letter down, relieved they no longer desired contact. It was best for all. She grieved at the direction her friends were taking, yet rejoiced to know she had the love and assurance of God and His Spirit to guide her.

Karen's Mennonite friends saw her Christian life blossom after breaking ties with the college group. She was encouraged to apply for church membership and did so, giving this testimony:

It is hard for me to look back on all the experiences I have had since I became a Christian. I don't know how I was able to go through some of those dark valleys. It still saddens me to know that not one of my college friends supported me while I was a proving member of the church. It also saddens me to think of the many other struggling Christians who are seeking Christ, but do not have the foundation of a strong local church to support them as I do.

The Savior cares about every one of my trials. I rejoice in the promise Jesus gave me: "Verily I say unto you, there is no man hath left house, or brethren, or sisters, or father, or mother, or lands, for my sake, and the gospel's, But he shall receive an hundredfold now in this time, houses, and brethren, and sisters, and mothers, and children, and lands, with persecutions; and in the world to come eternal life" (Mark 10:29, 30).

I can testify of receiving the blessings of being in relationship with God and you as my brothers and sisters. I can truly say I am glad for the hardships God sent. I hope I have learned to have a more compassionate, understanding heart.

The relationship I have with James and Ruth has helped me bridge the gap between being a nominal Christian and a Biblical Christian. Their home and friendship is a shelter of safety for me. My prayer is for others who are convicted in wearing the veil, of non-resistance and non-conformity, and against divorce and remarriage, to find a safe place of refuge in a Scriptural church like I have. I am thankful I believe the words of Apostle Paul, "There is therefore now no condemnation to them which are in Christ Jesus, who walk not after the flesh, but after the Spirit" (Romans 8:1).

———

Some months after becoming a church member, Karen felt God leading her to move with James and Ruth to another state with hopes to evangelize in their new community.

One evening several years after the move, Karen walked into her backyard to breathe in the fresh night air. A star-studded canopy stretched on and on into the heavens as far as she could see. *I'm a mere speck, less than mere, yet God knows all about me!* She took a deep breath, loving the dry, earthy scent rising from the sun-baked landscape prevalent in this semi-arid community.

She loved this time of the day when she was free to lay aside her work and commune with her Father in heaven. "I am so blessed!" she murmured, recounting her move to this place. "God has given me the desire of my heart—a fulfilling, challenging ministry of presenting the

Gospel to those enslaved by darkness.

"Thank you, God, for answering my prayers for my dad." She smiled into the darkness, marveling at how God had restored their relationship. "I never dreamed he would ever be glad and accepting of me as a Mennonite. Thank you for giving me the opportunity to visit him." She would keep praying for her family. She longed for each to know the blessings of a relationship with Jesus.

"Lord Jesus, you provide everything we need," she murmured. Then she prayed her simple yet heartfelt daily prayer. "God, I give you my life. I want to know you more fully and point others to salvation through the blood of Jesus. Amen."

A breeze swept across the yard. Karen inhaled the sweet smell of her neighbor's blooming shrub. She shivered as the dropping nighttime temperature reminded her it was time to retire to her bedroom. Tomorrow would arrive soon enough. Tomorrow—it would be another opportunity to serve her righteous, merciful, and compassionate God.

Karen smiled shyly at Nathan, the man seated beside her. *Today! Today is our wedding day!* her heart sang. She looked over at her father seated on her left, and her smile grew as he turned and smiled into his daughter's shining eyes. She felt his love wrap around her heart, knowing he gave his blessing to her and Nathan today. Dad and Mom were sitting beside each other, albeit stiffly. Then Kelly, and Ken and his wife. Her heart overflowed as she took in the faces of her loved ones who had come to share this special day. Her face beamed. Once more she caught Nathan's eye, his happy gaze washing over her.

Today! her heart whispered. *Today I begin a new life with a Christian husband in a Christian home. Today!* Overwhelming joy and thanksgiving bubbled up. She turned a beaming face to where James and Ruth sat on Nathan's right. Beside them were his parents and family—her family before the day would end.

She could think of only one appropriate response. Bowing her head, she prayed, *"Lord God, I am yours. Use me. Help me be a faithful companion in our home. I feel surrounded by a sea of divine love! It is your love flowing out to me through all these dear people!"* Once more she looked up at Nathan. Once more his steady gaze met hers and her heart quieted. She turned to the podium as Brother James opened the service.

"Dearly beloved, today we are gathered to share in the joy of our brother and sister . . ."

Emergency Landing

*E*arly morning silence blanketed the sleeping household as pilot Richard Good dialed phone numbers to get the latest weather conditions for flying.

"Good morning! I'd like to know weather conditions for Boston."

"Clear, fair, temperature 10 degrees, wind speed 5 knots," the voice gave him the needed information.

"Thanks! Sounds great!" Replacing the phone receiver, Richard picked up his air maps, slipped into his jacket, and dimmed the dining room lights. The clock showed 6:00 a.m. Time to meet his passengers and copilot at the airport in Lima, Ohio.

A dining room chair was pulled out from the table where his daughter had left it the evening before. Richard, a forty-year-old father of five, owned a construction and heavy equipment sales company. He had also been a pilot for ten years and did not think it unusual to drop to his knees beside this chair and pray.

"Lord, thank you for this beautiful winter day. You know my passengers flying with me are not believers. Help me fly the plane safely. Give me an alert mind as I handle the controls. Thank you for your presence." He ended his prayer, reassured that God held the day and he would not be alone. Taking responsibility to fly unbelievers caused a twinge of discomfort when he thought of the many lawsuits people filed each year.

Closing the house door, he stepped outside into a frosty January morning where glittering stars studded the darkened sky, giving promise of sunshine to follow.

An hour and a half after Richard left, the remaining household was astir with activity. "Mom, I need you to help me with my spelling words," Cathy wailed. "I have a test today. These fifth grade words are so hard!"

"Why don't you study them yourself?" Clint piped up. "That's what I do."

" 'Cause you're in third grade and third grade words are easy," said Cathy.

"Come," Leona called her daughter to where she was putting lunches together. "I'll give you your words out here. And Clint, would you tell Jenny and Andi to be down at 8:15 for breakfast?"

"Looks like Dad has a good day to fly," seventeen-year-old Ed remarked as he slid onto the bench for breakfast.

"That's good," his mother remarked absentmindedly. She hadn't even had time to look outdoors yet. A brief glance out the kitchen window confirmed her son's words.

Ring, ring! The phone interrupted their hurried morning, and Andi walked over to answer it.

"Mom, it's Don and he wants to talk to you," she handed the phone to her mother before sliding in beside her brother on the bench.

"Leona, your husband wanted me to call you," said Don, the pilot mechanic at the airport where Richard often flew out of. "Just wanting you to know he's having some plane trouble, but please don't worry, everything will be all right. Maybe just a little sheet metal torn when he lands."

"Okay, Don," Leona said, half nervous and half joking. "What's going on this time?" Both she and her husband knew the mechanic— and his love for playing pranks.

"Leona, I really am serious." His tone convinced her immediately that he did mean what he said. "He's having trouble with the nose gear and isn't going on to Boston. But don't worry. As I said, everything will be all right. He's planning to land here at our small airport at 11 a.m. It will take that long to lighten his load by burning up extra fuel."

Turning from the phone, she informed the children, "Dad's not going to Boston. He's having trouble with the nose." *What did Don say? Maybe some skinned up sheet metal?*

"Let's pray and eat or you children never will make the school bus," she admonished. In her prayer, she prayed for safety for her husband, asking God to give him a safe landing.

As the children ate, she explained further. "Don said not to worry. Dad's going to fly around until the fuel is nearly used up, then he'll land at eleven o'clock. Ed and I will head in around ten o'clock so we can be there."

"Bus coming!" Clint yelled, making a dive for his coat.

"I'm walking," Jenny announced, taking another bite of cereal.

"Then I will too," said Andi, content to do whatever her older sister did.

Clint and Cathy dashed out the door and down the lane to meet the approaching bus. Though school was less than a half mile away, riding the bus was still a novel experience for the two youngest.

Walking to school, fifteen-year-old Jenny and thirteen-year-old Andi discussed their father's dilemma. "Dad's a good pilot," Jenny said, readjusting her backpack over her shoulder. "He's been in tricky places before."

"I know," Andi said. "I'm just glad I don't have to fly around in circles all those hours. I would be sick for sure!"

As the girls entered the school, Jenny's best friend grabbed her. "Jenny, I'm so scared for your dad! We heard it on the scanner," she cried. Before the bell rang, the entire student body knew about the crippled plane circling overhead. When morning devotions commenced, Mr. Martin, the school principal, asked God to bless Richard with a safe landing. Many prayers ascended as the students prayed with him.

Upon leaving the house at six o'clock, Richard had stopped at his father's place to pick up his two Indiana passengers, and John, another local pilot who planned to go along as copilot. At seven o'clock, the two pilots and passengers boarded the fueled and warmed Cessna 411 twin-engine plane. The mechanics had recently finished an annual check-over on the plane, and this was only the second flight since then.

Down the runway raced the Cessna. Ever so gently, its nose lifted and the plane was airborne. Pulling up the landing gear to recycle, Richard felt nothing move. Three green lights should have been on to indicate that the gears were recycled, but the center one was off.

"I have a problem. The nose gear won't recycle," he spoke to John through their headphones.

John reached for the plane's manual. "Emergency gear," he read. Carefully both pilots went over the procedures outlined in the manual before them. John reached for the emergency landing gear crank and cranked the gear down. The gear held solid, so they knew it was down. Why couldn't they get it to retract?

"Couldn't you have two people crank using both hands?" one passenger suggested.

"Sorry, it wouldn't work. It would just break off the crank," Richard answered.

"We have a problem," he said to the ground personnel. "We will do a fly-by so you can see what is amiss with our nose gear." Twice they circled with the plane flying low over the airport, and each time the ground personnel used a video camera to take pictures. Both times the pictures showed the nose wheel dangling at a forty-five degree angle instead of the normal ninety degrees.

"Do you think we should try doing a stall?" Richard asked John after hearing the results from the fly-by.

"It might lock out the gear," John agreed. "Let's try."

Up, up, the Cessna climbed to 3,000 feet before the pilot cut the engine and the plane dropped free-fall. Several more times Richard sent the plane climbing, then stalling, sending it into a sharp drop. It was the first time either of the passengers had taken an airborne roller-coaster ride. With each stall they wondered if the plane would come out of it, but neither said a word. Both were keenly aware their lives were in the hands of the pilot and he was doing his best.

"The landing gear doesn't budge," John spoke the fateful words.

"We'll circle until Don comes in at eight," his pilot answered.

"Don, what should I do?" Richard was glad to get his mechanic's advice a short time later. Together they considered the options: fly on to Boston and emergency land; fly to Dayton with its bigger airfield; or stay here in their home area.

"I think I would rather stay here and land," Richard radioed Don after considering the options, none of which seemed satisfactory. "John is agreed. The wind direction is good and we have a good mechanic. I don't think we need to go anywhere else."

"Okay," his mechanic agreed and the men discussed what would be the best landing procedure.

After deciding, Richard went over the process with his mechanic. "Once the main landing gear is on the ground, we will shut off auxiliary fuel pumps at the left side. Close throttles. Feather the props. Cut the mixture. Shut off the four electrical switches, and hold the nose up as long as possible."

"Correct procedure," Don said when Richard finished.

The plane's occupants had three more hours to circle and reduce the aircraft's weight by burning more fuel. Three hours to think, plan, and prepare to land. The copilot and passengers watched with respect as Richard Good bowed his head in the pilot's seat and prayed audibly for a clear mind and safety in landing. He did not pray for his airplane. A damaged airplane wasn't his first concern. He was responsible for three other lives, men who did not confess to know Jesus Christ. It was for these three he prayed, asking God to spare their lives.

Three hours is a long time to fly within a fifteen-mile radius. Copilot and pilot used some of this time to practice training and do holding patterns. There was no danger in flying; the danger lay in landing.

When Richard first reported his trouble, the announcement went across the scanner in five townships. Unknown to him, it was also announced far and wide. People in the next state were praying for his safety. Dayton and Columbus news helicopters flew into Lima. Eight fire trucks pulled into position along the airstrip, and five rescue squads, ten state patrols, and forty rescue personnel were also on hand. Tension filled the airport. The parking lot was jammed with cars and people while worried airport workers waited for the landing.

No one knew what was keeping the nose gear from recycling. What everyone did know was that a normal landing would be impossible if the nose gear was in an incorrect position.

"We will send out another aircraft," Dayton airport offered Richard. "If we fly close, maybe we can see what the problem is."

"Thanks," Richard acknowledged, "but no thanks. I feel that's too dangerous."

Several more times Dayton called just to see how he was doing. Richard appreciated their concern. Time moved on. The fuel was almost gone and while their pilot calmly prepared to land his crippled plane, the passengers felt far from calm.

"We need to distribute our weight," John informed the passengers as he left the copilot seat, taking the seat directly behind. "You two take the back seats for added weight in the back. Good!" he said as they complied. "Now we should be set."

Set to crash, or set to die? Set for injury, or set to walk away? Those grim thoughts held precedence in the minds of the three as they took their new seats and buckled in.

On the ground below, Leona first began to sense how serious her husband's position might be when she arrived at the airport to find the entrance blocked by police cars. The officers were doing their best to keep back throngs of people from the already jammed parking lot.

"My dad's the pilot in the plane." Ed volunteered this essential information, which allowed him and his mother access to the airport. Ron, a minister from their church, had also come along and his presence was calming. Reporters were swarming over the area and the police immediately whisked the family members into a back room so they wouldn't have to face the media.

A chill clutched Leona. *This looks serious!* The closer the minute hand ticked to eleven o'clock, the more her fear mounted. Her mouth went dry. She had difficulty swallowing, and it seemed the air was almost too thick to breathe.

"Let's pray." Ron broke the silence of the three in their secluded room. All bowed their heads in prayer. Calm replaced Leona's fear. She could breathe again. God was in control!

Jumbled thoughts raced through Ed's mind. *What if the plane flips or catches fire?* He visualized the plane torn up like the one he had seen in a wreck recently. Shaking his head, he dismissed the picture. *Both Dad and John are good pilots and God is with them,* he reminded himself.

"Want to talk to your dad?" One of the airport personnel came into the room and handed Ed the two-way radio.

"How's everything?" His father's voice sounded normal and Ed relaxed.

"We have a big welcoming party for you, Dad," Ed answered. "How's everything up there?"

"I'm ready to bring it down, son. Don't worry. We are in God's hands."

With the minute hand almost at eleven o'clock, mother and son walked out onto the tarmac.

"Who are you?" A reporter quickly approached them.

"I'm the pilot's son," Ed answered, his eyes on the plane.

"Hey! We got the son over here!" the reporter called.

With a prayer in his heart, pilot Richard Good made the final approach at one hundred and ten miles per hour. *"God, you will have to take control,"* he prayed. *"I have done all I can."* He felt the presence of God in the calmness and peace within himself.

With a steady eye he watched the gauges. At two hundred feet before the runway, he shut off the auxiliary fuel pumps so his hands would be free to operate switches. Six inches above the runway, at a speed of eighty miles per hour, he leveled off until he felt the main wheels touch down. Upon touching down on the runway, his impulse was to pull the nose up. The plane bounced slightly and he felt a surge of adrenalin for the crucial moment ahead. *Keep calm. Keep in control of what you are to do. God is ultimately the one landing this craft.* At thirty-five miles per hour, with props barely turning, he gently brought down the nose. The plane shuddered, slowed, and coasted to a standstill.

Richard turned in his seat toward his passengers, a smile spreading across his face. "Praise God!" he said with reverence, and opened the door. He was stunned to see all the emergency equipment and personnel surrounding his plane. He hadn't even seen them while he was landing!

A sigh of relief swept through the school when they received word of the safe landing. Jenny found herself wrapped up in a big bear hug by her friend and Andi was finally free to concentrate on her studies. One of her classmates had lost his father a year earlier, and that had been nagging her. *Will I experience the same loss?*

When Richard stepped from his airplane, he turned his back on reporters to inspect the nose. The retracting fork was dangling, completely severed. Landing the plane with such a nose wheel defied all laws of nature.

"God was good to us," he told the reporters. "It's a miracle. We had a lot of people praying for us. God gave us a light load and perfect weather. There was only so much I could do. The Lord did the rest." He seized the opportunity to leave a testimony for his Savior. "This is a present-day miracle! The safe landing defied navigation laws, but not God's goodness to us!" As Richard Good left the tarmac, he was awed by the fact that God had chosen him to be part of His work.

Fear in the Jungle

Whack! Whack! The sharp machete blade bit into dense undergrowth, severing the lush, thorny vines that choked the footpath. Twisting through the hot, steaming Belizean jungle, the path ran under a canopy of branches arching overhead, but they were of little help to block out such oppressive heat. The afternoon downpour had ceased, and the low-lying tropics turned into a giant steam oven.

Manfred worked steadily, swinging his machete in a slow rhythm. *Whack! Whack! Whack!* Each dull thud left one less thorny vine to trip or snag everyone who ventured down this shortcut to church. Sweat dripped from Manfred's forehead and trickled down his neck and arms. He stopped to wipe his face and grinned at the mental image of vapor rising from his soaking wet shirt and the top of his head.

"How's it going?" Joel called as he came up the trail with a thermos of cool, sweet lime drink. "The women will surely appreciate your hard work! My wife informed me that going to and from church has become an obstacle course for them." He chuckled as he handed the drink to Manfred. "Yes, this looks wonderful!"

"Thanks for the drink," said Manfred, filling his cup for the third time. "It hits the spot. I have to drink three times more here than I had to on a hot day in Montana! Even haying never drained me as much as this does."

"Don't overdo it," Joel cautioned. "Rest when you need to, and pace yourself. I would help you if I could, but you know the doctor's orders. I'm thankful I am feeling better, but malaria is unpredictable and I would hate to have a setback."

"And we wouldn't want that either." Manfred replaced the thermos cap and picked up his machete. "I'm getting back to work, but feel free to stay. I'm glad for people who keep me company, even if they don't help!" He grinned and resumed working. His mind drifted to his Montana home with its gently rolling farmland. Sparsely wooded, the vast expanse of open country offered no obstruction to the wild wind sweeping across it. *How could I have ever complained about the constant wind?* he thought, longing for even a little breeze to waft through this stifling jungle.

But I am glad I am here, Manfred reminded himself, determined to enjoy and accept a country different from his own. He had prayed that he could know God's will, and he felt certain God had led him to come here, so he didn't want to question or complain.

Joel and his wife are truly examples of a committed mission couple. Selfless, positive, content, and forever interested in those around them. Since arriving at the mission three weeks ago, he had been challenged by the many outstanding qualities shining forth from the young mission director and his wife. This country was primitive, harsh, and taxing, yet Joel embraced each day with a zeal for humble service.

I want to have those characteristics. Renewed commitment throbbed in his heart. *By the grace of God, I will trust and work with an uncomplaining spirit. The needs of the people here are so many!* He attacked the vines with a burst of energy. *Whack! Whack! Whack!*

With a smile, Joel observed the vigor with which Manfred swung his machete. He had noticed the array of emotions displayed on his face. Conflict? Discouragement? Submission? Joel had no idea what deep thoughts Manfred was weighing, but the determined swing of his machete gave evidence that he was ready to face whatever challenge called him.

Suddenly, Joel caught the sinister movement of a yellow-brown patterned snake slithering directly between Manfred's legs. The snake stopped. Joel froze, waiting for the snake to sink in its deadly fangs.

"No, Lord!" was his silent plea as he stood rooted, unable to utter a sound.

Manfred had his arm raised, ready to cut a vine, when he sensed movement. Looking down he glimpsed the poisonous snake beneath him. He too froze, waiting for it to strike. Instead the snake stealthily continued its forward course, unmindful of its surroundings. As it disappeared into the dense underbrush, Manfred's arm fell limply to his side.

"A miracle," Joel whispered. "Thank you, Lord!" Taking another breath, he took a few steps toward his shaken friend. "Manfred," he said, "yellow-jaw snakes are one of the most aggressive and deadly snakes in Belize. Usually they strike instantaneously when startled. The slightest disturbance can get them riled up, and . . ." he paused. "And the victim doesn't always survive."

Awe at God's protection filled Joel's soul. *"We place our lives in your hands today."* The words Joel had prayed at breakfast flashed through Manfred's mind. *"We trust you for guidance, wisdom, and protection."* Manfred was humbled, aware that he could now be struggling for his life. Yet God in His great mercy had seen fit to spare him.

I have work for you, the quiet words of the Master echoed in his heart. *Trust me. Fear not.*

By the end of the week Manfred was finishing the trail. Each day while he worked he kept a vigilant eye out for danger. *Is the yellow-jaw snake around? Will he reappear? What other dangers are lurking in the jungle? How did I trust before this?* Since his brush with death, he constantly found fear threatening him, wanting to take hold. Many times throughout the day he needed to seek God and commit his life into God's keeping.

"Glad that's done!" he said quietly, gathering up the last of the cut vines. The sun was almost overhead as he strolled back to the mission house on the unobstructed path through a natural arbor. Danger seemed distant as he walked in the middle of the wide, clear path. For the first time he slowed his steps and took in the beauty surrounding him. Huge fronds drooped, and birds called and flitted from above. An iguana blended into the tree trunk. How easily he would have missed it, had he allowed fear to paralyze him. He swatted at a mosquito and hardly noticed the ever-present whine of insects, so intent was he on seeing what the jungle would reveal.

Upon entering the mission house clearing, he saw Joel and Maria's two small daughters, one-year-old Jessie and four-year-old Joanna, playing in the sandbox. For two days Joanna's tunnel building had been the main topic at mealtimes. Last evening she was quite discouraged when she informed them, "Jessie smashed my biggest tunnel when she fell down on it!"

I'll help her until lunch time, Manfred decided as he headed for the porch to put his machete away. Just as he reached the porch, he saw it—a gray snake head rising slowly behind the sandbox. In horror he watched it examining the children. Manfred was sure he heard rattling as he raced toward the sandbox. Then another snake head popped up. One, two, three times he swung his machete as he kept the children back with his foot. Two full-grown rattlesnakes lay dead, right beside the edge of the sandbox where the children were playing.

Scooping up both children, Manfred held them tightly against his

Destiny *by* Choice

pounding chest.

"Why did you do that?" Joanna's big blue eyes looked trustingly into his.

"I didn't want the snakes to hurt you." He took a deep breath to still his shaking voice. "Those snakes hurt people and we must get rid of them," he explained as he set them down.

She looked at the dead snakes and then at her unfinished tunnel. "Can Jessie and I play in the sand now?" she asked.

"Yes," he answered simply. Like an arrow, her trust pierced his heart. She had no fear. The danger, which had been so close, was gone. He had removed that danger, and now she wanted to finish her tunnel project.

He had worked all week in fear that the yellow-jaw snake would return, or something equally dangerous. He had missed out on so many of the wonderful sights and sounds in the jungle. Where was his simple, trusting childlike faith?

Just as God had been watching over the children in the sandbox, so He had protected Manfred when the yellow-jaw snake slithered away without striking. He too needed to trust, or he wouldn't be able to effectively carry on the work required of him.

I'm sure these children have learned trust from their parents, Manfred reflected. *What a lesson they are to me!* The words of David the psalmist came alive as he joined the little girls in the sandbox: *The Lord is my light and my salvation; whom shall I fear? the Lord is the strength of my life; of whom shall I be afraid?* (Psalm 27:1). The verse would be a good motto to live by, he decided. Whether he lived in the jungle or in another land, he was determined to remember it.

Tempered Through Trials

Part One
War Bonds and Questions (1939)

**WAR BONDS SOLD HERE.
BUY YOUR WAR BONDS NOW.**

Jacob Friesen read the bold signs posted in the post office window as he tied his horse to the hitching post one Saturday in September 1939. A cluster of locals huddled under the lone shade tree outside the entrance. He walked over to join them, hoping to learn more about the war posters. He had heard rumors of Canada joining forces with Great Britain if war were declared on Nazi Germany. His church was concerned about the possibility of another world war.

Would a war affect him, a seventeen-year-old? Would joining be compulsory across Canada, or would the government provide an alternative to military training? War against Germany! He and his parents were Germans. Would that pose a problem even though they had naturalization papers? What of his decision to join the Mennonite Church?

His family had German background, but Jacob had been born in Russia. His mother would not talk about it. She would shake her head and change the subject whenever someone questioned her. "It's too hard," she would say. But today his interest in the country of his birth was piqued. He wanted to know more about it. What had it been like for his parents living in a communist country?

"We'll give them what they deserve!" A harsh voice jerked him back into the present. "Those dirty Germans aren't even human!"

Jacob took a step backwards. Did these men know he was German? If they heard his last name, would they assume he was part of the big Russian settlement five miles to the west? Foreboding gnawed at him. The air felt charged with hatred.

Jacob eased away from the group. Slipping into the post office, he collected the mail for his boss, Adam Myer, and went directly to the hitching post. Stowing the mail in the saddlebags, he swung himself into the saddle and cantered down Main Street. A trail of powdery dust settled in his wake. He wished the hatred and unrest he had just heard would settle so easily.

The mid-morning coolness soothed his mind. The coolness would soon dissipate under the sun's rays in the cloudless expanse overhead. Jacob felt the touch of fall in the air. *I am ready for a change of season! All of us farmers are ready for an end to these long, hot summer days. It seems as fast as we irrigate, the winds suck up the moisture like a giant mop!* It had been a good summer, but he was ready to retire his irrigation tarps and shovel. It felt good to know the days of sloughing through the mud as he dammed water ditches were over for the season.

Yes, I am ready for harvest, he thought as he looked over the acres and acres of brown-gold wheat, waiting to be swathed and threshed. The threshing crew was coming Monday to Adam's farm. He would be tied to the farm for weeks. Jacob spurred his horse into a smooth gallop. His mind was made up. He would ask Adam if he could get off early tonight. He normally went home each month after receiving his paycheck, but that was three weeks away. His time at home was often just long enough to deliver their monthly groceries. Surely, Adam would grant him permission for a visit home before harvest started.

I want more time than that! I want to know why my parents came to Canada. Why doesn't Mama want to talk about it? Why did none of their families come with them? Why doesn't my father share my mother's faith in God? Was he that way in Russia, or only here?

Jacob pushed the questions away as he turned in at Adam Myer's farm. Although he had been attending the same church as his boss for almost a year, they never discussed spiritual or personal subjects. Their conversations were limited to giving and receiving orders.

"Lord, make a way for me to visit Mama this evening. The future looks unsettling. Lord God, for some reason I feel the need to know about my parents' early life. Prepare Mama's heart, so she will be willing to share with me if that is thy will. If it isn't, Lord, I want to accept that. My desire is to serve you as faithfully as Mother does."

"Jacob! What a surprise!" His mother Justina's face lit up as he stepped inside the kitchen. "You are just in time to eat a bowl of soup with us!" She took down another bowl, setting it at the empty spot at the head of the table.

"That's what I was hoping to do," he grinned. "Dad not here?" he questioned.

"No. He left a week ago today." The sadness in his mother's eyes belied her calm answer, and Jacob almost wished he could put off the talk he planned for tonight.

"But you are here, and that is a treat!" Mama's sincere words and smile told him his visit was special.

"Yes, I have this evening." He hung his hat on a hook near the door. "Mama, could you and I have a good talk after supper? I don't know if you have heard, but Britain has declared war on Germany. The news is saying this could be World War II. I have a lot of questions, and I think you are the only one who can answer them."

A shudder ran through his mother's slight frame. She clutched her heart, walked heavily to a chair, and sat down.

"Mama, are you alright?" Jacob asked. "I don't want to alarm you, but I think you need to know what we may have to face. Britain is our mother country."

"Give me a few minutes, son. It brings back so many memories."

"That is why I came tonight!" Jacob paced the small kitchen. "Mama, I have questions—it is like I suddenly need to know things! Things about Russia. Things about Dad. Can we talk, Mama? Can we?" he pleaded as he stopped by her chair. The stricken look on her face made him step back.

"I'm sorry, Mama, I don't want to upset you. If you can't, I will try to understand." He started to tell her what he had heard at the post office that morning. Then he grew silent as the haunting words smote him. "Mama, I don't want to even tell you!"

"Tell me, son. I need to know."

"They said, 'The Germans aren't even human.' " He ran his hand through his hair, making it stand up as if in defiance to the words.

Neither spoke. The wood in the kitchen stove snapped as a piece settled into the hot coals.

Suddenly, laughing voices drifted in as the children flung open the door. "Jacob! We saw your horse, Mac, and knew you were here!" They beamed in delight to have their big brother home.

"Wash up for supper." Mama smiled at them. She turned to Jacob. "Yes, son. I will have time tonight. It is God's time."

That evening after the younger children had gone to bed, his mother moved the lamp to the table and picked up her knitting.

"We young men at church are wondering how the war is going to affect us," Jacob began. "Some say all men over twenty will be the first to be drafted. But how long will this war last? The nineteen-year-olds could be called next, and I will soon be eighteen." Jacob heard his mother's sharp intake of breath, but he had to know. "Mama, did Dad ever face something like this in Russia?" He watched her eyes fill with fear and turmoil as she struggled to keep her composure.

"Jacob," she faltered, "the pain I feel in my heart right now—makes me think of my father—sawing trees." She stared out the window and far off, across the darkening landscape. "My father used a big crosscut saw. Back and forth, back and forth it would screech, protesting each cut as my father and his brother sweated to pull in unison. It was hard work to cut down a tree.

"Trees were an important part of my childhood in Russia. We needed them for firewood and building. Many trees were hauled from the forests surrounding our home. They came from the base of the beautiful, rugged Ural Mountains near our village. I loved these trees, but they killed my father." She took a deep breath and looked at her son.

"I still miss my family. After all these years, my heart still weeps for them. But I will try to tell you about Russia. It is a land I sorely miss. I loved it there, but God has brought me here, and I am learning to love these flat, treeless prairies too."

She laid her knitting on the table and blew out the lamp. "Come, let's go sit outdoors on the bench. I think if I am outside where I can smell the earth and see the heavens, it will give me strength to share with you. It is not easy to bring painful memories out in the open, but if it will help you to be faithful to Christ, I am willing."

Hardships in Russia (1905–1924)

"I will try to start at the beginning," Mama said. "I have kept these thoughts and memories in my heart for a long time. So many things are crowding into my mind. This is hard to do, but I will try.

"Russia is a beautiful country. Our village was built close to the wide, swift-flowing Volga River. Everywhere we looked we saw hills, forests, farmland, or towering mountains.

"Your father, Jacob John, and I both lived in the same Mennonite village called Ischalka, or the Neu Samara Colony. Our colony was one of the last ones established in 1890 in the middle-Volga region, which was farther inland than the crowded Mennonite colonies in the Ukraine. For years, prosperous farmers had bought up large tracts of land in the Ukraine, leaving none for the less privileged. This had forced the poorer Mennonites to move inland to the Volga region in Russia.

"It takes hard work and much money to begin a new settlement. These new colonies were considered very poor by the standards of the mother colonies. My grandfather told me when the mother colonies were established, the Ukraine was a wonderful place to live—favorable climate, religious freedom, many opportunities for earning a living, and no political interference. In 1786 when the Empress of Russia invited the Mennonites to move there, she made them promise they would not mingle with the native Russians or teach them Mennonite beliefs.

"My papa—your grandfather—lamented this promise. He said it caused God's people to forget Him. By the time I was born, many of our people did not give God first place in their lives. The Bible tells us that the love of money is the root of all evil. Grandfather grieved for the church. He said, 'Our people call themselves Mennonite, but they have not all received salvation through Christ. So many do not love the Lord or obey His commandments.'

"Son, our leaders were lax. They were caught up in accumulating wealth and living the good life without opposition, without persecution. They forgot to love God with their whole heart. We were a strange people in a strange land, and the Russians did not feel kindly toward us.

"Your grandfather, my papa, was a gentle, godly man who loved and raised horses. I was nine years old when he was killed in an accident. That was in 1905, and it was a beautiful June day. He and several other men were bringing home a load of logs when the chain broke. A log slipped, Papa fell, and the load went over him, crushing his chest." Mama paused to steady her voice.

"After my papa died, my grandfather helped my mother to care for us. Grandfather was also a gentle, godly man. He too, loved and raised horses—before the war destroyed everything.

"As I said, before the war came in 1914, it was a good life. I had a happy childhood even though our village was small and poor." Mama paused.

"What was your village like?" Jacob asked.

"Our village had twenty-two homesteads," Mama said. "Most families owned only thirty, forty, or fifty acres, but before the war, we could always raise enough food to eat."

Justina smiled up at her son. "I loved our village! As a young girl I would run along the wide, dirt- packed street. This road ran east and west with the village houses close together in a row, mostly on the north side. All the houses were built the same—one long building with the barn attached to the house. Both the barn and house had thick sod roofs." Mama's smile widened.

"Garden plots were directly behind each family home, with the fields beyond those. Across the street from our houses were the school, the mill, the miller's house, and a few more homes at the eastern edge of the village. Jacob, as I talk to you I can see my parents' home so clearly! Three houses down lived our good friends, the Willens. I have often wondered what has happened to our village. Are the mud brick walls of our homes still standing? What about the sod roofs?

"But then the war came. Famine, hunger, and death were all around us. I have only one sister and brother still alive. Three years after we emigrated to Canada, they moved to Siberia. I had a dear friend, Katherina. Where is she today? Alive, or gone? So much suffering. So much.

"But I am getting ahead. As I said, our village was very poor. Everyone had to work hard to raise enough food. Before your father, Jacob John, and I married in 1919, our country experienced lawless times. The government was overthrown. It was a time of extreme suffering, constant hunger and such terror. I hope we never have to see terror like that again. Armies and marauding bandits raided our villages, taking our horses, cattle, grain, and violating human life. We were left without animals to work our fields and without food to eat." Justina quit talking and gazed into the starry heavens.

Pounding hoof beats and shouts had filled the street as bands of soldiers raided Ischalka. The neighbor had fled on horseback, trying to save his horse. But then the gunshot sounded, the horse had screamed, and the neighbor fell lifeless in the street. So much death.

A tremor ran though Justina. "Many died," she whispered. "My younger brother Gerhard died, or at least we think he did as he never returned from the forestry camps with the other boys. The memory is sharp, as if it just happened." She shook her head, as if to dispel the memory, and continued.

"Because of our non-resistant beliefs, the young men in our scattered Mennonite villages were assigned to alternative service. They were sent to work in Siberia's northern forests at Hierman Nyatchkary under the Forestry Service Commission. The Russians despised our German boys and referred to them as 'bush monkeys.'

"The Czarist government was overthrown in March 1917 and in September the Bolsheviks took over. The Russian army withdrew from its war with Germany. Law and order quickly broke down, throwing the country into chaos. Unrest reached the forestry camps. The boys feared for their lives and quickly escaped camp, hoping to reach home and hide before officials came looking for them. Jacob John was nineteen and had been at the camp only six months, and we were not married yet. He made it safely back, but not Gerhard. We assume Gerhard was caught and probably shot—we never heard anything of him again. So much sadness . . . that is why I have not wanted to talk about it."

"Mama, I'm sorry it is so painful, but you are answering questions I have been struggling with for a long time. Please go on." Jacob sat riveted to the bench. He had no idea his mother carried so many sorrows.

"Jacob, I need to tell you something. It broke my heart, and I—I have never brought myself to speak of it before. Your father—made it home alive when war broke out, but—" her voice faltered, "but it came with a price." Jacob leaned toward his mother so he would not miss her halting words.

Justina sat with bowed head. "I did not know this until after we were married, but your father did not stand true for Christ. The Russian soldiers were given first chance to get on the overcrowded trains. 'I was able to get another soldier's uniform and a paper with a blue stamp!' I overheard him boasting to some of his friends. 'I could ride most anywhere!'

"The officials were often illiterate and it didn't matter what was on the paper, or who had signed it, as long as it had a blue stamp," Justina explained. "Your father boasted of how he outsmarted the officials and the Russian people. 'No one knew I was a good little Mennonite German boy!' He had to be careful not to talk German, as the Russian people who fed him thought he was one of their boys returning from fighting the war.

"Oh, son, I was shamed and sickened by what I heard. It was then that I realized your father was a Mennonite by name, not a born again Christian. We grew up in the same village and I had never before had reason to doubt his character. He loves to talk, and you know how good he is at entertaining. Before we were married, I admired the good cheer Jacob John brought to a group by his stories. I guess I don't have to tell you, as you know fully how things are with your father." Her voice was etched with sadness.

"But God is always faithful—always, son. Don't ever forget that. I know you, too, have suffered because your father does not serve Christ. I hope you are praying for him. I pray every day for his salvation. I pray God will open his eyes and heart to his need for Christ. I have been praying for years—in Russia, and now here."

Several minutes passed in silence. Why had God allowed his faithful mother to marry someone who was not a true believer? Jacob wondered.

Justina sat in the evening quietness, gathering her thoughts. "After we married, we lived with your father's widowed mother and family," his mother picked up her story. "I was expecting our first baby and wanted to be in the privacy of our own home before its birth. Your father found other things to occupy his time, so I made most of the mud bricks for our house. He did help put up the mud walls and the roof, but I plastered the inside walls alone. I mixed pails of plaster made from clay, cow dung, and straw, and lugged them to the building site at the end of the village. Once I had our little house plastered, I whitewashed it, and we were able to move in just before your sister was born. I hoped that if your father had his own home he would take better responsibility, but the hard work almost cost me my life.

"Things did not go well for me that summer day in 1920. Both the midwife and my mother prayed, giving me into God's hand. I will never forget my mother kneeling by my bedside and praying, 'Lord, we can do nothing more. Thy will be done.' God extended His hand of mercy to me. I lived, and your sister was a healthy baby.

"Son, I remember another incident of God's mercy and loving care. The year you were born, 1922, was the third summer of drought and grasshopper hordes. We had no crops. We couldn't even eat the chicken's eggs—they tasted terrible because all the poor chickens had to eat were grasshoppers. The government ordered all landowners to go to the fields and pick up grasshoppers. We women dug trenches and buried sackful after sackful of grasshoppers in them, but it did not help.

"The men asked permission from the officials to make drags out of planks. They wanted to use horses to pull these wooden drags across the fields in order to crush the grasshoppers. Permission was granted, and the men built over a hundred of these drags. Someone would sit on the drags for weight as the horses pulled them across the fields.

"The officials designated a certain day they would bring horses for all farmers to use. Everyone was to be at the fields early in the morning when the grasshoppers were still in the ground. Round and round the field the men drove the horses and drags, scraping the land, killing millions of grasshoppers burrowed in the soil.

"We all thought this was working, but as the days of dragging continued, the more grasshoppers the men crushed, the more they seemed to multiply. We discovered that in scraping the ground to crush the grasshoppers, we were also burying the eggs so more would hatch. It was fruitless. The men wanted to give up, and finally the government officials agreed that it was not working, there was nothing to do.

"The village was desperate. But Jacob, there *was* something we could do! We gathered at our school house and prayed. You were about five months old—a strong, healthy baby even though I had no milk for you. All I had to feed you was water thickened with a little mashed potatoes.

"One day in the beginning of August, a terrible hailstorm pounded our settlement. I was afraid our roof of straw and sod would give way, but it didn't. That storm was a direct answer to our prayers. The torrents of rain washed the land clean and the grasshopper plague was over.

"Many times I remember God's mercy during those years of famine. We saw death everywhere. People were starving, beggars roamed the countryside asking for bread, but there was no bread. No wild animal was too small to snare. Gophers, crows—even rats—were gladly eaten.

"One time your father was hunting in the fields for gophers when one of his younger brothers came by and begged him for one of the gophers he had caught. 'I'm so very hungry,' he cried. 'Could you give me one of yours until I can catch one?'

"Your father gave him a gopher. Jacob, his brother was so hungry he ate that gopher raw as he walked back to the village. Such hunger!" Tears stood in Justina's eyes.

Jacob could not speak. He knew of the pain that gnawed at his insides and the weakness that made him tremble. He knew of going to bed and wondering if he could sleep because he was so hungry, but he had never eaten a raw gopher. Real hunger—near starvation—must be terrible.

But he had been hungry! Many times! And so had his mother. He thought of the times they had nothing to eat and Mama had sent him to the butcher shop to ask if they had cracklings they were going to throw away. Or the times he had asked the neighbors for their potato peelings. At one farm where he had worked, he had learned to drink milk from the cows while he milked, and to suck raw eggs. Eating what he found in the barn had given him enough nourishment to keep at his work when he did not receive regular meals. But to eat warm, raw, wild meat? No, he didn't know what it was to be starving.

"Our church leaders went to Siberia," his mother continued. "In Siberia the harvest was plentiful. They were able to bring back several railroad cars of grain. With twelve villages to feed, this did not last long, but it did help. Then the North American Mennonites sent food parcels to be distributed by someone in the village.

"Son, it saddens me to say this, but the help that came did not benefit everyone as it was intended to. Without strong faith in God, without a determination to live close to His teachings, suffering people will do things they would never think of doing before.

"Some were like Esau, who sold his birthright for a mess of pottage. Some families in our village starved while other families bragged about their fat children. But God is the judge. Someday, we will all be judged for our actions.

"In the spring after that terrible winter, North American Mennonites sent tractors for the villages to share because there were no horses left to do the work. Horses that hadn't been taken by the army or bandits had been eaten. The American Mennonites said they would sponsor Mennonite families wanting to immigrate to Canada. They would pay our passage, and after we settled in Canada we were to pay the money back. Most everyone wanted to go.

"Although your father feared rejection because he had malaria, he went ahead and applied for immigration. The Canadian government sent Dr. Drury to Russia to inspect the emigrants. Dr. Drury told your father not to worry—Canada accepted malaria patients. The doctor gave him a prescription to take to the Red Cross so he could get quinine.

"But no one else in our families was accepted for immigration. I have often wondered, why us? Why not my sister Marie who wanted to come so badly? Why not your father's brother? He was never given a reason why he was rejected.

"I didn't want to come. I didn't want to leave my family because I knew I would never see them again. I didn't pray to be accepted, but I did pray, 'Thy will be done.' Son, it was hard, but I believe our acceptance into Canada was the will of God. That is what has sustained me all these years.

"On Sunday, October 19, 1924, the Ischalka community had a

farewell service for all the families emigrating. Monday morning we left home by horse and wagon to meet the train, fifty miles away." Justina paused again, lost in thought as she relived the parting.

When the time came to say good-bye, Justina's only sister wept inconsolably. Justina held Marie close, memorizing the feel of her arms and the scent of her hair.

"Pray for us. Take these to remember that I am praying for you," Justina said as she handed Marie her precious Bible and songbook. She felt she had to be strong for her weeping mother and sister. "Oh God, give me strength. This parting is so hard!"

Justina's mother-in-law begged to keep her four-year-old granddaughter. Justina finally pulled her crying child away from Grandmother's arms and climbed into the wagon, feeling as bereft as the weeping family left behind.

Who will I go to when I need a sister or a mother to talk to, or to ask advice? Who will my daughter turn to when she has no Aunt Marie nearby?

Justina could not turn and wave as they left the village. So great was the conflict raging inside. If she looked back, she was afraid her strong family ties would draw her too strongly, and she would let her husband go to Canada without her.

"It is hard to share this, son. So many emotions are crowding me and I need to sort out what I should say," Justina finally said in a quiet voice that seemed far away.

"Thank you, Mama, I know this is hard, but please tell me," Jacob said. "What happened after you left your village?"

"We took the train to Moscow where our documents were processed and had further medical checkups. From there we took another train to the port city of Riga, in Latvia.

"When the train stopped at the Russian border check point, everyone in the train was under extreme tension—so thick it seemed we could hear it. We stood or sat like statues as the train waited. Tension pressed in from all sides, making it hard to breathe normally. I prayed that your frail baby sister would not cry out and bring attention to us as the uniformed customs officers boarded the car. I didn't worry about you or your sister sitting on the floor. You were only two, and both of you were so exhausted that you were leaning against each other in a stupor.

"To still my anxiety I began praying. I prayed for the other people traveling with us. I prayed for calm, and for God's will to be done. I prayed for the officials who were often ruthless. They might pull someone off the train for no reason at all. They might confiscate things a family treasured. As I prayed, I felt my tension leave. I could hear our baby's even breathing and marveled at God's presence. I imagine most everyone on the train was praying as the officials thoroughly, painstakingly checked each passenger.

"I'll never forget the change of atmosphere in our train car when the engine was unhooked at the Russian border and a Latvian locomotive took its place. Our train crew was replaced with a Latvian crew while the Russian Red Army stood by. The army started singing a farewell song called 'The International' when our train crossed under 'The Red Gate' that marked the boundary between the two countries.

"Suddenly, someone in our train car burst into song—'Grosser Gott, Wir Loben Dich.'[1] We had passed from communism into freedom! Tension left our car and we all rejoiced. At Riga we stayed at the air force base. The people were so kind, giving us food and clean bedding."

But the next day's rigid cleansing, delousing, and disinfecting by the British had been harsh and humiliating. Justina would not mention

---

[1] Holy God, We Praise Thy Name.

Tempered Through Trials

that awful experience to her son.

"We boarded the ship *Baltara* and crossed the Baltic Sea and the North Sea. Your father was impressed with the Kiel Canal, which crosses Denmark. At first, it seemed as if our ship would sail right into the bridges crossing the canal, but as we drew close to the bridges they would automatically swing aside, or lift up, as we passed through. It was an amazing sight. Never had we seen such a happening!

"On the North Sea a violent storm came up and most of us were sick as our ship tossed up and down on the rough water. When we arrived in England, we had to wait for eight hours at the London Bridge for the tide to come in before we could dock. From the ship, we took a train to Southampton where we went through a final cleansing before boarding our ship to Canada.

"English workers combed our hair with aluminum combs to check for lice or nits," she explained. "Every time the lady combing hair thought she saw a nit, she would snip out that chunk of hair. Ladies and children were crying, begging for mercy, as the combers were not gentle. Your father did not want your sister to suffer so he cut her hair off to the skin. Others did the same, but I did not want my hair cut off so I suffered through the ordeal. I couldn't help the tears running down my cheeks, but I didn't try to resist as some of the others did. I saw those who rebelled to the combing get slapped and tortured for hours under the combs. The English lady combing my hair would look at me with my tears and pat my cheek. I think she tried to be as gentle as she could because I sat meekly and let her do her job. But my, did those aluminum combs hurt!"

Jacob sat silently beside his mother. The hardships his parents had endured gripped his soul. He had no memory of leaving Russia. He wondered how many other things his mother had suffered that she was not telling. So many times she had stopped, lost in thought, before she told him more.

"I saw my first iceberg," she continued, her voice growing light at the remembrance. "It was towering bluish-white floating ice that glittered in the frigid ocean air.

"We ran into other storms, but not as bad as the one in the North Sea. I think it was because our ship to Canada, the S.S. *Empress of Scotland*, was much bigger than the first one. High winds drove waves over the deck during those storms at sea and we had to stay in our cabins.

"Many got seasick, and we heard reports of deaths and burials at sea, but God spared you three children. In Russia two of my siblings had died before three years of age, and many families lost more than that. God was good to me. I brought all my children to Canada and He has given me nine more.

"We lived in Saskatchewan when we first came to Canada. We traveled west by train along with 400 other immigrants after we left the ship in Quebec."

Mama paused to organize her thoughts again. She smiled as a random memory came. "I remember the heavy buffalo coat a Jewish neighbor gave your father."

"Yes, I remember that coat." Jacob smiled too. "Each winter when Dad wore it he would say, 'I would have surely frozen to death without this gift.' "

"Jacob," Mama said, "your father came to Canada with high hopes of finding an easy life, but life is never easy. The only peace in this world is found at the feet of Jesus. Your father cannot read well and says he does not understand what the Bible is saying. My father, and then my grandfather, taught me from the Bible. I love God's Word, and I thank God that you, too, have found peace through Jesus Christ.

"We have faced much hardship in Canada, but we have always had the freedom to worship God. I don't know what trials are ahead if our country is entering war. But son, be faithful to God and His Word. I would rather you die like my brother Gerhard, than to blend in with the enemies of Christ. Right now I am thankful to have ten daughters, instead of ten sons. I give thanks that my other son is only three."

Jacob was glad his sisters did not have to worry about enlistment. He had longed for a brother to share in the hard work. His sisters suffered because Dad often expected too much from them. But now he was glad his siblings were mostly girls.

He looked over his mother's darkened garden. She lovingly tended it, and flowers grew here and there among the vegetables. His mother was a special person, strong spiritually, yet tender by nature. He had always sensed that but had never put it into words before.

He rose from the bench and stood beside his mother. "Thank you, Mama, for sharing your story with me. Some of the boys my age at church believe we will be called to serve now that Britain is at war. Samuel said he wonders if we won't face persecution. He said we need to be prepared, so when and if that time comes, we are not caught by surprise." Jacob paused. "Mama, did the Mennonites suffer for their faith when you lived in Russia?"

"We suffered some, but more persecution came after we emigrated. Russia was in political upheaval and got worse. Many Russians hated the Germans. They felt we had taken land that belonged to them, and they took advantage of the unrest.

"My sister Marie married a widower with three children after we left. In 1927 they moved to Omsk, Siberia, with my mother and brother Nikolai's family. They believed the harsh climate in Siberia provided greater religious freedom for them.

"We got very few letters and the ones we got were censored. One letter my sister wrote said, 'Work is my lot on earth.' I think it was very hard for them in Siberia. We will probably never know what persecution they suffered for following Christ.

"Son, no country is safe from the enemy of our souls. Obeying God and His Word is the only place we will find safety and rest." Mama rose heavily from the bench. "It is late. Tomorrow is Sunday and morning will come quickly."

Destiny *by* Choice

"Thanks again, Mama. Yes, I need to go. I do pray for Dad and all of you." He watched his mother go inside and close the door before he untied his horse and headed back to the Myer farm. He was glad for what his mother shared, but there were so many gaps. He was sure she had only grazed the surface. Had his father's family stayed in the village? Had his paternal grandfather been a harsh man like his father? Mama said her father and grandfather were godly gentle people. How could she not have sensed the difference in their interests before they were married?

Part Three

Hardships in Canada (1924–1933)

Even though Jacob would have to get up early to chore, he was in no hurry to get home. He allowed his horse, Mac, to amble along the dark road. He needed time to think, and his thoughts went back to his childhood. He had helped his father, and he had worked and boarded at many places since he was nine years old. His mother's prayers had helped him many times. Had her faith and courage helped give him strength to do right?

"Jacob, I need some tools to fix this chair I found at the dump," his father called from the small shack behind their house where he kept the things he tinkered on. "Go over to neighbor Hans's barn and get me a wire cutter and a pliers with long pointed ends. They are in church, so don't bother stopping at the house to ask. I will tell him sometime."

Ten-year-old Jacob did as his father asked, but he felt uneasy about taking the tools without asking permission. Hans had a lot of tools and it took Jacob a while to find what his father wanted. When he returned his father was upset. "What took you so long?"

"Hans has so many tools I couldn't find them right away," he innocently answered.

His father calmed down. "You did alright." It was a bit of rare praise.

Jacob did not give the incident another thought until the third time he was sent over to get tools when Hans was not at home. Suddenly it dawned on him. The first tools he had borrowed were still in his father's tinkering shack. He had seen them the other day and asked his father if he should take them back.

"Nah, Hans doesn't need them," his father answered.

Jacob felt sick to his stomach. His father did not intend to return the tools! His father was using him to steal. "I won't go," he said, facing his tall, strong father without flinching. "Taking Hans's tools is stealing, and I won't steal for you."

His father flew into a rage. Grabbing a stick nearby, he gave Jacob a severe beating.

"Now, you *will* go!" his father panted, his face red and perspiring.

"No. I won't steal," Jacob cried through lips quivering with hurt. "You can beat me as much as you want—but I won't steal." His father didn't say anything. Instead, he walked away, but it was the last time he asked his son to "borrow" tools. Jacob had never told his mother about the tools or the beating.

The next summer, Dad hired out ten-year-old Jacob to rake hay for a neighbor whose rakes were not in good working order. The old rake had high wooden wheels and a row of huge curved teeth behind the seat. A team of horses pulled it. Jacob's job was to watch the teeth scoop up mowed hay until the rake was full, then pull the lever to leave a bunched-up mound of hay behind.

Jacob's arm ached dreadfully, but he drove those horses around the field until he noticed the tongue coming apart. Back to the barn he went. The owner gave him another rake to use, but it too had a faulty tongue. "Will this tongue hold?" Jacob asked.

"Yah, it's nailed. It's okay. Take it and get back to work." The owner waved his hand in dismissal. So back to the field Jacob went! It wasn't long until the strain of pulling heavy bunches of hay snapped the nails. The tongue broke loose from the axle, Jacob's seat dumped him forward, and the horses kept going, pulling the rake over him.

When Jacob came to, he was under a pile of hay in an irrigation ditch near the main canal. He remembered nothing that had happened after his seat tipped. Every bone in his body felt bruised. He was so dizzy he could hardly walk. But once he made it back to the barn he was met by an angry boss.

"What do you think you are doing by beating my horses!" Jacob winced at the angry voice. "Now don't talk yourself out of it. My neighbor told me what you did. You beat the horses and that sent them off toward the canal. You get right back out there and finish that field!"

When Jacob tried to return to the field, hurting not only from the accident, but also from the unjust accusation, he walked only a short distance before his legs gave out and his stomach heaved. His boss took him home, and he never did go back to that farm to work. He could have easily been killed or badly hurt, yet God had protected him.

Jacob was eleven when Jacob John had moved the family to this irrigation community in southern Alberta. School was not a priority with his father, and Jacob often got only two or three days of schooling a week. He repeated fifth grade twice as he missed so many days. Fifth grade was the extent of his school education.

An accident occurred the first summer in Alberta. Jacob was helping Dad get the seed drill ready for planting. They were trying to lift the drill when it fell off its block, wrenching Jacob's back in the process. He lay on the ground, helpless, unable to move, completely paralyzed.

"*Mein Gott! Mein Gott!*" his mother cried out in German, then fell on her knees, pleading with God to restore her son's health. When neighbors finally took Jacob to the doctor, the doctor shook his head. "There is nothing I can do to help him. Take him to Mr. Porter, the chiropractor. He is the only one I know who may offer hope."

Lying in the back seat of the neighbor's car, Jacob felt no pain. He could hear and talk but he couldn't move. They went to chiropractor's house and told him what the doctor had said.

"Let's pray," Mr. Porter replied. After prayer, he checked Jacob thoroughly and gave adjustments. Jacob rode home in the back seat of the car without showing improvement, but three days later he was able to walk. Young as he was, he knew God had miraculously touched his life.

At twelve years old, Jacob learned the ins and outs of irrigation. Farmers depended on irrigation for consistent seed germination. As soon as planting was finished, water sets for flood irrigation had to be made every six to eight hours. It was a challenge to dig straight ditches while keeping them on a slight downhill grade. It was backbreaking, yet rewarding, to gauge and control the amount of water flowing into the smaller ditches crossing the fields. Carrying a shovel and ditch canvases, and wading mud day after day under the relentless sun required stamina, but he soon learned.

Jacob had been fifteen when he approached the local police for advice. "Is there any way I can keep my father from collecting my wages?" he asked. "I need to support my mother and siblings."

"We know your father collects your wages and then disappears," the officers answered. "The law requires you to bring your wages home until you are twenty-one, but there is a legal way you can be exempted from this law.

"If you leave home for a year and are able to take care of yourself, it will show the law you are not a dependent of your father. When you return, we will make sure your father understands he cannot collect any of your wages. Then you will be able to support your family.

"Our advice is that you avoid telling people where you are going," they cautioned. "This will keep your father from finding out where you are and coming to get you. Also, don't worry that your family will go hungry. We will make sure they have enough."

Jacob studied the problem and decided to act on their advice, though it had been terribly hard to break the news to his mother.

"Mama, you will need to trust me. You won't hear from me or see me for a year," he began. His mother's hand flew to her mouth but he pressed on. "I can't tell you the details, but I want you to know I am going with the blessing of the law. Keep this information to yourself. When I come back in a year, I will tell you why this is necessary.

"Pray for me, Mama," he finished, voice husky with emotion.

Tears swam in his mother's eyes. Jacob was sure she sensed this situation was because of his father's negligence, and she did not question him. Instead, she nodded wordlessly as she put her trembling arms around him. "I will," she finally whispered, stepping back and looking up at him. "I do pray for you every day."

"Good-bye, Mama. Don't worry about me." Jacob's voice broke. "The police have promised to take care of what you need. I will be back in a year, Lord willing."

With that, Jacob left behind all that was familiar. Was he doing the best thing? Would his family really be taken care of? But it was too late to change his plans. He took the bus northwest to a little outpost named Westward Ho. He was used to taking care of himself, so striking out on his own had not seemed difficult. His biggest concern was to keep it up for one year without his father hunting him down.

Exactly one year later, Jacob said goodbye to Mr. Semen, his employer in Westward Ho, and boarded the bus for home. He had learned to respect the man who had hired him and given him a place to live. Mr. Semen had become a father figure, giving him the stability and encouragement he needed.

Getting off the bus in his hometown hadn't been easy. Sooner or later he would meet up with his father, and he did not want that confrontation to take place without the police knowing. He took Mr. Semen's advice and went directly to the police—and God took care of things. "We'll go right out and talk to your father," the officers assured him. "We have been keeping an eye on him and he is at home."

Arriving at the house, the officers said, "Jacob John Friesen, your son Jacob did not run away from home. We knew what he was doing this past year! Since he has proven he is capable of taking care of himself, you may no longer collect your son's wages or claim him as a dependent." Thankfully, his father agreed without a fuss.

While the police talked with his father, Jacob went to the grocery store and bought a hundred-pound bag of flour. Oh, the look of shock on everyone's faces when he walked up to the door carrying that big sack!

"For us?" his siblings gasped. They had never seen such huge bag of flour come in the door before. "Mama! Look at all the bread you can make."

"Yes, it's all for you!" He grinned and handed his mother the Sears Roebuck catalog. "I want you to write out an order for winter clothing. All I need is a winter coat. The rest of my wages are for *your* needs."

"This is better than when the police came when you were gone!" His siblings gathered around him. "They brought us food, and sometimes clothes, but never this much."

"Most families would be afraid if a policeman showed up at their place, but these youngsters jump for joy when one comes," his sister whispered to him.

That summer Jacob's siblings were invited to attend summer Bible school at the Conference Mennonite church in town. His mother and siblings began attending Sunday morning services. It wasn't long until his mother had told him, "These Mennonites preach and live the Bible. I wish you and your sisters would always go with these young people instead of the other group. It is sad, but the German Mennonite Church here is just like my childhood church."

"What do you mean?" he had asked, but his mother did not explain. Now he could understand what she meant. He and his sisters had enjoyed the fun-filled, rowdy evenings with the German group.

Smoking was prevalent among the boys and he had willingly joined them. *It sure wasn't an atmosphere conducive to God's people.* He shook his head in regret at the things he had taken part in before his year in Westward Ho and since his return.

But now Jacob had a place at Adam Myer's farm. It was one of the largest irrigated farms in the community, and the Myer family was part of the Conference Mennonite church. Before Adam had hired Jacob, Deacon William had given Adam a favorable report. Jacob was a good worker, dependable and gifted. Adam was pleased with his work. Jacob accepted his job as an answer to prayer. But he sometimes worried about the extra work he caused Adam's wife, Noreen.

As Jacob rode toward the Myer farm, remembering these incidents from his childhood and early youth, he thought of his mother's prayers, her faith, and her love for God. *That must be what helped me break loose from the boys I considered friends in my teenage years—friends with the wrong influence. Is God reminding me of these things for a reason? Does He want to strengthen my faith?*

He chuckled as he thought of the dump rake again. Mac tossed his head, jangling the halter as if letting him know he was listening. "Well Mac, it is one accident I don't ever want to repeat! You know all about a dump rake, don't you?" Jacob patted his horse's neck and let his reigns hang loose, assuring Mac it was okay to amble along at will.

I do enjoy living here. In the six years since his parents had moved to this community, he had rarely lived at home. Thanks to the Canadian Pacific Railroad, his parents had been able to rent a half-section with a small four-room house. The railroad company had built these small houses to put on unsettled land. Their idea was to attract settlers by offering both a house and acreage that could be either rented or bought.

"Thank you, Lord God, for answering my prayer tonight. Thank you for giving Mama strength to share her past. I realize how unworthy I am for all the blessings you give." Praise rose from his heart and trembled on his lips. No human ear heard, but the Father in heaven rejoiced to hear the prayer of His child.

"Lord," his heart cried, "save my father! How I have longed to be able to live at home like other boys, but you have had other plans for me. I have often felt my hardships are too great or not fair, but as I look back, I can see your goodness and your hand of mercy. Lord, are you preparing me for trials yet to come?"

He put Mac into his stall. *What lies ahead? Will I be tried for my faith? Tried with fire so my life will bring praise and honor and glory to God?*

"Lord, what of the problem I'm wrestling with now?" He frowned as he watered and fed his horse. "Lord, I feel you want me to wear a plain suit coat for baptism. But how is that to be?"

Mac nickered, and his ears flicked to let Jacob know he was listening, but he kept right on eating his oats.

"That's okay, Mac. Go ahead and eat, I should know better than to worry! Hasn't God always provided?"

As Jacob exited the barn, peace settled over him. He needed to trust, and God would provide a way.

Part Four

Standing for Truth (1939)

As he rose from the Sunday dinner table, Jacob addressed his employer's wife. "Thank you for the delicious meal, Noreen. I appreciate your hard work."

Leaving the big farmhouse, he made his way to his bunkhouse tucked into a corner of the yard. "Thank you, Lord, for this job." He rejoiced at the close proximity to his mother's home, and that he was able to financially support his family.

God did answer my mother's prayers! he reflected. God had provided a good place for him to work, and Mr. Semen had helped him think of the future in light of eternity and his standing with God. Jacob had needed to make choices concerning a church and friends.

It had been hard to break away from his former friends. The more he had mingled with the Conference Mennonite church, the more his actions at the parties with his German friends condemned him. Before the year was over, he knew he had to make a choice if he wanted peace. Two months before his seventeenth birthday, he had responded to the call of God during the December revival meetings. In October he would be baptized and taken into church fellowship. He did not have much longer to wait.

Jacob had tried to keep ties with his old friends after his conversion, but when he refused to smoke with them, they were determined to change his mind. "Weakling! It won't take much to break your sissy intentions!" they had boasted. "Just wait! We'll help you lose your salvation!"

Several months later he had been invited to one of their parties. He had headed to the party in hopes of giving a testimony to his old friends. *I don't consider myself better than them, but I want them to understand that God has changed my life. I am serving Him, not sins of the flesh, and I want them to seek God too.*

I sure never expected their reaction! Jacob stood at his bunkhouse window remembering the ambush. His so-called friends had jumped him along the road as he walked to the gathering. Pinning him to the ground, they forced a cigarette between his teeth. "You will smoke! You will give up your salvation!" they had hooted, expecting him to give in.

He had not fought back. Instead, he had called on God for help. He had clenched his jaws as the boys ground the cigarette into his teeth. Expecting resistance, but finding none, their fun changed to disgust, and they soon deserted him. He had returned home, sickened and saddened.

In the ten months since his conversion, Jacob was learning to know Christ. He treasured the opportunity to sit under the sound teaching of God's truth in the Conference Mennonite church. He cherished the memory of his mother's tearful happiness. She had clasped him in her arms crying, "My son, my son! God bless you and keep you. How I have prayed for this day of salvation!" Her careworn face had lit up with joy at God's mercy that day he had gone home to tell her about it.

Home. Where is my home? he asked himself now. *Is it this bunkhouse at the Myer farm? Did I leave my home in Westward Ho? Or is home the house where my family lives?*

For the past five years, he had lived with whoever could give him work and a place to live. He had grown up in many different homes. Some had treated him well and others heaped unfair work on his young shoulders. But he had survived! He had done his best and learning all he could about each job had proven to be a godsend.

"Lord," he said as he bowed his head to commune with his heavenly Father. "I would have chosen a different upbringing if it were possible. But I do thank you for bringing me to this place. Thank you for my mother's steadfast faith. Her cheerful acceptance of daily hardships has helped me choose the way of holiness."

He closed his eyes, treasuring a memory of his hardworking, uncomplaining mother on one of the rare occasions he had lived with his family. Mama sat alone by the kitchen stove, knitting a pair of socks in the dark winter night to save precious lamp oil. "How can you see?" he had asked.

"I don't need too see. I let my fingers feel by memory." A beautiful smile lit up her face as she added, "It is when I talk to my God."

Jacob pushed his nostalgia away when he realized it was chore time. He had planned to ponder the suit coat problem but time had run out. *I will think about it after church,* he promised himself, weary of the indecision.

Several weeks ago Jacob had asked Noreen about a suit coat. Three days later, she stopped him as he left the main house. "Jacob, did you get yourself a coat?"

"No, not yet."

"Wait here. I have one for you." She returned in a few minutes and handed him a coat. "It is a double-breasted suit coat. I came across it the other day and I think it will fit you. Coats made double-breasted are the easiest to change as you can cut them straight down the front and have plenty of fabric left to make the collar," she explained.

"Thank you!" He had reached out in eagerness for the suit, never suspecting he would not find anyone willing to alter it for him.

Noreen had protested when he had asked her advice later. "There is no time on this farm to change a suit! Just go without one! It's not necessary for your salvation!

"Besides, it's canning season!" she went on. "I'm sure there is not one woman in church who has time to sew. I don't know why the church didn't take that into consideration when they planned this baptism," she vented.

And she had been right. He had asked two other women in the church, but neither could do it.

Noreen's unconcern had shocked him, but the longer he worked for Adam the more evidence he saw of spiritual laxness. Money seemed to have preeminence. Jacob was used to taking care of himself, but getting a suit altered baffled him.

"I don't know what to do!" Jacob cried out in frustration. "Lord, do you want me to wear a plain coat for my baptism? Or is this just something I want to do—without your blessing? I know the church doesn't require a straight-cut coat, but Lord, you know what is on my heart." No answer broke the quietness. No bolt of lightning. Nothing but stillness.

"God is always faithful. Always." His mother's words sent a jolt through him. *If I truly believe that, then why am I so troubled?* He raked his fingers through his hair. The minutes ticked by as his soul wrestled. Finally he knelt by his bed in surrender. "God, I do believe you are always faithful. I guess my biggest fear is what I might have to do. You know of my desire to wear a plain suit for my baptism. Thank you for the suit coat Noreen gave me, but no one in church has time to change the collar and I don't know how. If you want me to wear a simple, plain coat you will have to show me what to do." He stayed on his knees, seeking the will of God, until quietness replaced his agitation. He slipped under the covers and slept peacefully.

Jacob awoke as dawn spread its finger of light across the horizon. As he stepped into the barn to begin milking, his bedtime prayer and surrender were fresh on his mind. In three weeks was his baptism. Not all the men in church wore a plain coat. Though the church taught and encouraged the importance of wearing the style that separated them from the world's fashion, many did not. "Lord," his heart communed as milk pinged into the pail. "I still feel convicted to wear this mark of distinction when I make my vows to you and the church. I know it will set me apart when I am in public, but I feel I need the reminder to keep you first in all my actions. I want to bring honor to both Christ and the church. Unless you take this peace away from me today, I will take it as your will to wear a plain coat."

Monday dawned with cloudless skies and Adam Myer itching to be in the harvest field. As soon as chores were finished the horses were hitched to the rake. The swathed wheat needed to be turned so it could dry, as tomorrow the threshing crew would arrive. All through the hectic workday, Jacob felt the steady presence of peace. When he retired that evening, he knew what God wanted him to do. He was to change the lapel coat himself.

Maybe I should have asked Mama to knit me a plain coat! Muffled laughter escaped, but he sobered as Noreen Myer's earlier statements came back to trouble him. That evening he approached Noreen with some apprehension.

"Do you have a good sewing scissors I can borrow?" he asked. Noreen looked sharply at him, started to say something, but decided against it. With a shrug, she nodded. Jacob waited in the gathering darkness for her to return with the scissors. *Surely it can't be that hard! God will answer my prayer!*

"Here is my sewing basket in case you need other things," Noreen said as she handed it to him, her expression doubtful. Was Jacob actually planning to change the coat himself?

"Thank you." He smiled as he took it, looking as if he had received a treasure instead of a woman's simple sewing basket.

He started for the bunkhouse. "Well, tonight I begin," he said dryly as he looked down at the sewing supplies he carried.

But as he held the suit coat, a feeling of complete hopelessness washed over him. *You can't do it!* the devil taunted.

No, I can't do this by myself. "Lord God, I want to wear this coat for my baptism. I'm at a loss. I need your help and guidance. Show me, Lord," he prayed.

Picking up the scissors, he looked at his big calloused hands. Cutting would be easy, but changing the lapel to a straight front with a standing band that fit around his shirt collar was not an easy undertaking. His hands were at home handling horses, using an irrigation shovel, pitching hay, or swinging an ax. Using a needle and thread to mend his clothes was not a foreign task. He had done so many times. But this—this was definitely uncharted territory!

As he studied the suit, God reminded him of the things Noreen had said. "You cut a double-breasted suit straight down and have plenty to use for a new collar." He tried on the suit, measuring with his hand how much he would need to cut off the left side to make the front centered. Taking the suit off, he laid it on his bed and measured again from what he had estimated.

"Better leave a little more so I have plenty to turn under," he murmured as he moved the oil lamp closer to the edge of the shelf above his bed.

Busy harvest days followed. Each night Jacob took time to work on his suit. Every evening it looked a little bit closer to what he thought it should look like. By the third week, he had done all but the buttons and buttonholes. *How do I make a buttonhole?* he agonized. *Oh well. Who looks at them anyway! I doubt anyone will notice. I sure don't!*

It was late Friday evening when he laid his finished suit coat on the bed. A sigh of relief escaped as he inspected his handiwork. "It does look wearable! Thank you, Lord!" Praise filled the bunkhouse as he hung it on the hook beside his Sunday shirt.

The next morning Jacob filled the wringer washer with water and started the motor, as he did each week. He was surprised when Noreen peered through the washhouse doorway. "Did you get the suit coat done?" she asked with a flush of embarrassment. She had seen his lamp burning late in the evenings and had known he must be sewing. "I can press it for you today if you did."

"Yes, it is done. I was going to press it under the mattress tonight, but an iron would do a much better job. Thank you!" Jacob answered, touched by her offer.

Mattress! So that's why his clothes looked passable for church. Noreen's mouth nearly dropped in shock. When she held Jacob's suit in her hands she was surprised at how well it looked. All sewing was done on the inside, and though it was not as a woman would sew, he had done an amazing job of leaving the outside unmarred. Once it was pressed, it would do! She shook her head in admiration, but laughed aloud at the stitches whipped round and round the slits for buttonholes. Yes, pressing would smooth out a multitude of mistakes. Was there anything this young man was not afraid to try?

When Jacob saw his mother in church that beautiful fall Sunday morning in 1939 he was filled with mixed emotions—glad that his mother was able to attend his baptism and sad that his father was not with her. It did seem as if God was giving him a special blessing. First a suit coat, and now the presence of his mother who had to walk two miles to church.

"Will you be coming home for dinner?" Mama wondered as she met him at the side door after service. "Dad is not home and the older girls are invited away."

"Yes, Mama, I hoped I could. I'm glad you could be here this morning." His mother's careworn face lit up as they moved outdoors.

Part Five

The Call to Service (1942)

Three years elapsed before the war with Germany affected every Canadian young man between the ages of twenty and twenty-four. "Did you receive your draft notice?" Samuel asked Jacob as they sought shade beneath the cottonwood trees surrounding the church.

"No, did you?"

"Yes," his friend answered as he ran his hand through his thick, dark hair. "I must return my notice by July 15. Did you know they are calling those twenty years of age first? I wonder if we Mennonite boys will get exemption as conscientious objectors, or if we will be drafted." Silence hung heavily between the friends as they contemplated the question.

"I have heard that Canada has agreed to supply a large army," Jacob broke the silence. "It doesn't make the future look too hopeful. I mean, are the officials going to take kindly to us able-bodied boys just because we believe it is wrong to fight and kill? I don't think so."

"It is facing it alone that worries me. I have heard rumors of prison, camps, labor farms, even forced enlistment," Samuel confessed. "They are bound to separate us COs."

"We needed the encouraging message Brother Hess brought this morning. 'Be thou faithful unto death, and I will give thee a crown of life.' "

"Yes," Samuel acknowledged, his voice firm with conviction, "That is my desire. The unknown future is what is hard." The two friends parted, promising to keep each other informed. Uncertainty lay ahead, but the God they served was unchanging.

Jacob thought of his mother's life in Russia. Coming to Canada had not freed her from trials, just given her different trials. His heart ached for her. His older sister had married a neighboring bachelor with a five-bedroom house. His father had lost their farm, and the family had been living with his sister. Conditions were less than ideal with two families under one roof. His mother had given birth to another girl only seven months before he became uncle to his second nephew.

Jacob had been doing all he could to purchase a two-hundred-dollar CPR house. He had saved half the money needed and one of his sisters had fifty dollars to contribute, but they still lacked another fifty. That August, the church stepped in with the needed money to purchase the house, and one of the church brethren gave his parents a rent-free corner of land on which to place their house. When fall harvest was finished, Jacob helped his father enclose the long, narrow porch, creating two more bedrooms.

Losing the farm had made Jacob's father a very angry man. Jacob's sisters became the victims of their father's verbal abuse. Outside the home, Jacob John was a sociable person. He loved to tell stories that got "better" with each telling.

Jacob John was quite skilled with his hands. He had dug wells and cased them. He built cardboard-covered sleighs to protect the family in winter's cold. He built buggies from salvaged scrap wood and iron. He could cobble worn-out shoes or boots for his children. But he did not work at repairing his relationship with his family. He did not seek to know God's peace.

Jacob grieved for his siblings. He understood their suffering and prayed for grace to honor his father. He channeled all the earnings he could spare into purchasing the bare necessities his family needed.

Who would take care of them when he was drafted? That burden was heavy. He had to remind himself what his mother had said, "I accepted it as the will of God and that has sustained me through the years." *I must do the same. God and His promises never change.* Knowing his mother now had a house she could call her own would make it easier to leave.

While Jacob waited for the inevitable arrival of his draft notice, Cornelius, a friend he had associated with before becoming a Christian, came to visit him. Cornelius shared his testimony of salvation.

"Would you be interested in studying the Bible together?" Jacob asked. Cornelius readily accepted, and several of the young men from the English[2] Mennonite church met with the new Christian for Bible study.

One day Cornelius arrived in distress. "I received my draft notice, but I don't know if it is right for me to enlist or not. Can you give me advice? My parents don't know how to advise me, but they said they thought your church had strong teaching against it."

Jacob scratched his head. Where should he start? "We do receive sound Biblical teaching through the church, but the most important thing is not that our *church* teaches against enlisting, but what *God* teaches in His Word. Would your parents consent for me to come to your place and show them what the Bible teaches?" he asked.

"They would be glad if you would come," Cornelius said. "They are the ones who told me to ask you."

That Sunday evening Jacob left to visit Cornelius and his family with a prayer for God's leading. "Open their eyes to truth," was his plea.

"I would like to begin with prayer." Jacob's request took the family by surprise. They were not used to praying aloud, even at mealtimes. But they bowed their heads as Jacob prayed aloud.

"Our Father which art in heaven, hallowed be thy name. Thank you for freedom to read the Bible and pray. Thank you for your guidance

---

[2] The German churches referred to the General Conference Mennonite churches as "English" because the preaching was in English.

as we make choices to honor you. Be here in our midst tonight as we seek answers of truth. Bless this family. Especially bless Cornelius with understanding and wisdom as he faces this grave decision. We pray in thy name, Amen."

Cornelius's father cleared his throat. His mother pushed back her chair. They looked at each other. This—this wasn't what they expected! They had never heard a young man pray like this before. He must be used to doing so. He did it so naturally and wasn't embarrassed at all.

"I told Cornelius the most important thing in making a decision about enlisting, is to know and do what God commands," Jacob began. "I haven't received my draft notice yet, but I know that when I do, I will not enlist. I want you to understand why I have decided this, based on the Word of God.

"Let's begin in Matthew 22:37 where Jesus says, 'Thou shalt love the Lord thy God with all thy heart, and with all thy soul, and with all thy mind. This is the first and great commandment.' Verse 39 says, 'And the second is like unto it, Thou shalt love thy neighbor as thyself.'

"Now, in Matthew 5:14 and 16. 'Ye are the light of the world. . . . Let your light so shine before men, that they may see your good works, and glorify your Father which is in heaven.'

"Do you see any place in these verses that gives us God's blessing to go and fight? To kill other people because they are considered our enemies?" Jacob asked.

Cornelius shook his head. The verses spoke of love and good works—not fighting.

"This is just a beginning. We could spend hours on this subject but we won't. Verse 39 instructs us to 'resist not evil: but whosoever shall smite thee on thy right cheek, turn to him the other also.'

"In verse 44 Jesus becomes more explicit: 'Love your enemies, bless them that curse you, do good to them that hate you, and pray for them which despitefully use you, and persecute you.' Jesus finishes up the chapter with the command, 'Be ye therefore perfect, even as your Father which is in heaven is perfect.' Do you find any allowance in these verses for taking another life?"

Cornelius took a deep breath. He had no idea all this was in the Bible. His church never addressed subjects like this. Is this why Jacob had not resisted when the boys had tried to force him to smoke?

"Let's look at Romans 12:19–21," Jacob continued. " 'Vengeance is mine; I will repay, saith the Lord. Therefore if thine enemy hunger, feed him; if he thirst, give him drink; for in so doing thou shalt heap coals of fire on his head. Be not overcome of evil, but overcome evil with good.'

"I have one more verse for you if there is still any question about taking part in war. Let's turn to Matthew 19. We all know the Ten Commandments, one of which is 'Thou shalt not kill.' In the New Testament Jesus gives us the same commandment. The rich young ruler came to Jesus and asked what he could do to have eternal life. Jesus said, 'Thou shalt do no murder. Thou shalt not commit adultery. Thou shalt not steal. Thou shalt not bear false witness. Honor thy father and thy mother. Thou shalt love thy neighbor as thyself.'

"Obedience to the Word of God comes after hearing," Jacob encouraged. "Obedience—even if we don't fully understand why. God will bring understanding when we yield to Him in obedience."

Jacob left their home, burdened for Cornelius. *How can a church drift so far from God's truth and still believe they are serving God?* Cornelius was confused because he was receiving the opposite counsel from an older, respected member in his church.

"I can see why your church is against enlisting," Cornelius confided, "but Isaac told me it isn't wrong to enlist as non-combatant. He said I would not be going to fight.

"And what about the benefits of enlisting?" Cornelius continued. "I'm told I will get free education and will be taught a trade. That is not fighting." Cornelius had spoken as if his mind was already made up, but then he hesitated.

"I just can't be sure which is right. What you say seems right, but how can it be wrong to enlist when I won't have any part in fighting? Maybe I will be helping the wounded, showing compassion."

"It is what God says, not man's reasoning," Jacob insisted. "If you enlist you would still be a part of the military operation. You would have to wear the uniform, which identifies you with the military. Church and state can never mix. They are opposites. The faithful church of Jesus Christ is one following after holiness and righteousness; the state is run by ungodly men.

"Jesus calls us to come out from among them and be separate. Psalms 141:4 reads, 'Incline not my heart to any evil thing, to practice wicked works with men that work iniquity: and let me not eat their dainties.'

"Cornelius, don't sell your soul for thirty pieces of silver as Judas did. Eternity is forever."

"I know. Maybe I won't go," Cornelius backed down. But he would not commit himself either way.

In January 1943, Jacob received an official letter stating he was to appear before the tribunal in Edmonton. Since he had already registered and claimed conscientious objector status, he felt this summons was the last hurdle he faced before being drafted.

Taking the bus north, he prayed and rested in God's presence. "Lord, I come to you. Grant me exemption from the military if that is thy will. But what of my family's needs if I am sent to prison? I know you promised to care for them. I do trust you; forgive me for doubting. Lord, stand with me today so I will not falter or fail. Give me the words to say that will bring honor and glory to your name."

Jacob's heart was heavy as he thought of what Cornelius had said before he enlisted. "I talked to Isaac again and he told me, 'At least you will have a future!' I know you do not agree with my choice, but I am enlisting in non-combatant service. I am allowed to come home during training and will talk to you then."

Cornelius had come home during his training. He was shaken, but resolute in his decision to return. "Jacob, there is no such thing as non-combatant training in the military. I am being trained like any other soldier. But I will never kill another human!"

Two weeks after returning from Edmonton, Jacob received his military letter. His fingers fumbled with the seal. Would his answer be the same as the one Samuel had gotten saying, NO EXEMPTION? Would he be sent to prison like Samuel? "Thy will be done," he breathed as he reached into the envelope and pulled out the single sheet of paper.

Qualified to obtain CO exemption.

His heart beat joyously, "Thank you, Lord God, thank you!"

Report to your local office on Wednesday, February 19, 1943, to obtain your four-year farm service position.

"Farm service! Praise God! But why me?" The question tempered his happiness. *Why is Samuel in prison when his life has always been one of dedication? He never did wrong. Even as a young boy his dad said he was obedient. Why isn't it me being sent to prison?*

Jacob sighed. He got upset so easily! Frustration seemed a huge battle. He fought constantly against bitterness. He did try to do right, to do his best, but God must often be grieved with his failures, his impatient thoughts and his quick temper that seemed always to be lying in wait. How he battled that!

I'm probably the only young man who needs to ask God repeatedly for grace to accept what comes and for strength to overcome. I fail so often! "Lord, I am not worthy of your goodness to me." He bowed his head, humbled by God's answer to his heart's cry.

The Canadian government paid those in farm service sixty dollars a month. He would need to give the Red Cross thirty-five dollars, but could keep the remaining twenty-five. Those who were sent to camps in the forests received fifteen dollars a month as pay to keep.

Twenty-five dollars to keep! If I save every penny I can, I should be able to help my family and still pay off my parents' debt to the Mennonite Immigration Board. The board had sent notice that all debts should be cleared by 1946, and it had been a huge burden weighing on him. Even though the interest had been reduced to three percent, and all interest after 1934 had been canceled, it still seemed an insurmountable amount to pay. His father had paid fifty dollars, but two hundred and twenty-five remained. Now, God was granting him a way to clear the debt.

Several days later Jacob had an opportunity to go home. He wanted to share his exemption status with his mother. As he drove home, a conversation with Samuel's father lay heavy on his mind.

"Pray for Samuel," his friend's father had said. "He is allowed a visitor once a month and we were able to go visit him." He had stopped talking, overcome with emotion. "Samuel told us his cell is small—four confining walls, a window too high to see out of, and a bed bolted to the floor. He said the barren room isn't so hard to bear, but the overhead speakers play songs of patriotism, immorality, and corruption for twenty-four hours a day, and that wears him out. He tries to block them out by praying, singing, repeating Scripture, or recalling sermons or Bible subjects.

"Samuel suffers from cold, lack of sleep, and not enough to eat." Tears clogged the father's throat. "Jacob, I was shocked at the physical change in him. But I was encouraged to hear him say that his prayer is, 'Lord, keep me faithful for this day.' He told me he is ready to go, and even prays for God to take him home.

"Samuel had just gotten out of the hospital when we visited him. The doctor kept him in as long as he could and even apologized for not being able to keep him longer. When he returned to his cell it was the same—damp, cold, and barren—but it didn't have the same impact as the first time he entered it. Samuel feels his sickness has drawn him closer to God. 'Dad,' he shared as we prepared to leave, 'My life is in God's hands, not man's.' "

"Praise God! I am sure that means much to you." Jacob clasped the older man's hand, promising to pray for his friend. "I covet your prayers too. I will find out on the nineteenth of this month where I will be doing my four years of farm service."

The house Jacob had helped to buy for his parents sat like a lost lump on the flat, snow-covered prairie. Not a tree was in sight to stop the drifting snow or buffer the howling winds. The weather-beaten house did not have the feeling of 'home' because he had never lived in it, but it was wonderful to know his mother and siblings had a place to call their own. Jacob pulled up to the door, immediately recognizing the faded yellow flour sack curtains at the kitchen window. They seemed to welcome him.

This was his mother's home! Home—with the same curtains and a purple violet blooming at the window. Mama could make plants grow anywhere. He smiled, wondering what the place would look like after four years. Probably Mama would plant a big vegetable garden, hardy cosmos from which she saved seed each fall, and clumps of prairie flowers or wild sweet clover she would dig up and transplant.

"You came home!" His mother greeted him at the door. How frail she looked! Yet what gentle peace radiated from her. Jacob marveled and rejoiced, knowing his mother rested in the Father's care.

"What brings you?" she questioned, searching the face of her first-born son. The son who had needed to carry heavy responsibilities since he was a small child. The son who had worked away from home more than he had lived at home. The son whom she had not been able to guide and teach as he grew to manhood. The son she committed to God each day. Had her son been drafted? Is that why he was here?

"Did you—? Are you—?" She stumbled over the cruel words that were tearing homes apart across the country.

"Yes, Mama," Jacob answered. "But do not fear, I have been granted exemption."

"Praise God. Praise God!" she whispered as she reached for her apron to wipe tears of relief. She had feared her son would receive the same notice as Samuel.

"How are things for you, Mama?" It was hard for Jacob to think of leaving for four years. "Do you have enough coal and food for the winter?"

"We will manage," his mother assured him. "It does help to live closer to town. Some of the girls have work. We will manage. It is you I am concerned about, Jacob. Four years is a long time." She searched his face as if to read his thoughts.

"I know, Mama, it concerns me too, but I am reminded of the courage Samuel shows in prison. He prays each day for strength to be faithful to God for just that day. He told his father that it is all God asks of him—to live one day at a time. I want to do the same. Samuel's example is a tremendous inspiration."

On February 19, 1943, Jacob entered the local military office to receive his instructions. When his turn came, he laid his exemption paper on the desk.

"Just what does this mean!" The question thundered across the office. Instantly, silence settled over the room of milling young men.

"It means, sir, that our government is allowing me to do four years of farm work instead of serving in the military. Sir, I cannot go against God's commandments in the Bible. God commands us, 'Thou shalt not kill.' " Jacob paused, unaware of the confident, earnest ring in his voice. "All human life is sacred before God. His Word instructs me to love my enemies, to do good to them that hate me, and to pray for them."

Jacob no longer felt alone. God's presence was with him, and ministering angels were lifting him above the hostility that pervaded the room.

Without a word the officer put his glasses back on, took up his pen, and scrawled a name on the destination line. He handed the paper to Jacob. "Your officer in charge is at the desk over there." He waved his hand in dismissal and barked, "Next!"

"Thank you, sir," Jacob said as he took his paper and turned to walk through the line of waiting young men.

Several men waiting in line hissed.

"Coward!"

"Traitor!"

"Yellow!"

Their obvious hostility ignited into action. Who did this man think he was? Well, he wasn't going to get off that easy. They would make him pay. Such cowardice! Who cared what the officers thought. They would show this coward what they thought of his stripe. He would be crawling, begging for mercy before he got to the end of the line.

A foot flew out. Another kicked him in the shins. Jacob stumbled but kept walking. Laughter erupted, egging others to take part. A fist caught him on the shoulder. Another sent his head reeling, but he did not fall. He felt supported by unseen hands, as God's presence walked with him through the fire of hatred. Suddenly, he was through the line and standing at the desk where he had been directed to go.

"Lord, have mercy on them," he prayed. "They know not what they are doing." Compassion, not hostility, burned in his heart for these young men. They believed they were giving their best by giving their lives to serve their country, yet they were blinded and filled with hatred for the enemy and for conscientious objectors.

He looked at his paper. It couldn't be! That was his hometown written on the destination line. There had to be a mistake!

He handed the officer his paper, expecting to hear the same. Instead he heard, "You will be working for a local farmer, Mr. Roth, who meets the requirements. Since we were told you support your family, we have placed you in local service.

"You will begin work immediately. I will be your officer during your service. My name is Perry and I will check up on you periodically. The first time will be within the next month or two."

"Thank you." Jacob found his voice in time to express his thanks.

Picking up his paper and his packed bag, he left the office. He could hardly believe he would be working close to home. He knew nothing of Mr. Roth except he was considered a prosperous farmer and a hard driver. To think—he should be able to attend church on Sundays!

Winter held the land in a firm grip. The bus shook whenever wild gusts of wind caught it broadside. Its motor rumbled in protest, lugging down as it plowed through deep snow drifts. Cold seeped through the frost-covered bus windows. It swept across the floor and inched its way up the bus walls and into his heavy parka.

The Roth farm should be coming up, Jacob gauged, peering out of the small frost-free area he had scratched off. Sure enough, the bus slowed as the driver downshifted. Lifting his bag from the overhead bin, he made his way to the front of the bus and up the lane to the house. Four years. Four years of service at this farm. *What will I find?*

Jacob found a crude bunkhouse waiting for him. It was neither tar-papered nor chinked. Dismay filled him as he brushed snow off the bed before setting down his bag. Wind whistled through the cracks. It wasn't hard to see that the bunkhouse had been hastily constructed with green lumber which had shrunk as it dried under the summer sun. *At least I have a stove,* he thought grimly as he started a fire. That night he woke up many times to add wood to the stove, but he never got warm under the scant covers though he slept in his clothes and even wore his coat to bed.

Employer Walter Roth was not inclined to visit. He gave Jacob his work instructions but said little else. Meals consisted of a plate of food waiting for him on the kitchen table after the family had eaten. Seconds were never mentioned, and though Jacob ate three meals a day, he was always hungry. Milking began at four in the morning and evening work concluded at seven.

Winter continued with no letup through March. Night after night Jacob huddled beside the stove, wearing all the clothes he owned, wrapped in his sole blanket. Many mornings his bed and the floor were coated with snow. The numbing cold and lack of sufficient food began to wear him down physically.

As much as he dreaded to ask for another blanket, he knew he had to.

"I have none for you," came Mrs. Roth's curt answer.

"Lord," Jacob prayed, "I know this is a small trial. Give me grace to show the Roth family the love of Christ. Keep me physically well. My body is tired and cold all the time. I feel myself weakening. Thank you for your care thus far. Thank you that I have not gotten sick. Lord God, if it is thy will, send relief from this cold."

One month after officer Perry had assigned Jacob to the farm, he came to check on him. Without the Roths' knowledge, he inspected Jacob's bunkhouse. Shaking his head at the appalling sleeping conditions, he strode purposefully to the house.

"Mrs. Roth, the bunkhouse Jacob Friesen is using is not acceptable for human habitation. I need to see immediate improvement or I will move him to another farm. Tell your husband I give you two choices. Move him into the house today or put tar paper and siding on the bunkhouse by tonight," he instructed the startled woman. "I will be back tomorrow to see that you have complied." His clipped tone and set jaw left no room to argue.

"I will tell him," Mrs. Roth replied, afraid to say more. Grudgingly Mr. Roth moved Jacob into a storage room with its own stove. Officer Perry had left him no choice and he did not want to lose his cheap labor.

That evening as Jacob lit the fire in his stove, his heart filled with thanksgiving. It didn't take long for the crackling fire to reach him with its comfort. No bitter wind whipped through this room to drive out the heat as soon as it left its firebox. Tonight he would be warm.

Several months passed. Warm weather arrived and Jacob moved back to the newly tar-papered bunkhouse for the summer months. Whenever he could attend church services he heard how life was going for other young men. He heard about Allen, a young man from another congregation. Allen had not received CO exemption and had been sent to the army. Because he refused to do any military work, he was physically mistreated and ended up in the hospital.

Jacob prayed often for Allen. He rejoiced when Brother Hess announced, "The doctor has given Allen a medical discharge and he is back home. Allen feels the doctor was sympathetic to his CO stand and this was the doctor's way of getting him home before something worse happened. We don't know for sure if that was the reason, but we do know God answered prayer for Allen's protection."

Conditions for Samuel in prison remained the same. Jacob pondered the information he had received from Samuel's father. Samuel's mother worried that he might not survive the two years, but that was easier to bear than the pain Cornelius's parents must be experiencing. Not one word had they heard from Cornelius. Was he missing in action?

Cornelius! When he had come home during military training, he had told Jacob in distress, "You were right. There is no such thing as non-combatant service. I am being trained as a soldier."

Jacob had tried to encourage Cornelius not to go back. "Whatever consequences you will face for backing out, will be worth it if you chose to follow Christ's way," he had pleaded. But Cornelius had returned to the military.

Cornelius's family received notice that he was considered M.I.A. Missing in action. Dead? Or a prisoner? Jacob felt as if a knife were plunged into his heart when he heard the devastating news. If Cornelius was a prisoner, what must he be going through?

"Why did you spare me, Lord?" Jacob prayed. "My prayers were answered so quickly and I was warm for the rest of the winter. I'm not worthy of your blessing, but I do thank and praise you. Bless Samuel, oh Lord, bless him with your presence, and relieve his sufferings, if it is thy will."

That evening Jacob told Mrs. Roth, "Don't fix me a supper plate. I received some news yesterday that lays heavy on my heart. My friend was not granted exemption from serving in the military as I was. He is in prison and is not being treated well. I want to spend the evening in prayer for him."

Mrs. Roth looked at Jacob in astonishment and nodded mutely, letting him know she would do so. Not eat supper? Give up food for prayer? Not once had Jacob complained about the scanty portions they had been dishing out for his meals. Why, Mr. Roth ate twice as much! Why would someone voluntarily skip eating to pray? Mrs. Roth shook her head in confusion.

The next morning a full bowl of hot cereal and a thick slice of bread waited for him at the table. Jacob's eyes widened, and a smile spread across his face. After asking a grateful blessing for the food he picked up his spoon and dug in. Conditions improved at the Roth farm. He almost felt guilty for having enough to eat when Samuel continued to suffer.

After three years of working for Roth, Jacob finished his last year of service with a farmer from his church. By the time his four-year term ended, he had repaid the immigration debt, been able to assist his family, and had started building his own house on a corner of land his last employer had given to him.

His thoughts were often drawn to certain young lady who had captured his heart. Wilma Weber had promised to marry him, and the wedding was planned for November 16, 1947. Lord willing, he would have a place to call "home."

Samuel survived prison. He was married the year before Jacob finished his service.

Cornelius's family grieved for their son. They had given up hope that he was alive.

Two years after their wedding, the church asked Jacob and Wilma to consider moving to Smith, a small logging town where the church sponsored a mission. The couple took it as a call from God and they were willing to go. Selling their cozy home, they packed up their belongings and infant son. On a cold December day they moved into a drafty log house in a backwoods community.

Childhood privation and hardships had prepared Jacob for the rigors of the harsh north country. He dug into the challenge of clearing land and planting crops in the virgin soil. He raised sheep in bear country. He bought a sawmill and sold fence posts to supplement their income. God blessed Jacob and Wilma with six children. By harvesting his own trees and milling them into rough lumber, Jacob was able to build a barn and a warm house for his growing family.

The mission church ordained Jacob as deacon, an office he filled for fifteen years before the Lord called them back to the community where he had lived as a teenager. The family began attending a small conservative congregation that had begun in the area. Jacob again filled the role of deacon, and preached regularly until a minister came to fill that place.

In September 1967, Jacob stood at the graveside of his mother, knowing she had reached her eternal rest. She had lived a life of faithfulness till death, and he had no doubt that she received her crown of glory.

In February 1967, twenty-four years after Jacob left to do farm service for his military exemption, his father suffered a stroke that left him permanently paralyzed on one side and with reduced mental capacities.

Jacob John was cared for in a nursing home. Jacob visited his father and read Scripture to his father from his own Bible. God's Word calmed Jacob John, and in time he looked forward to having his son read and explain the passages. Year after year Jacob read God's Word and prayed with his father.

Then came the day when he asked, "Dad, do you understand why Jesus died for you? Salvation is the only way we can inherit eternal life. The thief hanging on the cross recognized Jesus, and Christ shows us plainly that the saved go immediately into Jesus' presence after death.

"Dad, are you ready to meet Jesus? I've read you the account of Jesus' death and resurrection many times. Do you understand the plan of salvation?"

Jacob's aged father slowly nodded yes from his seat in his wheel chair.

"Dad, do you understand that you need salvation—that you need to ask Jesus to forgive your sins in order to enter heaven?"

Tears trickled down his father's face as he whispered, "Yes."

That day, Jacob left the nursing home with hope. His father had seemed to understand and had prayed after Jacob did, asking God to forgive his sins. He would need to leave his earthly father in the Heavenly Father's righteous hand. He had never known an earthly father's care.

But he had known the love of a mother who loved the Heavenly Father. A mother who had been a shining example of one who faced the fires of life with an unquenchable spirit. A mother who had brought the love of Christ with her when she immigrated. A mother who had passed on to him the peace that comes from abiding in the love of Christ. A mother who gave this testimony:

"For I am persuaded, that neither death, nor life, nor angels, nor principalities, nor powers, nor things present, nor things to come, nor height, nor depth, nor any other creature, shall be able to separate us from the love of God, which is in Christ Jesus our Lord" (Romans 8:38–39).

By God's grace, Jacob's father could now claim the same promise.

Part Six

What Future? (1996)

"Did you see the article in the newspaper? It's unbelievable!"

The comments circled the community when headlines in a southern Alberta newspaper electrified the older population.

"Imagine! Finding Cornelius's bones after fifty years."

"And by a hunter deep in the jungles of Burma."

"Isn't it something how his watch survived all those years without any person or animal taking it?"

"I thought it incredible that the hunter took the time to take it to the military headquarters in Rangoon, Burma."

The news article was passed around and talked over. The public gave approval of a memorial service being planned in Ottawa. "I'm glad he is receiving the honor due him," was the common consensus.

"At least I will have a future!" When Jacob read the news clipping, he remembered Cornelius's words, echoing over time, mocking, yet fearsome. In his memory he saw Cornelius—a strong young man standing on the threshold of decision. A young man who had chosen a "secure" future offered by the world—in exchange for his soul. A future that left him rotting in a jungle. A false security that had no substance when Cornelius stood before God, his final judge.

Every hardship in Jacob's life seemed as naught when viewed in light of eternity. He had a glorious future promised by God Himself. A future which included a crown of life if he lived in obedience and served his Master—the King of kings and Lord of lords. A future incomprehensible to his earthy mind.

Reverently Jacob picked up his well-worn Bible. His future was mapped out. He had never had to go blindly into the unknown. God had clearly given him every tool he needed to secure his future. "Praise God for saving my soul!" he rejoiced as he turned to 1 Timothy 4:10 and read Timothy's challenge to God's people.

"For therefore we both labor and suffer reproach, because we trust in the living God, who is the Saviour of all men, specially of those that believe." Turning to 2 Timothy 2, he scanned the chapter until he came to verses ten and twelve. These too, had given him courage many times. "Therefore I endure all things for the elect's sakes, that they may also obtain the salvation which is in Christ Jesus with eternal glory. . . . If we suffer, we shall also reign with him: if we deny him, he also will deny us."

What opposite futures he and Cornelius had chosen! What a vast difference. One held eternal death. The other held joy—peace—rest—and eternal life.

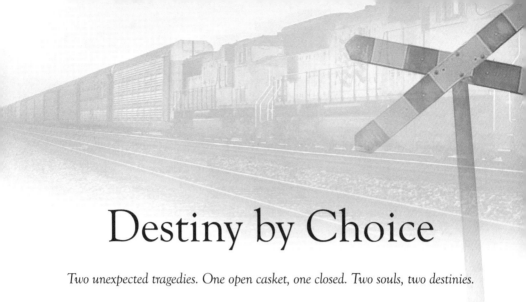

Destiny by Choice

Two unexpected tragedies. One open casket, one closed. Two souls, two destinies.

Part One
Ellen

"*Danke schoen!*"[1] Gina's gratefulness flowed across the telephone wires as she spoke in her native German language. "My heart is already lighter."

"Dear Mama Ellen," she whispered with a smile as she replaced the receiver.

"Thank you—for let me use—telephone." Gina spoke the broken English words to her neighbor as she buttoned her worn jacket firmly and left the warmth of the beautiful, spacious home. Thrusting her hands deep into her pockets, she flew down the snow-covered lane to her two children waiting on their sled beside the road.

"Mama Ellen is coming, precious children of mine!" She sighed with relief as she smothered their cold cheeks with kisses. "Dear Mama

---

[1] Thank you!

Ellen will send someone out to fix our heating, and we will soon be nice and warm again!" She smiled as their little faces brightened. How they loved Mama Ellen!

Would Mama Ellen bring a special treat for them? Maybe she would bring her picture book and read them a story in German. Maybe she would help with the work and sing the songs of their native tongue, or tell them stories of when she was a little girl. It didn't matter what she did with the children, they just wanted her to come.

"I don't like this cold." Carl's lips trembled as he studied his mother's face. Tears stung Gina's eyes as she wrapped both children in a quilt and hugged them to herself. "Soon," she soothed. "Soon we will be warm. Mama Ellen is coming right now."

Gina longed for the warm sunshine that flooded the hill country of her old home in Mexico. There it had never been cold and snowy as it was in this new country, Canada. Here, everything was strange—the language, the climate, the customs, the people. Her heart ached for her own mother and father. When would she ever see them again? *They will never leave the old colony*, she sighed. *But then neither would we have left if it hadn't been for the drought.*

"Now we are here—in Canada," she spoke softly to her little ones. "Mama Ellen is just like a mama. God is so good to give her to us, isn't He? Life will be better for us after a few years. At least that is what Mama Ellen tells me. Your papa has work here and we have food to eat," she rambled on, trying to keep them from thinking of the cold creeping in through the worn blanket.

"Mama Ellen says the winter is always like this, so we must make the best of it!" She contrasted the neighbors' modern house down the road with their own. Of course she and Henry were grateful for the protection of the sturdy walls and the four rooms furnished with bare necessities from the second-hand store or someone's cast-offs.

"Someday we will have a big fine house!" her Henry had promised, his eyes glowing. "I'm strong, and I have work. We will save, save,

save, and someday Carl and Andrea will forget we lived in a poor little shack. Why, they aren't even five yet. It won't be many years before they will be able to speak English as well as our neighbors."

Gina hugged her children tighter. *Such a good father the children have. And so full of dreams!*

A car motor broke the stillness. They all hurried to the window. High snow banks bordered the road where the snowplow had pushed back the drifting snow. It wasn't until the car nosed into the driveway that they could see who it was. Carl and Andrea squealed excitedly at the car floundering through the deep snow. Then they watched as Mama Ellen's husband Daniel backed up the car, stepped on the gas, and roared through the drift blocking the driveway.

Laughter filled the cold living room as the car zigzagged crazily. Sending up sprays of powdery snow, it came to a stop in front of their house. A truck pulled in behind Mama Ellen's car. "Who is that?" they asked in wide-eyed wonder. No one but Mama Ellen and her husband ever came to their house.

"We brought someone to fix your heater." Mama Ellen's German explanation sent relief coursing through Gina's numb body.

"You always bring hope," she whispered, her eyes glistening with tears.

Mama Ellen wrapped her arm around the young mother's shoulder, giving it a squeeze. "That's what God wants me to do," she said simply. "He wants all His children to bring hope to others."

"Come, Carl and Andrea. Mama Ellen needs a hug from two sweet children." She bent to catch their outstretched arms. Knowing the children missed their previous home, Mama Ellen tried her best to be a friend and grandmother to them.

"Now I feel young again." Her laugh bubbled and she planted a kiss on each forehead. "If Mama says it is all right, let's have some of the hot tea I brought, while the men are fixing the heater."

Ellen laid out thick slices of bread and cheese while Gina poured the steaming tea. "Henry and I woke up around four this morning. Brr! The house was so cold!" She smiled and touched Ellen's hand. "Henry and I would be sad if we did not know you and your husband. You are like a grandmother and a mother to us. Our friends who have moved here from Mexico all say the same.

"They say, 'Without Mama Ellen, no one understands what we say!'" Gina laughed. "It's true. You translate our German so the Canadians know we are not stupid people!"

"You will learn English," Ellen encouraged. "Little by little. It takes hard work, but you are hardworking."

"Do you need buns?" Gina asked eagerly, wanting to repay the kindness.

"Yes, please!" Ellen answered. "It is only a little over a week until Christmas and all the children and grandchildren will be coming. Make five dozen buns and I'll order two dozen cinnamon rolls also. Will that be all right?"

Gina nodded happily.

"That will help me so much, Gina. I hardly knew when I would get it all done! I know you're offering to do it for free, but please let me at least pay for your expenses," she said, reaching for her purse.

Daniel entered the kitchen. "The propane line was blocked, so no propane was getting to the stove," he explained. "We have it fixed and the heat is now on. You shouldn't have any more problems."

"*Danke schoen, danke schoen,*" Gina kept repeating as Daniel and Ellen prepared to leave.

"Goodbye, Carl. Goodbye, Andrea," Ellen said as she gave them each a lollipop. "Look for me in three days, after your mama has baked the buns. I will bring a Christmas story to read," she promised.

Carl and Andrea hugged the windowsill, their noses plastered against the glass as they waved goodbye. Gina stood behind them, her face wreathed in smiles and love for her friends.

"Mama, they can't go." Carl pointed to the car as its back tires spun

Destiny *by* Choice

in the snowy lane. Gina held her breath as Daniel rocked the car back and forth. She sighed with relief when it inched forward then backward, forward then backward, each time making a little more progress.

Inside the car, Ellen said, "I wish Henry and Gina's house wasn't perched on top of this hill! These high snowbanks make it doubly hard to see if any traffic is coming. I can watch the road for you if you want to focus on getting us out of the lane," she told her husband as he wrestled the car back and forth to make a packed track so they could get out.

"It's clear!" Ellen called as Daniel gunned the motor, throwing it into reverse. The car almost made it through the drift by the entrance before it bogged down. Once more, Daniel drove the car up to the house. Again, he backed up, this time gaining more momentum as he kept the tires in the packed track. The car shot through the drift.

Watching from the window, Gina and the children screamed in horror. At that precise moment, a semi-truck crested the hill, plowing into the car. Grabbing her children, Gina sank to the floor, too weak to stand. Suddenly her own screams and those of her children brought her to her senses. "Mama Ellen! Mama Ellen! No, God! No!" She sobbed uncontrollably.

Bang! Bang! Bang! She opened the door to a white-faced truck driver talking in rapid English. Gina understood "telephone" and shook her head, pointing down the road to her neighbors. The driver left. Numbness crept over her. Each breath she took pounded painfully. She held Carl and Andrea tightly and they waited, unable to tear themselves away from the window. In a haze, she saw a police car and an ambulance arrive, followed by more cars and trucks. Gina's heart felt like lead as she watched two stretchers being loaded into the ambulance and rushed off toward the city. *Can anyone live from such a smashed car?*

The news came late that evening. Gina wept when she heard Mama Ellen was gone, but her heart gave thanks to God when she knew Daniel would be alright.

"Dearly beloved, our hearts are grieving with the passing of our sister, wife, mother, grandmother, and friend. She was snatched from this world where we feel she was still needed. We are here because Sister Ellen was called home to keep her appointment with God." The minister paused. He swallowed and wiped his eyes.

"Knowing that she is in the presence of our Savior Jesus Christ where all is bliss, incomprehensible to us, gives us peace in our sorrow. Sister Ellen, or Mama Ellen as her German friends called her, has received her crown of life that God has promised to all that love and obey Him."

Tears coursed down the faces of the family, friends, and relatives sitting in front of the casket. Yet joy filled their hearts because they knew Mama Ellen was in the presence of Jesus. How different from those who die serving the kingdom of darkness.

How different from the funeral of Ellen's nephew Todd.

Part Two

Todd

"I'll get a job in hell! I'll carry water to the boys!" Todd's arrogant reply sent chills through William's God-fearing heart.

"Todd," William pleaded earnestly with the seventeen-year-old youth leaning nonchalantly on the counter in his shop. "Rethink your answer! God may honor your words.

"Where would you be, Todd, if you hadn't made it? If the careening car with its lost wheel hadn't been brought under control?"

For one fleeting moment, William saw the young man's shoulders slump, a frightened expression flitting across his face. In that short time, William sensed the young man's fear of death.

But the next instant Todd squared his shoulders and a hard look filled his eyes. "I'll never be a hypocrite!" he spat out. "Never! When I serve God, I won't be like so many others who don't live what they say they believe.

"Are you going to fix my car?" he asked evenly in the next breath as if that were the only thing they had been discussing.

"Yes," William nodded. "I will."

Todd strode from the shop, slammed the door of his borrowed pickup, and spun out of the parking lot. William could hear the floored engine as it roared out of town.

"God, have mercy on that boy's soul," he whispered. A cloak of heaviness engulfed him as the truck's roar became fainter and fainter. *How can he be so hardened?* William shuddered as he thought again of their conversation.

"Have you ever thought of what it would be like to spend eternity in a Christless grave?" William had asked him. Pain enveloped him as he recalled Todd's shocking answer. *"I'll get a job in hell! I'll carry water to the boys!"* A harsh laugh had followed, a mocking laugh that still sounded in his ears.

Young Todd knew the consequences for sin. He had been raised by parents who upheld Bible doctrine, or at least they had at one time. As a boy, Todd always attended Sunday school and church services, sang Gospel hymns, and knew numerous Bible verses and Bible stories by heart. In Todd's early teen years, their church had drifted with the world. Television entered their homes. The church encouraged its people to support, and participate in, the local sports and entertainment groups. "Think of the wide-open audience we can impact! These people need firsthand examples of what Jesus meant when He said, 'Love thy neighbor as thyself,' " was the consensus of the church.

"Dressing the same as our neighbors makes it easier for the community to feel accepted as we mingle with them," the leaders reasoned. Gradually the members traded simple, modest clothing for casual, more fashionable clothing styles.

Todd's church friends mocked the more traditional church where several of his childhood friends still attended. Even his parents held contempt for the strict rules the church people kept, rules considered too old-fashioned for the modern world.

"Customs have changed; we are enlightened. God is a God of love," they claimed. "He wants us to enjoy living in this beautiful world He gave us. How can we love our neighbors if we look and act so different? They will feel we are judgmental by setting ourselves apart. We don't want them to be offended! We must meet on the common ground of

God's love." These were the teachings expounded from the pulpit where Todd's parents attended but where Todd had stopped going.

For years, Todd heard and saw partial truth lived and spoken by his parents and the church. He saw confusion in the church because obedience to God was left up to individual interpretation. A shallow philosophy seemed to prevail in the church: "If we love God, we will want to do what God desires. And if we love our children they will want to obey us. Obedience comes naturally when there is true love!"

In time, Todd observed differences in the lives of his childhood friends compared to those in his parents' church. "Why don't we associate with each other anymore?" he asked his parents, noticing the blameless lives of those in their previous church. His parents became upset with his questions and insisted he spend less time with these people.

"Their views are too narrow. God doesn't require all that of us. Look at the love we offer our community!" Their words dripped with disdain for their "suppressed" acquaintances. Todd had complied with their wishes, but he also stopped attending church. He began running around with a group of rowdy boys from town. It appeared his parents did not care what he did. Instead of providing discipline and guidance, they determined to love him enough to overlook his faults, believing he would settle down when he was older.

Though William attended Todd's previous church, it did not keep Todd from visiting the repair shop, often bringing his friends with him. Fascinated with the shop work, he frequently came to William for help when he ran into a problem while fixing something at home. William was an able teacher and Todd a fast learner.

William was grieved to notice the change in Todd's character. Stories filtered into the shop and around town of the trouble Todd was getting into. "Is it true?" William asked Todd the previous fall, when he was in the shop. "Are you really burning neighbors' haystacks?"

"Yes, sir!" Todd boasted. "Just for fun! Did you know I'm considered the leader?"

William had used every opportunity to befriend the youth, but as time continued, Todd found less and less reason to stop in at the shop. But William's customers didn't hesitate to share their views of Todd and his friends.

"The gang is breaking into homes and stealing money!"

"Put padlocks on your gas tanks. They'll come and take gas when you are in church if you don't!" William was warned.

"Todd is the worst," was the news circulating through the community.

"Something has to be done!" The community grew upset with the parents. "The roads aren't safe anymore! He drives one-hundred plus most of the time!" Rumors ran rampant, some exaggerated but most quite accurate.

Finally, when Todd's license was suspended for drunk driving, his parents paid attention. "How will he get to his job at the Douglas farm?" his mother tearfully appealed. "He's really a good boy—just got in with the wrong crowd. It won't happen again. We promise."

The judge relented. "This license is strictly a daylight work permit. If you are caught driving any other place than between your house and the Douglas farm, it will be revoked."

Todd nodded, acting outwardly repentant while inwardly smirking. *I knew Mom would bail me out. I'm her good little boy.*

At the Douglas farm, the mid-August sun blazed down on the long rows of swathed summer wheat. Heat waves shimmered endlessly across the acres of grain with nothing to break the monotony.

"Can't see why old Douglas put me alone in this desolate field," Todd grumbled as he maneuvered the combine along the wheat rows. He reached for a can from the cooler at his feet. "Ahh! Nothing like a cold beer on a hot day!" He took a deep swig of the Budweiser he had stolen the day before. For several hours he continued combining, helping himself to another can whenever he wanted to. The second semi-trailer was nearly full when Todd shut off the combine and climbed unsteadily down.

"Can't miss the dance at Fort Jackson," he mumbled. He was hoping to be early enough to catch a ride with his friend Burt.

Fort Jackson was twenty-five miles away, but the two boys made it in fourteen minutes. Though the last of Todd's six-pack was finished on the way, the boys found plenty more at the dance.

"Get lost!" several older boys shouted menacingly. "Get back in your truck and get lost! You are both dead drunk and we don't need you here!" Burt couldn't even walk by himself, so the boys carried him to his truck and shoved him into the passenger's side. Todd took the wheel.

"Don't know what the fuss is," Todd slurred. "Gotta get home. Gotta combine." With a roar Todd flew down the road north of the river. The needle on the speedometer reached ninety. One hundred. One hundred ten. One hundred twenty. Then it no longer registered their speed. The wide gravel road dipped then climbed a hill with a river under it. Cresting the hilltop way too far to his left, Todd plowed right into an oncoming car. Metal exploded. Vehicle parts and people lay meshed together in a twisted heap. Burt groaned unconsciously. Everyone else was deathly silent.

Three lives had been hurled into eternity. The two young people killed in the oncoming car were friends of Todd and Burt. They were on their way to the same dance the boys had just left. Burt lived—scarred, crippled, and bitter.

Only three weeks earlier Todd had proclaimed those fateful words in William's shop. *"I'll get a job in hell! I'll carry water to the boys!"* Todd's boast rang in William's ears as he stood beside the closed casket. Like the casket, his destiny was sealed and dark. And it had been by his own choice.

Who Will Be My Daddy?

Dear, precious baby! How can we face life alone? Tears fell as the young mother clutched her newborn baby, sobbing softly against the infant's pink flannel blanket. Her daughter's tiny heartbeat fluttered as the baby found her breathing rhythm, oblivious to the anguish of her mother.

The tread of nurses busy with their daily routine, the muffled voices, the carts being wheeled down the corridor, a buzzer going off, a friendly greeting to someone getting a visitor—the noises created a background for Esther's mind, but they did not soothe her. Instead, they heightened her sense of being alone with little Mary Beth. Wayne did not even know he had become a father. She was forsaken—bereaved though no one had died.

"Daddy would love you! Don't you think so?" she whispered the haunting question. Would this be what it took to soften her husband's heart? She sobbed quietly as she spoke to him in her mind. *How could you just leave?*

Her bedside clock silently displayed each passing minute: 11:02, 11:03, 11:04. Suddenly the passing time penetrated Esther's grief. "It's almost lunch time!" she gasped. "I should comb my hair and decide what to order for lunch."

Pushing aside her troubles, Esther studied the tiny face cradled in her hands. Perfect mouth; long, dark eyelashes; and enough black hair to make a soft curl on the top of her head. "Precious, precious darling." She planted kiss after kiss on the velvet cheek and murmured, "I love you so much. Oh, how I love you!"

"You have your daddy's dark hair," she whispered to the infant sleeping contentedly in her arms. "I wouldn't be surprised if you will have his dark brown eyes too." She hugged her daughter protectively. *Will I be able to be both mother and father to this innocent child?*

By the time the lunch cart arrived, her tears had been dried and her husband's rejection had been pushed into the background. She was actually amazed that she could laugh and smile with other people when her heart ached fiercely for her husband. How she longed for him to return home! She had dreamed of it happening. She had fantasized his homecoming so often that it seemed the incident had taken place.

In her dreams she saw the two of them sharing the happiness she had had when they were first married. She reveled in the thought of serving God together like other happily married couples. But all she had was her dreams. It had been six long, lonely months since she had last seen or heard from Wayne.

Esther had trouble going to sleep that night. After spending time in prayer, she fell into a fitful sleep. The next day greeted her with returning discouragement as husbands came and went in other rooms.

Holding tiny Mary Beth in her arms, she reached for her well-worn Bible. "Little daughter," she confessed, "Mommy has to stop pitying herself! All Mommy gets is one big headache! We certainly don't need that, do we?

"Dear little Mary Beth, I want you to grow up knowing that Jesus is always with us. Don't you think Mommy needs to start trusting Him right now? I'm glad I can whisper my thoughts, my longings, whatever I need to say, and you will stay right beside me." A tear splashed onto the blanket, but the sleeping infant did not stir.

"Our Father which art in heaven, I need you today," she began. Raw, ragged emotions threatened to overtake her prayer, but she swallowed and pressed on. "You will have to be my daughter's Father. You know where her earthly daddy is. You know where he has been these past long months, even if I don't.

"Thank you, Father, that I can claim your promises." Her voice broke. "Help me to remember them. Remind me to apply them to my life and to teach them to my daughter.

"Wherever my husband is, keep him safe from harm." Fresh tears fell. Each heartbeat felt like a sharp twisting pain, driving a wedge deeper and deeper into her soul's peace with God. "I can't do this on my own!" she finally cried in brokenness. Feeling calmer, she continued praying.

"Father in heaven, bring to Wayne's remembrance the truths he was taught as a child. Send the Holy Spirit to bring conviction. I give Wayne to you. As much as I want him to be a husband to me and a father to Mary Beth, I pray not for ourselves, but for his salvation. My prayer is that he will find peace with you."

Esther laid her baby on her bed and went over to the window. She felt forsaken, despite the flow of traffic below, the honking horn of an impatient driver, the ambulance siren, and the people walking to and from the parking lot.

Is this how each day will be from now on? Time stretched endlessly before her. The longer she contemplated the future, the more despondent her spirit became.

Leaving the window, she opened her Bible and read John 14. "Let not your heart be troubled." She finished the chapter and began reading the next.

"Abide in me, and I in you. As the branch cannot bear fruit of itself, except it abide in the vine; no more can ye, except ye abide in me. I am the vine, ye are the branches . . ." (John 15:4-5). The Holy Spirit spoke to her: *Esther, I will be with you, but you must abide in me. Keep my commandments. Abide in my love.*

She drank in the message, reading several more chapters. Mary Beth stirred and whimpered. A bird landed on her windowsill, pecking the glass. A lusty cry broke the stillness, and Esther picked up her daughter.

That evening, Esther's aging parents and sister made the forty-five minute drive to the hospital so she would not have to spend the evening alone. "Thank you for coming and caring," she said, making a great effort to be cheerful in spite of the ache she felt as her dear family prepared to leave.

"Rest in the Lord, Esther. Don't worry. We as a family will help all we can." Her mother's compassion gave her renewed hope.

As best as she could, Esther adjusted to life as a single parent. Though her family and the church helped out financially, Esther began sewing from home as a way to provide for herself and keep herself occupied.

Mary Beth turned two, and Esther still had not received word from her husband. Even Wayne's parents did not know where he was. *Has something happened to him? How could he simply disappear?*

Their wedding picture still held a cherished spot on the bedroom dresser, in case he returned home. She wanted him to know she had not given up on him. Pausing one evening after tucking in her daughter, she gazed at the happy, smiling couple who had promised to love and cherish each other till death.

Taking the photo out to the living room, she set it on the stand beside the couch, reliving their courtship. The longer she studied the picture, the more it dawned on her that she had not really known her husband's character when she married him. She had not really known him after marriage either.

I think he always checked to see where I stood on an issue and then hurried to agree. He never stated his own convictions.

"You were quiet and reserved," she spoke to her husband in the picture. Images from their first days together at Bible school flooded her mind. She sighed, thinking of Wayne on the fringes of the group, looking ill at ease as though he wished to be elsewhere. She had felt sorry for him, and being an outgoing person, her heart had gone out to him.

She cringed as she remembered walking up to him and introducing herself on that fateful evening. "If you need a partner for this Bible quiz game, I'll be glad to help you." Esther had noticed the lost puppy look on Wayne's face, a handsome face that had caught her attention.

If she was honest with herself, she had come to Bible school in hopes of finding a boyfriend. The fact that she initiated the first conversation did not keep her from exulting in the thrill of having a boyfriend. It did not matter that she was four years older than Wayne.

Letters arrived several times a week. Her heart had quickened in gladness when he wrote that he was lonely, that he missed her tremendously and he didn't feel life had much to offer unless he got a letter from her. When he had written those words, she was so sure that he loved her.

She shook her head at how easily she had believed what she wanted to. Several months later she heard the "three little words" she longed to hear, followed by the wonderful letter telling her he wanted to get married! *Please, Esther, let's get married. I'd like to get married right away,* he had written.

Though she was caught by surprise, she was more than willing to make an ideal home for him. He was tired of the tension in his home and could not take it any longer. *Poor Wayne! If he came from a poor home situation, it is no wonder he holds himself aloof from others.*

Who Will Be My Daddy?

"But, Esther, you haven't even met his family!" her parents had voiced in concern. "And he has been here to see you only twice." She had been too dazed with happiness to listen to their concerns. She was getting married! She was to be a bride like her friends had been! She and Wayne would have a lifetime to get to know each other.

Though she did not think twice before giving her answer, it did bother her that she had not met his family. "What if your parents don't approve of me?" she asked her future husband.

"That is no problem," Wayne assured her. "They don't really approve of me as their son, so why should we be concerned about that? As I told you, there is a lot of tension in our home. But don't worry, we won't be living with them!

"You will meet them at our wedding," he added. Six weeks of planning and preparing kept Esther busy. Wayne moved to her community and she had laughed when he complained, "This wedding is taking too long. All you do is work and I never have you to myself."

"But you will!" she had teased. "What are these few weeks in light of a lifetime together?" Wayne had been extra quiet for a number of days but had not brought the subject up again. She took his quietness in stride and blamed it on his upbringing. *He'll learn. I'll teach him to communicate. I'll show him by loving him.* And she had brushed off his moodiness.

"Why didn't I suspect anything?" she asked now, in the stillness of the room. No one was there to answer, but the question continued to echo until she whispered, "I wanted to get married. Nothing else seemed as important as that. I didn't want to suspect anything negative." Her admission filled her with sadness as she recognized how shallow her relationship with God had been.

Her eyes caressed the small country home they had bought together. This house was all she had left of her shattered dreams of a happy married life.

It was exactly six weeks from the day Wayne proposed until she met her in-laws. The wedding, although simple, was everything she had always dreamed of, and she could hardly contain her happiness. Their week-long wedding trip to the mountains passed in a blur, and she remembered the feeling of wonder and joy upon returning to take charge of her own place.

"What fun I had fixing up our cozy home! Oh, Wayne," her voice trailed into the emptiness, "was it only me who loved being married? Was I so blinded by having what I wanted that I didn't notice you were only enduring our marriage? Did you find married life too restrictive? Did you leave me for the same reason you wanted out of your parental home?

"That certainly sounds harsh and judgmental," she finished sadly, "but I'm afraid it is true. I'm sure I failed too—failed in meeting my husband's expectations." Her mind returned to the days she spent decorating their home. Her new husband had not asked if she needed money for shopping, but since she had her own bank account, she hadn't bothered asking him how he wanted to take care of finances. She had simply gone out and bought whatever paper and paint she liked. She had bought new curtains, rugs, pictures and knickknacks. She had purchased whatever she wanted until each room was matched to perfection. *Oh, I asked him if it was all right after I did something, and he always agreed, but what had he really thought or wanted? How much did I contribute to his discontent?* Tormented, unreasonable guilt assaulted her.

Esther continued to gaze at their wedding picture. Five or six months after they were married, Wayne started driving a logging truck for the local mill. His hours soon lengthened and he was unable to make it home every night. He got a truck with a sleeper and began hauling long distance. Before three months had gone by, Esther routinely found herself at home alone all week. "I had a husband only on the weekends. He still went to church on Sunday, and I acted like everything was going well," Esther confided to a friend. "I was so scared someone would find out we were not living like normal married people."

Would it have helped if I had not kept silent? I certainly wish I had done things differently.

She recalled the time she had complained to Wayne. "I hate it when you are gone all week. Can't you go back to your old job?" Her husband had pretended not to hear. A suffocating silence had hung heavily between them. By then, conversation between them was almost nonexistent.

She thought of their first anniversary. Though she had spent the day alone and sad, she thought of the good that came out of it. *It was the first time I asked God to search my life, so I guess there is some good to remember.* She surrendered her life to God more fully that day, and a peace settled on her that had not left since then.

Picking up the photo, she let her mind travel back over the heartbreaking years. First it was one missed weekend, then it became two or three in a month, until he was rarely home. Then came the time he was at home for the weekend, and she could wait no longer to tell him the news—although in some ways she dreaded sharing something so personal with this stranger she called her husband. She prayed the news would soften his unapproachable shell.

"Wayne, my dear husband," she repeated the words over and over in her mind until she felt sincere. He was her husband, after all. She had vowed to love him.

"Wayne . . . I have something to tell you," her voice faltered and she tried smiling, but his stoic stare killed her smile. Her tongue seemed to stick to the roof of her mouth. Gathering courage, she rushed on. "We are going to have a baby. Won't you . . . won't you be happy with me?"

A hard glint darkened his face. Without a word he had turned from her and strode out the front door. She had collapsed on the couch, this very couch, too heartbroken to go after him. She remembered hearing a vehicle start up, but she had been too crushed with grief to rise. Later that night he returned. She heard a drawer open and close. She heard each footstep her husband made, but he had not spoken to her, and she did not have the energy to confront him.

"It seems so long ago since he walked out the front door and never returned. So long since I heard his truck motor start or his rig pull out of our lane. So very long." Esther picked up the picture, returning it to her dresser. *Oh Lord, will our daughter ever have a daddy?*

Another year passed. Another anniversary alone. Another year without any contact with Wayne. One night she was ready to retire when her telephone rang.

"Hello?"

"I'm sending divorce papers for you to sign." Her husband's voice sent chills coursing through her body.

Click. The earpiece hummed in her ear as the connection was broken. Numbness washed over her, and she never knew how long she stood holding the silent receiver in her hand. Her marriage was over. Mary Beth was just three years old. Already, her daughter had asked her, "Mommy, where is my daddy?" Esther had not been able to answer the haunting question.

Wayne had never seen his daughter. He had never wanted to. Years of emptiness stretched ahead of her. The evening of Wayne's call, she removed their wedding picture from the dresser and fell on her knees in prayer, seeking solace at the feet of her Lord and Savior.

"Lord," she confessed, "I never sought your will when dating Wayne. I took everything to be okay because I wanted it to be. I thought I was serving you because I didn't do anything bad, but now I realize that I never gave you first place in my life. The reaping is hard, but I place my life and my daughter's life into your care and keeping.

"I need your wisdom. I cannot teach and train my daughter without your guidance. Lord, direct me as I face life as a single parent. I need words of courage and comfort when Mary Beth asks the painful question, 'Who will be my Daddy?' I need her to know you have promised to be a Father and help the fatherless."

Esther clung to that promise. Though she would always carry the scars of her own decisions, she had the confidence that if she lived in faithful obedience to God, His Word, and the church, she would be a continual recipient of the joy of the Lord.

As is the case with all of us, Esther had to interpret the events of her life as best as she could. Perhaps the reader will think she was too hard on herself. Perhaps she was carrying guilt that was not hers to carry. Yet on the other hand, her story contains a lesson for all young people: Marriage is a big decision. It is never wise to rush into an irrevocable vow.

Granted, even when both parties take lots of time and ask for advice, a marriage can fail. But as Esther's story shows us, there is surely another level of regret in failed marriages that were undertaken hastily.

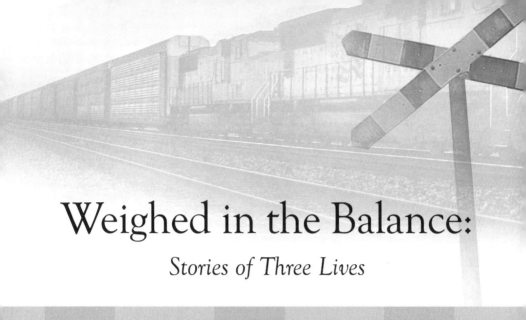

Weighed in the Balance:

Stories of Three Lives

Part One
Galen

*E*nd over end the oil truck rolled as it crashed into the steep ravine. Skidding sideways, it bounced over a dry, boulder-strewn creek bed before it slowed, coming to rest against the side of the embankment. Fresh tracks veering off the sharp curve of the gravel road were still visible in the twilight gathering over the barren mid-summer countryside.

Dust settled over the silent wreckage. The four occupants inside the mangled truck were unaware they had left the road. The headlights beamed upward at a crazy angle, alerting other travelers that something was not right.

A coyote loped across the grassland. He stopped uneasily as his nose picked up the scent of man. Sniffing the air, he swung in a wide detour around the ravine. Galen moaned, his twisted, lacerated leg trapped under the lifeless body of his seatmate. A shattered bottle had spilled its foul contents inside the cab.

Though it was nearing eleven o'clock, darkness had only begun to settle over the land. The truck's headlights dimmed as the battery grew weaker. Another truck roared along the desolate stretch of road, spewing loose gravel in the driver's eagerness to reach the next town forty-five miles away. *Don't want to miss all the fun!* he fumed. Suddenly, the dim, oddly angled light shining from the ravine caught his eye and he braked hard.

"Someone didn't make the corner!" He whistled. "Just my rotten luck! Tonight of all nights." His truck fishtailed as he brought it to a stop by the fresh tracks disappearing over the edge of the road. Shutting off his ignition, he made his way down the embankment. *Doesn't look good. Not good at all.* He shook his head, a chill sweeping over him as he approached the silent wreckage.

When the four occupants in the truck had left the oil-drilling site, they had stopped at the nearest town to cash their paychecks and fuel up on both gas and drink. Six long, hot days of drilling with nothing to relieve their thirst for alcohol—it had been nearly unbearable. Drinking was off limits at work, but with two days of free time, the young men intended to make the most it. Grabbing a cold six-pack to tide them over, they headed to the big town to celebrate. Three of the four had not grown up in homes free of alcohol. They had never been taught to consider the serious consequences of drinking and driving.

But Galen knew better. God-fearing parents had raised him in a Christian home. He had older brothers and sisters who loved him and prayed for his salvation. The young man had chosen to leave this haven for the allure of the world where he could do as he pleased.

Abandoned at birth by his alcoholic mother, Galen was placed in the Yoder home soon after birth. Love and care had been lavished on the beautiful baby boy with big brown eyes and a dimpled smile. Three years later the courts officially gave the Yoders the right to call him their son.

Galen had a happy, secure childhood. He was a respectful, quiet young boy who became a pleasant teenager, but he never yielded his life to Christ. Once his older siblings married and left home, he chafed under the house rules of his parents. *I'll never know freedom unless I live life on my own,* he decided as he enviously watched the neighbor boys doing things he was not allowed to do.

The world beckoned. Galen found a group of local young men to move in with, but friction arose. He moved again. Since Galen had been taught to work, it was easy for him to get a job with an oil crew. The pay was excellent, but the workers were rough men moving from one oil field to another. Most of them had no time for God.

Galen discovered it took a lot of money to live in the world. The only way to have friends was to freely spend money on them. Instead of finding freedom, he became enslaved. Drink crazed him. For six days he would thirst and sweat, the burning desire for a drink becoming stronger and stronger. Drunken brawling became the norm on his days off. Broke, he would return to begin six more grinding days of work, his swollen eye bearing witness that the cycle of sin was a hard taskmaster, one so opposite that of his parental upbringing.

Making his way down to the wreck, the truck driver found it hard to imagine how anyone in the vehicle could be alive. He was astonished to hear groans coming from the cab. God, in compassion and mercy, had spared Galen.

His life hung in the balance. After examining his patient, the doctor did not give Galen much hope of saving his leg, or even his life. But although recovery was excruciating, the leg was not amputated. "Galen," his family pleaded when they visited him in the hospital, "God is giving you another chance. We could be having a funeral for you instead of visiting you. Even the doctors say you should have died from all the blood you lost."

Galen had plenty of time to think. "I'll never drink again," he told his family, and he meant it. But still he was not willing to yield his life to Christ Jesus. After he left the hospital, his good intentions to stay free of alcohol evaporated under the influence of his former companions.

Today Galen makes high wages in the oil fields but has no real home, no trusted friends, and no peace with God. Galen's life is still hanging in the balance. Will he be found wanting?

Part Two

KENNETH

The yellow bows dotting the tiny rural hamlet proclaimed the unspoken message: "We support those serving in the Gulf War!"

Donning his uniform, Kenneth Sauder looked at the huge yellow bow proudly displayed in his own home. Nancy Sauder smiled bravely through her tears as she hugged her son goodbye. Broad-shouldered, good-looking, kindhearted, and dependable—this son she dearly loved. *Kenneth is all I ever wanted in a son.* Her heart beat with pride as he left home to defend his country.

"God, bring him safely home!" Her lips moved in prayer as he disappeared from sight in the airport terminal. Her brow puckered as she contemplated how best she could convince God to keep her son safe. Maybe she could convince her husband they should go to church again. Would he listen to her? Well, she would do everything in her power. And she would definitely say a prayer for Kenneth each day.

"I know." Nancy brightened. "I'll ask Harvey to pray for Kenneth. He's a Mennonite preacher. God would definitely hear his prayers!" Kenneth would surely be safe if his Mennonite uncle was praying for him. She felt relieved at the simple solution, but a sense of guilt nagged her. Would God think she was using her brother-in-law for personal advantage?

"No," she reasoned. "I hold nothing against Harvey. He and Jennifer are friendly and easy to talk to. It's just that they are so peculiar about their Christianity! It doesn't make sense to me!" Uneasiness lingered as she recalled Kenneth's questions several months earlier.

"Why is Uncle Harvey against my enlisting?" he had asked. "Even my boss is against it! But, I suppose it is because they are both Mennonites," he answered his own question when she remained silent. Nancy didn't care whether Harvey was Mennonite or not, but she thought his prayers would count for something. She asked him to pray for Kenneth.

Many people prayed for Kenneth. Uncle Harvey repeatedly mentioned his nephew's name in the weekly Wednesday evening prayer service. Intercessory prayer rose for Kenneth's soul as the saints of God banded together, pleading for his safety in the midst of a war zone—and that he could know God.

Kenneth's boss, Merlin, felt a keen loss at his absence. He appreciated Kenneth's hard work and honesty, but he also longed for the young man to find the peace that only God can give. Numerous times Merlin had steered the conversation to God. Kenneth only listened and nodded in polite agreement.

"It is the only thing he is lacking," Merlin told his wife. "In the ten months he worked for me, he displayed an excellent character."

Time moved on, and finally newspapers carried the exciting headlines: GULF WAR OVER! OUR BOYS COMING HOME! While the hamlet rang with rejoicing, Nancy vowed to invite Harvey and his wife for Kenneth's homecoming party. *After all, it is probably their prayers that brought him safely home.*

"Kenneth! We are glad you made it home again." Merlin gave his former employee a warm handshake when they chanced to meet. "We have no promise of the certainty of life, but I praise God for answered prayer in your safe return."

"I'm glad to be here," Kenneth answered, his voice husky with feeling. "I know you don't believe it is right to participate in war, and I'm inclined to agree with you now."

"Praise God!" Merlin replied. Then he asked the probing question, "How is your relationship with God?"

"Well, uh, I do believe in God," Kenneth stammered, not sure what Merlin was driving at.

"Your personal relationship, Kenneth," his former boss's voice held no reproof, only genuine concern. "Do you believe all men are sinful, and that we each need to personally acknowledge Jesus Christ as our Savior?"

"It makes sense," Kenneth answered hesitantly.

"Take that step, Kenneth. Don't delay," Merlin urged. "Don't put it off. If you know you need to confess Jesus as your Savior, do it now. Will you choose Christ today?" he asked.

Kenneth knew Merlin was right. He liked his no-nonsense approach and respected him highly. Instead of beating around the bush, Merlin came right out and said what was on his mind. Kenneth knew what he should do, but it was not as easy as Merlin suggested.

Does Merlin know what effect my decision would have on others? What would my girlfriend say? If I confess Christ, will God ask me to change and be like Uncle Harvey or Merlin? He just couldn't! What a scene his parents would make! I just can't do it right now. There are too many things at stake!

Someday, he tried to convince his conscience. *Someday, later.* Until that someday he would live a good life. Maybe that would suffice.

"Thanks, Merlin." Kenneth squared his shoulders. "I'll think about what you said."

Merlin watched the young man. He had felt the Spirit's prompting. *Now! Speak to Kenneth now!* Had he said enough? Should he have persisted? Merlin's heart was burdened for Kenneth as he continued praying for him.

Kenneth left Merlin, but a great longing to find peace with God filled his heart. *War was a terrible thing. What a relief to be home, alive! I hope I never have to go back.*

He pushed his unrest aside. Tonight his parents were having a homecoming party for him and he must get his girlfriend some flowers.

Pretty, popular Jamie would want only the best. All morbid thoughts fled when he looked at his watch and whistled. "I had better hurry! The best flowers are in the next town. I'll have to make tracks to be back for Jamie in time."

He purchased a bouquet of beautiful yellow roses arranged artistically in a sparkling crystal vase. Carefully he stowed them on the floor in front of the seat beside him where he could keep an eye on them. He eased his car into the traffic. Just before he reached the railroad crossing, the lights began flashing and the gates lowered. Kenneth checked his watch. Ten minutes left till he needed to pick up Jamie. He still had time if this wasn't a slow train. He tapped his steering wheel as if to hurry the train along, but the lights kept flashing, the bells kept dinging, and slowly a long line of boxcars started crossing the street. Then the train came to a standstill, blocking all traffic.

Motorists behind him were backing up and turning around, so Kenneth followed their example. He groaned, knowing it meant extra miles if he backtracked and took the overpass. If they were switching train cars at the yard, the wait could be lengthy.

"Finally!" he breathed in relief when he found himself free of traffic. "Hope I'm not too late!" He punched the accelerator and his faithful Mustang surged ahead, flying down the narrow country roads.

No cars coming, he thought as he scanned the sharp, upcoming curve before leaving his lane to drift over into the oncoming one. He did not have time to slow down!

He heard the flower vase fall and automatically reached over to set it up before the roses were damaged. His quick reflex jerked the steering wheel, sending him into a spin that caught the sharp drop-off along the edge of the road. The Mustang rolled over and over. Down the sharp incline it flew before wrapping itself around a tree. Kenneth Sauder lay still, crushed, with bruised broken roses strewn over his lifeless body.

"Someday" would never come for Kenneth. Someday was already too late. His life had been weighed and found wanting.

Part Three

Lamar

"Wake up! It's morning! Wake up!" the roosters seemed to say throughout the sleepy little village of Santa Rosita as sunrise tinged the still-darkened sky. Households stirred. They depended on this predawn call, which signaled the birth of the workday.

Twenty-two-year-old Lamar, a volunteer at the mission, awoke to familiar noises around him. Being the sole driver for the 600-kilometer trip to Guatemala City was weighing on him. If plans held, he would sell the full load of beans on his box truck, the proceeds covering the cost of renting a tent for the upcoming week of revival meetings in Santa Rosita.

Before leaving his room, Lamar fortified himself in God's Word and prayer. Robbery was a real threat to anyone hauling valuables, and his heavily loaded box truck held more than 6,000 U.S. dollars' worth of beans. He had hauled other loads, but never one worth this much. Fuel was expensive, and on each trip to and from the city, the missionaries took large amounts of cement blocks, medical supplies, or whatever was needed to make the trip worthwhile. It was the first time the mission was hauling beans and, given the plentiful harvest, the load was quite large. On the return trip, Lamar hoped to be hauling the new tent for the revival meetings.

Lamar walked around the truck, checking to make sure all was in readiness. *I'm glad Juan agreed to come along!* The nineteen-year-old from the village had been hired to help with the corn project Lamar had started. Hiring Juan and other young men like him had provided opportunities for establishing relationships. *Lord, may our time together on this trip help Juan see his need of a surrendered life to you,* Lamar prayed as he stowed his backpack into the cab.

"Ready?" Juan asked as he climbed in with a grin, depositing his backpack on the floor beside him. To him, it was a fun trip outside the village and he meant to enjoy every minute.

The large truck hadn't left the village when Robert, a local man, waved them down. "Hey!" he called as he strode over to the truck and peered into the cab. "Where you hiding your guns?" He gave a short laugh, knowing Lamar would not have a gun for protection. "You're hauling a money load. A real money load. Isn't safe at all without guns!" He shook his head to emphasize his feelings.

"Watch out for robbers. Anyone else with this load would have several guns before they even thought of leaving!" Though he did not understand the missionaries, Robert highly respected them, especially Lamar. He admired the way he worked to create jobs for the village boys. But this endeavor seemed risky to him. However, even if he gave Lamar a gun, he knew Lamar would refuse to take it.

"Be careful. Be on a sharp lookout," he warned as he backed away from the truck and waved.

Lamar drove to the edge of the village and then stopped. "Juan, I want to pray for God's protection. I did pray this morning, but Robert is right about the danger. I know the village thinks I am foolish, but we are far safer with God watching over us than if we had five guns." Juan nodded, and out of respect he closed his eyes and listened as Lamar prayed, asking God to grant them safety.

"And thank you that Juan is with me," Lamar finished. "Bless him too, Lord. Thy will be done. Amen."

"Eleven o'clock." Juan checked the time after they left the village behind. "When do you think we will get to Guatemala City?"

"I hope to be there before tomorrow morning's rush hour," said Lamar. "Let's see. We have four hours to Daniel's place. I told him we would stop and eat supper with him. If all goes well, yes, we should be there before heavy morning traffic."

Stopping for supper at their neighboring mission made for a welcome break. "We will travel through the night," Lamar said quietly to his older fellow worker. "I am not too worried, but robberies do happen. It is always in the back of my mind."

"I will pray for you. Trust in God. That is the most important thing we can do," Daniel encouraged the two men as they climbed into the truck.

On through the dark night the box truck labored. Because of the heavy load, the engine was maxed out. Hills and speed bumps kept them from maintaining speed for any length of time. Constantly, the danger of being robbed niggled in the back of Lamar's mind. *We do make an easy target. It would not take much for someone to pull in front of us and find out what we carried!*

They traveled mile after lonely mile through the darkness. Praying hard, Lamar fought to keep fear at bay. He knew he needed to stay awake and alert, and for that he also asked for the Lord's help.

Around 2 a.m. they ran into a construction zone. The road was completely blocked. Juan woke up enough to ask what was going on, then promptly went back to sleep. *Wish I could sleep too!* Lamar rubbed his forehead, thinking longingly of the mission bed waiting just an hour and a half down the road.

The traffic sat for almost two hours before they were allowed to move on. Juan kept sleeping. He had kicked off his shoes, and his bare feet were splayed across the floor and his backpack. *Here we come, Guatemala City! Right in rush hour traffic!* Lamar relaxed his vigil as they neared the city. *Who would dare to stop us now?*

Oh, for a bed! A yawn split his face as he slowed for a left turn. *One more turn after this. I will certainly be glad to see the mission!* Daylight was well on its way. His phone showed the time, a little after 5:30 a.m.

Just as Lamar began his turn, a car shot out in front of him, its doors opening even before the driver stopped the car. Instantly he knew what was happening. *No! Not a robbery! I'm almost at the mission!* "Juan!" he called.

Juan shot up, wide awake. "Hit them! Hit them!" he yelled as he locked the truck doors. But Lamar only melted back into his seat, unable to believe what was happening. Four men jumped out of the car with guns drawn.

"Open up!" they shouted.

Lamar unlocked the doors, and both boys were shoved to the center of the seat while captors entered on either side of them. The other two men jumped back into their car. As the new truck driver took off, the car followed.

Juan had a gun pointed to his head. He started fighting for the pistol and almost had it in his hands when Lamar realized what was happening and urged, "No! Don't do that, Juan! Don't fight." Relief flooded him when his friend listened and let the robber have his gun back.

Past the mission street they drove, and Lamar looked longingly at the mission house. Though it was a fearful situation, he felt calm. His concern was for his unsaved friend more than for his own safety. *Spare Juan,* his heart cried. *Lord, he is not ready to meet you.*

They drove around the block before the robbers stopped and ordered the boys out of the truck. They shoved them into the back seat of the car. "Heads down!" they barked. "Keep your heads down and no talking!"

Lamar tried to keep track of what was transpiring, noticing that the truck was taking off in the opposite direction from the car. With his head on his lap and a gun to his head, it was difficult to gauge the distance, but it felt as if they were going quite far. He felt the car slow down, then stop. Lamar and Juan were jerked out of the car beside a deep ravine.

"Get a move on!" The two captors prodded harshly as the four plunged down the ravine. Reaching the bottom, they were ordered to lie down. Lamar lay on his back, hoping he wouldn't be told to lie face down, but that was not to be. Turning onto his stomach, he cradled his head in his arms, grateful when he was allowed to stay that way.

What a secluded spot! Lamar thought of possible reasons why their captors had brought them to such a remote spot, none of which were encouraging.

He thought of Juan lying beside him. *If I could only talk to him! Lord, help him to think of you.* Suddenly an idea came to Lamar. "Can we pray?" he asked out loud, hoping his question would get Juan thinking of his soul's need.

Then after a moment: "Yes." The reply sounded harsh and rude.

Immediately Juan started praying. His words were not loud enough for Lamar to understand, but he knew God heard. Fervently, Lamar prayed for his friend. He prayed for himself, that he would be faithful, and that if God willed, his life could be spared. He prayed for his family, knowing the shock it would give them to hear about his capture. He prayed for the mission workers, for their protection and faithfulness. Finally, difficult though it was, he prayed for his captors.

Lamar thanked God for being with them in this uninhabited ravine. He could hear Juan praying on and on beside him. Far above him, he heard traffic. Resting in a deep inner calmness, he committed their lives to God.

"I will be praying for you," his friend in Ohio had told him when he had been home for several weeks in January. More names came to him—people from church, family, friends, and loved ones. He clearly recalled each promise of prayer for him. His heart quickened with thanksgiving as he clung to the promises. He wasn't alone! His loved ones at home were praying! Daniel and his wife were praying, and he knew other mission personnel were praying for him regarding this trip. In boldness he spoke aloud to his captors again.

"Gentlemen, I would like only two things. Could I please have my Bible and my billfold?" No answer came, but then he didn't really expect one. Mentally he surrendered everything to God. His passport, credit cards, driver's license, everything he needed to be able to stay in this country or to get out of it—everything was in his billfold. He rested, knowing the situation was in God's hands.

Time crept by before the captors got a call and talked rapidly. "Get up!" they suddenly commanded, and the two stiffly complied. "Your truck is empty. You are to wait here forty-five minutes. If you go before that, someone is watching and will get you," they warned.

In a more congenial tone, one said, "Because you did not fight, the Boss said we should let you live. He says if you fight, we are to shoot. The Boss says you will find your truck at this location," and they passed on the information before hiking out.

Lamar thought of the warning Robert had given him in the village before he left. How useless a gun would have been! It would have probably cost him and Juan their lives instead of protecting them. What if he had listened to Juan when he had yelled, "Hit them! Hit them!"

"Thank you, Lord, that I chose your way of peace. Thank you for your protection and care." Lamar's soul rejoiced. *I was ready to die, but I am thankful to be alive!*

Since Lamar and Juan did not know the time, they waited for a while before climbing cautiously out of the ravine. Once they reached the road, they stayed hidden in the brush, just in case they were being watched. Lamar noticed that Juan was gingerly picking his way through the bush and realizing his friend was barefoot, he offered him his shoes. "I have socks to protect my feet and you have nothing." Juan gladly took them and put them on.

"A taxi!" Juan yelled, and both boys dashed from the bush to the road. The taxi stopped, but locked his doors as the boys approached.

"What happened to you?" he called, seeing them out of breath, noting the missing shoes and their roughed-up appearance.

"We've been robbed," Lamar replied. "Could you take us to the MAM mission?"

"Get in." The taxi driver unlocked his doors. "I am taking my daughter to school, but I will take you there after I do that. My daughter speaks English. Tell her what happened," he instructed. So Lamar told her about the robbery and she relayed the information to her father.

Once they were at the mission house, Lamar told the driver to wait until he went inside and got money for fare. "My billfold is in the stolen truck," he explained.

Lamar found Larry Martin, the mission administrator, and told him what happened. He checked the time. Only two hours had passed since they got stopped, the longest two hours of his life.

After paying the driver, Lamar called Daniel to inform him of the robbery and their safety. He then gave the phone to his administrator who was waiting to make a call. "I'm calling Ed," Larry told Lamar. "Having a national brother with us when we fill out a report will certainly be helpful."

Ed met them at the police station. Once the report was completed, Lamar expected the officers to take charge but all they said was, "We will not look for the truck until tomorrow."

Disheartened, the men left the police station. "The robbers gave me information about where they parked the truck," Lamar told Ed. "Do you think we should go check it out?"

"Yes, let's go," Ed agreed. The two men drove away in Ed's car, finding the truck exactly where the captor had said. A white car was parked in front of the truck, but it drove away when they stopped, and neither thought anything about it. Lamar stayed in the car while Ed checked to see if the keys were in the truck. As he was checking, the white car drove by. A man opened the window and pointed a gun at Ed.

"Guards," Ed said breathlessly as he slid back into the driver's seat of his own car and pulled out onto the road. "I'm sure they are guarding the truck."

After they returned, the administrator called the police and informed them the truck had been found, but that the robbers still had guards stationed there. "Go back to the vehicle again. We will be there to meet you," said the police. So back they went, with the police writing up a notice that the truck was found. When that was done, Lamar opened the truck door and spied his Bible and billfold on the seat. With a glad heart, he retrieved them and headed for the mission.

"Thank you, Lord, for taking care of us! I can replace my clothes, but I would be in real trouble without my documents." Juan was not so fortunate, as both backpacks were missing, and everything Juan had brought along was in his backpack.

When God weighed Lamar in the balance, he was found ready and complete in Christ. Someday, each of us will be weighed. Will we be as the ungodly ancient Babylonian king, Belshazzar, who was weighed in the balances and found wanting? Or will we hear the words of Jesus, "Well done, thou good and faithful servant . . . enter thou into the joy of thy lord" (Matthew 25:21)?

Trust–Prayer–Praise

*M*ary picked up a towel, gave it a sharp snap and pinned it to the wash line. *What a perfect August morning!* Happiness bubbled up inside her until even the humdrum task of washing the family's mountain of dirty clothes took on new meaning. *Fifteen more days and I will be Mrs. Truman Yoder!*

Dreams of the future were constantly invading her thoughts, even when she should be concentrating on the job at hand. Reaching into the basket for a clean piece of laundry, she pinned it to the line while mentally checking over her wedding work list.

> *Wedding dress: pressed and hanging in the closet*
> *Wedding cap: sewn*
> *Table decorations: all completed*
> *Wash early on Monday*

"That job turned out easy! It is not even 8 o'clock and I am almost finished!" Mary felt a mixture of relief and satisfaction at the progress. More work was planned for this week but there was no reason to rush today.

She spied a row of birds sitting on the roadside telephone wires. Laughter rippled across the yard as she imagined the little birds gathered to serenade her as she hung out the wash. *Who knows! Maybe they feel my happiness spilling out. Maybe this is their way of letting me know that they, too, are thrilled with all my plans!*

She laughed in merriment, but then sobered. Her hands grew still while she studied the morning choir. *No doubt about it, those birds are singing their hearts out. I know they are praising God! As my beloved says,* "Prayer and praise should be a part of our faith and trust in God."

She paused to reflect on the implication of those choices. *I know if I sing as heartily as the feathered choir, my mind won't have time to race from one thing to the next.* She thought of a verse in Psalms. "But I will hope continually, and will yet praise thee more and more" (Psalm 71:14).

A prayer filled her heart. "Thank you God, for leading me to a godly man. I want to be a faithful wife and live each day with a song on my lips and a prayer in my heart."

Gazing up at the birds, Mary remembered how a visiting minister had expounded on the Sermon on the Mount recently. His remarks had left a deep impression on her.

"We are far better than birds and flowers!" he had said, referring to Jesus' familiar words. "God knows each of our needs. It is as if Jesus is saying, 'Why do you even doubt my care for you?' We need to examine ourselves. Do we have faith? Do we trust God in all things? We can't be praising God and doubting Him at the same time. It doesn't work!"

She had asked Truman, "Am I doubting God when I feel incapable to be your wife? I am only eighteen, so young and inexperienced, and I don't always feel good enough for you."

"It is the devil trying to put a wedge in your happiness, Mary. The devil does not want us to begin a home where Jesus Christ is the Head. It takes faith and trust on our part to live above doubt. I believe that if we are committed to prayer, God will give grace. Mary, make a conscience effort to live each day in prayer and praise. Just as faith and trust are a choice, so are prayer and praise."

It had been easy to agree, but harder to put in practice. She found herself struggling in her commitment. God clothes the grass of the field; did she trust God to provide for her in the same way?

"Trust needs to happen in the big and little problems we face," Truman had encouraged. "Trust will produce prayer and praise in our lives!"

"God in heaven," she prayed. "I do want to trust you in everything. I want to praise you and be a blessing to those I am with." Mary forgot the little birds as she communed with the Father, committing the coming event to God.

Her mind skipped back to Truman's promise of last evening. "I'm working only this week, then I plan to take off and help with the wedding preparations. Everyone tells me Amish weddings require a lot of work!" He grinned. "I plan to heed the advice of my elders as I have no prior experience!"

Mary scooted the laundry basket under the clothesline, causing a dark trail in the heavy dew. *Snap!* Another towel joined the parading line of clean flapping wash. Mary's smile grew as her nimble fingers increased their tempo. A light wind blew merrily, causing the clothesline to sway back and forth while the laundry fluttered erratically. How she loved the sounds of washday!

Suddenly, a premonition of danger swept over her. She looked around. No one was outside. She couldn't explain her uneasiness, but it held her firmly, gripping her with urgency. *Pray! Pray for Truman! Pray now!* She heard the inner command as clear as if a voice had spoken right beside her. She grabbed the clothesline overhead with both her hands. Bowing her head she cried out, "Is Truman in danger? Oh God!

Something is not right. Be near to him. Watch over him! Protect him! Oh God, please spare him from harm!" Tears filled her eyes. Her heart pounded. She labored to breathe as a heaviness pressed in on her. Weakness claimed her limbs. "Be merciful. Spare him," she cried out.

What if God took Truman? Is that what is happening? "Oh God, I don't know what is going on! Lord in heaven, I know you can protect him and keep him safe. But Lord!" Tears ran down her face as she struggled to surrender her will for God's will. "I . . . I . . . this is so hard! Lord God, thy will be done," she finally whispered in brokenness, feeling as if her dreams were being shattered. "The cost, Lord, you know what is best, but the cost, I don't know how I will bear it. Help me, Lord, help Truman, but thy will be done."

Time stood still as she clung to her Savior. Calmness replaced her turmoil. Her heaviness lifted and she gazed heavenward. *God is up there. God knows what the future holds!* As tears streamed down her face, she suddenly felt bathed in God's love and sweet peace filled her heart. "It is going to be alright. I feel it in my heart," she whispered as she took in the familiar surroundings.

Once more, she bowed her head and prayed, "Thank you, Lord God. Thank you for hearing my prayer and giving me this peace. Thank you for being with Truman . . ." Awe filled her heart at the realization that God loves His children enough to speak to them through His Spirit. That knowledge gave her confidence that God was in control of whatever lay ahead.

Meanwhile, twenty-year-old Truman Yoder accompanied Willie Schrock to the job site where they would put shingles on the roof of a chicken barn. A bare electric wire was strung overhead, and to warn visitors of danger, an eight-inch CB antenna was welded firmly in the middle. It had been the first thing they noticed when they pulled into the chicken farm on Friday. Willie had laughed at the farmer's ingenuity.

"Guess it beats the cost of replacing a bare wire!" Truman's employer remarked.

Today, though, Truman had other things on his mind. *My last week of work for a while,* had been his first thought when he awakened this morning. *With such a busy week, time certainly won't drag!* He checked his watch—a few minutes before 8 o'clock. It was nice to get an early start.

Pulling an extended aluminum ladder off the ladder rack, Truman headed for the chicken barn. Behind him, Willie grabbed a non-extended ladder, and followed.

Walking behind, Willie saw blue flames arc between Truman's feet. In horror, he looked up to see the aluminum ladder caught against the live wire. Truman clutched the ladder, shaking steadily but unaware of what was happening. He seemed welded to the ground as securely as the little antenna was welded to the bare overhead wire.

At that instant, an unseen power released Truman's grip on the ladder. He crumbled to the ground as the ladder fell in another direction.

"Truman! Truman!" He heard his name faintly, as if called from a distance, though it was being shouted. Panic vibrated through the crisp morning air. "Truman!" He heard his employer's urgent voice closer and louder, but he was too weak to answer. "Truman! Answer me! Answer me!" The frantic summons aroused him, and he looked up.

"W-h-a-t?" he asked thickly, trying to rise. Willie grabbed him in relief and helped him sit up. In a few moments he was able to stand on trembling legs. Feeling his strength returning, he declined Willie's invitation to sit down.

He saw the ladder lying on the ground and remembered the bare wire. "I hit it, didn't I?" His voice still sounded thick.

"Yes, I thought you were gone." Willie shook his head before letting out a long, slow whistle from where he was examining the ladder. "I had forgotten all about the wire. Truman, come look at these grooves! The wire burned a good inch and a half into the ladder! It had to be held in the wire's grip for a good second." He whistled again as he gazed at the damaged ladder and then at Truman.

"This defies all logic. I mean, this should have killed you. When I saw the blue arcing flames between your feet I thought it was over. Usually, a person is pulled into electrical currents like this, not thrown away from it. Praise God, you were thrown out and the current was broken! Praise God you are still alive!"

An hour later when the couple talked by phone, Truman was awed to find out that his Mary had been praying for him at the very time he was at the brink of death. "I don't know what God has in store for us," he shared with Mary, "but where He leads I want to follow. The choice to trust God, to be instant in prayer and praise, holds a deeper meaning than ever. I am thankful God spared my life and I am thankful God saw fit to answer your prayer."

Mary's heart was full and overflowing. "Maybe God wants to show me, a young bride-to-be, how powerful prayer is," was her soft answer. *It seems God wants to instill in me the need to pray for Truman,* was the thought too precious to share with her soon-to-be-husband. *Maybe someday, but not now.*

It took Truman a long time to recover from his ordeal. He felt he never fully got back his previous zest. A specialist told him, "When you were thrown from the ladder you had a fifty-fifty chance to live. It depended on which pump your heart was using. One would not have started up, but the other would. Your heart was on the right pump at the right time. God had a purpose for you to live."

God did have a purpose! As the couple dedicated their lives in service to Christ Jesus, prayer and praise were an integral part of their walk with Him.

Living the Dream

Mark Nines looked over the sea of faces waiting for him to share his story of how he and his family came to know Jesus Christ as Lord and Savior—or, as he liked to say, "became Biblical believers." He wished to present more than his life story. He wanted to challenge the audience to live a life separated from the world. Opening his Bible to his theme verse in Romans, he began.

"My desire today is to glorify God, to be a living sacrifice for Him. I deeply appreciate Paul's instruction in Romans 12. 'I beseech you therefore, brethren, by the mercies of God, that ye present your bodies a living sacrifice, holy, acceptable unto God, which is your reasonable service. And be not conformed to this world: but be ye transformed by the renewing of your mind.'

"It is only by the grace of God that I am able to stand before you and share what He has done in my life and in the lives of my wife and family. Joining a church is not enough. We must have a changed heart and a living, personal relationship with our Lord and Savior. Nominal Christianity teaches salvation. They stress the importance of being saved and attending church, but they fail to teach the importance of separation from the world.

"Their message is one of false hope: 'You don't need to give up your worldly entertainment. God is not asking you to wear modest clothing. The old cultural command for a woman to wear something on her head is not expected for today. Denying yourself of things you love is bondage! God wants you to live in the freedom of His love. Only believe in Jesus Christ and you are saved!'

Mark paused to look over the audience, noting several rows of young men seated to his left. *God, help me speak your truth tonight,* he prayed inwardly, and continued where he had left off. "I was taught to believe this worldly form of Christian teaching. My mother was almost seventeen when I was born. She was a devout Methodist believer while my father didn't believe anything. He had no dealings with God. He loved alcohol and women, and his life was wrapped up in the things of the flesh. In spite of that, he gave me a great gift. Let me explain.

"Mom wanted me to be baptized. She was devastated when her pastor gently informed her, 'We can't baptize your baby because your husband is not a member of our church. We baptize babies only if both parents are members.'

"My father became a member of the Methodist church so I could be baptized. To me that was a great gift. In the seventh grade I had my confirmation ceremony and joined the church.

"My wife Susan was raised in a staunch Catholic home. In eighth grade she, too, was confirmed and joined her church.

"After meeting Susan, I attended her church occasionally, and I would ask her about some of her church's practices and why they practiced them. 'We have always done it that way,' she would answer, never questioning their many rituals. I wanted to know the reason why they were important. That search took us deeper into the Word of God."

Mark told of the close relationship he had with his mother's parents while he was growing up. Because he dearly loved them, he chose to go with them to the early eight-thirty morning service. By going, he got extra time alone with his grandparents. Mark's mother and his three siblings came for the nine-thirty Sunday school and the later service, so he stayed and attended those services with them as well. Because of his devotion to church attendance, the older women in church felt he would one day be a minister.

He smiled. "Maybe it will shock you when I say I am a pilot. To be a pilot in the aviation world is referred to as 'living the dream.' The general public considers it a great life. You get to fly all over the world. Our friends and acquaintances viewed us as being high on the social ladder, but they saw only the outward appearances of a young couple. They did not see the void in our hearts. By God's grace I am now living for Him, not living a dream. I have kept my job as a pilot, flying for Delta airlines out of Detroit, Michigan.

"In my upper teens and early twenties I turned away from the teachings of God. As a young boy, I had been exposed to things in the bars my father frequented, things that boys should never be exposed to. Mom would send me into the bars to find Dad, and while she waited outside in the car with my younger siblings, I tried to get him to come home. Sometimes my father refused to come out. He would buy me a Pepsi and tell me to wait with him. I would sit at the bar and drink my Pepsi while he had his beer."

In the audience, seventeen-year-old Craig Yoder found it hard not to squirm. He schooled his emotions, making sure his face was a mask even though he was sure his neck was turning red. This Mark Nines was getting personal. Turning away from the things of God, indeed. Was that all adults thought about? Where did youth and fun enter in?

Did the ministers suspect him? Did they hear anything of his week-end activities? Was that why they had asked this tall, forceful speaker to come?

No, they don't know a thing! I have been careful. Craig tried to appear relaxed, determined not to let the speaker get under his skin. *After all, you're only young once, and might as well enjoy it! Just because he is past his prime doesn't give him the license to condemn us.* Craig tried to dismiss the guilt he felt as the speaker's words bored into his soul.

"Over time my parents' marriage dissolved. One evening I went to the bar to spend time with my dad. I went with the intent of sharing a drink with him, and it was not a Pepsi. I got drunk, and as I stumbled from the bar that night, my father thought happily, *My son is just like me!* But when I arrived home, the pain on my mother's face told another story. *My son, my first-born, is going to run the same track as his father.*" Mark's voice cracked at the memory of his mother's countenance.

"I repented verbally to my mother and never again spent time with my father in the bar. But though I repented verbally, I did not leave alcohol alone. Why do I mention this? Because it is so easy to become involved in the sin of alcohol. You take a little, you dabble in it some more, and before you know it, you are hooked."

Craig clenched his jaw. Never! He would never get hooked. He would drink only enough to be accepted by the gang of carpenters he worked with.

Mark went on to say that when their children came, he and Susan gave up alcohol for good. Though some of his co-workers ribbed him about his teetotalism, he found it opened the door for him to tell them about living as a true, committed disciple of Christ. People respected him for it and it gave them a good taste for Mark's church. Inwardly, Craig found himself respecting Mark's actions.

"During my time away from God, I worked as a lifeguard at a swimming pool," continued Mark. "One of my duties was to walk around the pool making sure all was okay. I came upon two girls sunbathing on the upper deck. I had already met Lori, one of the two girls. The other girl was Susan, and that was the first time we met. I found out Susan was engaged, and I didn't pursue anything, but in my last year of college we met again. She had broken her earlier engagement and we began dating. We married the fall after my graduation and settled in West Virginia, where I took a job at the local airport as flight instructor.

Craig sat up straighter as Mark told them how, before marrying Susan, God saved his life twice. The first time was when he was practicing a solo stall just after he had learned to fly, and the other time was while he was riding his motorcycle. Craig hated to admit it, but the speaker certainly held his attention. He had come expecting to listen to a preachy know-it-all, but instead he was hearing the speaker elaborate on his close shave with death.

Though only seventeen and quite inexperienced, Mark had loved speed and was thrilled to be flying by himself. One evening he had time to take up a plane after he finished his duties of washing, cleaning, and fueling all the aircraft used that day. He was excited at the chance to practice a stall. He was intently focusing on the instrument readings, making sure he was doing the correct procedures.

"The plane entered a full stall, meaning the nose dropped straight toward the ground," Mark explained. "I broke out of cloud cover to find the ground rushing up to meet me. Cows grazed peacefully in my shadow, and I saw the propeller give one lazy turn and then another. I was at a much lower altitude than I thought, and on top of that, the engine had quit! Death stared me in the face. I was seventeen years old and had seconds to correct my error.

"As you see, I am here tonight." Mark smiled at his audience before continuing. "God had His hand on me that evening. I pulled the throttle back to idle position. The propeller started windmilling, the engine caught, and I skimmed just above the scattering cows and started climbing. Was I living my life for God that evening? No, I wasn't, but God in His great mercy looked down on me and saved my life."

Craig felt his arms tingle. *Seventeen! My age!* Without thinking about it, he was listening to a man of God speak, and he was not closing his mind to the message as he usually did.

"Another incident that impacted my life was, again, one where God intervened. I became a disc jockey for our local radio station before moving on to a rock-n-roll station. I loved my work, and I got caught up in the harsh, beating rhythm of ungodly music. But God said, 'Enough! I want you out of here!' And how did God send that message to me? By having my boss fire me for playing too much rock music on a rock-n-roll station! It sounds impossible, but that was the reason he gave. It was a low point for me. I did not understand it was God's mercy upon my life.

"When I asked Susan to marry me, we faced a major hurdle. She and her parents wanted the wedding to take place in a Catholic church, and to appease them I agreed to it. Her priest said he would marry us even though I wasn't a Catholic, but not unless we took premarital classes. When we were almost through with the classes, he told me I needed to sign a paper saying I would raise our children in the Catholic faith. I told him I can't do that. Maybe I was not living perfectly, I told him, but I was not going to lie.

"The priest was not at all happy with me and insisted that unless I signed, he could not perform the ceremony.

"I told him we would get married in the Methodist church, but he backed down and said only Susan has to sign the paper. I told him it is up to her if she wants to sign, but that our children would not be raised Catholic. Susan did sign the paper, with the knowledge that she was promising to do her best to raise her children according to Catholic teachings.

"I had warned Susan that if she married me, we would be moving around quite a bit as I gained experience in flying. My goal was to become a commercial pilot, flying overseas with a major airline, but I had a long way to go to reach that goal.

"We made four moves in the first two years we were married. One month after our second move to a different town in West Virginia, the boss at the airport went bankrupt. There I was with no job and Susan was expecting our first baby. Once again God intervened. I was asked to run the airport, which included a trailer house on the same premises where we were living. I had taken business management in college, and I knew how to fly an airplane. One mechanic stayed, so he and I took on the job of running the airport.

"We found we needed to generate more income. I made a down payment on a twin-engine airplane in Oregon with plans to bring it home and do charter flying. The mechanic and I flew out to Oregon to bring it back, but while checking the plane over, he found birds' nests in each engine and metal shavings in the oil filter. The plane's owner had flown the plane to where we met him, and unknown to him, the nests had been sucked into the engines.

"My mechanic insisted I should not buy the plane. Where was God in all this? I had withdrawn savings to pay for our trip and the down payment.

"The owner reluctantly refunded my payment by check, but it bounced. Now what should I do? We lost the chance to earn more income, not to mention the savings we had withdrawn.

"Then I got a phone call from a glider group that had used the airport in previous years. 'I'm calling to confirm our reservation in February,' said the voice on the phone. At first I was clueless, but I played along, asking them for their information to make sure we understood each other. They complied, and when I hung up, I had all the information I needed. A group of approximately thirty-five to forty gliders came every February for two weeks. My airport provided the best location for turbulent winds and gliding.

"We would get reimbursed for electricity, camper hookups, and the use of our airport. When I found out a local restaurant was going out of business, I purchased their equipment and we sold meals to the glider group. When the two weeks were over, we had made enough to keep us afloat for six months. God had blessed us tremendously. However, before the six months were up, I received a better job opportunity.

"A coal company that used our airport offered me a job flying one of their planes. To be closer to their company, we moved south to Summersville, West Virginia. While there, I gained experience flying a larger turboprop aircraft. About a year later, the coal company that employed us was bought out by a larger Tennessee company. We made plans to move to Bristol, Tennessee, but that door closed. God had other plans for us." Mark paused and looked out across the audience. "God wanted us to turn from sin."

Craig listened intently. *This man wasn't even a Christian, but he sure rolled with the punches!* Craig thought of how he exploded when things did not go as planned. Ears burning, he remembered how he had lashed out at his dad that very evening. He wanted to stay home. What would his crew buddies say when they found out he had attended church? Now he was here, listening and intrigued. The speaker continued.

"I contacted a Comair pilot I worked with while I was still a flight instructor. 'I'm looking for another flying job,' I told him. 'Does your company have any openings?' Then I got a call. I had two interviews as well as a job offer with Comair in Cincinnati. Three days later I was offered an opening in Pennsylvania. Not one, but *two* job offers in three days' time!

"We decided on the job in Pennsylvania so we could be closer to our families, and I would be operating familiar aircraft. Susan stayed in West Virginia and I went to Martinsburg, Pennsylvania, to receive more flight training for a turbo prop, the same aircraft I had been flying in Summersville, West Virginia.

"I knew it would be difficult to find a house. I wanted my family close, and I didn't want a long commute. The town of Martinsburg put out a weekly paper, so I went to see if I could buy a paper. It was almost closing time, and they let me buy the next day's paper that evening. God planned for us to move to Martinsburg. He planned for me to buy the paper a day early. You're probably asking, 'How can you say that? Did you ask God for direction? Were you following Him?'

"Bear with me while I explain. The reason I know the merciful hand of God was leading us is that there was only one house listed for rent in the whole paper. I called the number and said I wanted to know about the house they had for rent.

"Right away the lady wanted to know how I found out about the house so quickly. I told her I bought the paper a day early and would like to come out to see the house that evening if it suited them. She gave me directions and invited me out.

"The house for rent was close to the airport and owned by an Old Order Mennonite family. It was my first encounter with Old Order Mennonites. I rented the two-bedroom house, and Susan and our little daughter Eva joined me. Our landlord's family, whose house was only fifty yards from ours, impacted our lives tremendously in the ten years we lived next to them. We became friends and I spent hours in conversation with my landlord. He showed me many truths from the New Testament, such as nonresistance, modest dress, and living daily for God.

"Growing up in a patriotic family, I had planned on enlisting with the Air Force because I would get free flying lessons. Money was almost non-existent in our home, so that was a big draw for me. Mom was deeply opposed because she feared I would die in combat, and in the end I did not enlist. God put that opposition into my mother's heart. But nonresistance was a new concept to me, and it took a while for me to understand and accept God's teaching on this.

"Another teaching I struggled with was living daily for Christ. I went to church on Sunday—wasn't that all God required? Can you understand why I say God planned for us to move to Martinsburg? Like the rich young ruler in Matthew 23, we found out the most important thing in life was loving God with all our hearts. It all started with the influence of our landlord and his family."

Suddenly Craig's bench seemed extremely hard, and the air felt stifling. It was all he could do to sit motionless and act unconcerned. He focused all his concentration on Mark Nines, willing himself to relax.

"On our first Sunday in Martinsburg, we went to the only Methodist church in town, only to find out it was the last service they were having before closing. Our plan had been to continue alternating attendance between the Methodist church and the Catholic church. I asked my landlord, and he suggested a Mennonite church in town whose members drove cars. We began attending. It was more conservative than the Methodist church in some areas, but we were never challenged to change our dress or get rid of our television or jewelry. Today we would say they were a nominal Mennonite church, as they had lost many Scriptural teachings and practices.

"An older gentleman had come to serve as interim pastor. Finding out he came from West Virginia, only twenty miles from where I was raised, we struck up a friendship. When he found out we had attended for seven years already, he asked why we had not become members. I described our situation and told him about our different upbringings.

"He asked Susan if she had made a personal commitment to Jesus, and she asked him what he meant. It took a while for Susan to think differently from what she had been taught as a Catholic, but as the pastor gently showed her Scriptures, she understood and received Jesus as her Lord and Savior.

"He prepared us for baptism along with another couple who were also of different religious backgrounds but had been attending the Mennonite church. I had been studying the modes of baptism and felt strongly that believer's baptism meant immersion. It was a new concept to the Mennonite church, but they agreed to baptize us by immersion. On a beautiful, eighty-degree July day, near a gently flowing creek beside a church member's manicured lawn, we received water baptism as believing adults. In the sanctuary of that peaceful setting, we could sense God was leading us.

"As a co-pilot for U.S. Air, I was doing a routine landing one day as the captain communicated with the airport. Summer afternoons at this airport were often hazy, and I happened to glance up as I brought the aircraft around. Right in my path, in our airspace, were two helicopters. With no time to talk to the captain, I pulled back on the yoke and turned abruptly. Keeping the throttles up, I went over the helicopters.

"The captain hollered frantically, as he had not seen the choppers and did not realize we almost had a mid-air collision. While I circled again and landed, he got on the radio, reprimanding the two pilots in the helicopters. When our passengers disembarked, a few of them voiced their displeasure of our flying. One said, 'Next time you do aerobatics, why don't you let us know?' I wanted to say, 'We were saving lives! You should be thanking me!'

"Even though the passengers did not realize it, God definitely had His hand of protection on us that day. What if God hadn't made me look up at that second? How many times does God reach out His hand of mercy to us and we are not even aware of His salvation? Are we like the unhappy passengers, complaining about the rough bump they experienced, when in reality the bump made the difference between life and death?"

Craig's thoughts took off. Had God shown His hand of mercy the previous winter when he encountered a patch of black ice and narrowly missed getting hit by oncoming cars? He remembered the helpless feeling when he veered into the other lane, but he had never thought of God's hand being present in his near-accident. He pushed the unsettling questions away. He didn't want to miss what Mark was saying. Maybe he would think about it later.

"During our last four and a half years in Martinsburg, I worked for Northwest Airlines. I was constantly making the two-flight commute to and from Detroit. I spent a lot of time waiting at airports for available connecting flights, often on Sundays. God began speaking to me. I wanted to honor the Lord's Day. We could move to Detroit, but I had been there often enough to know I didn't want to be right in the city to raise my family. We now had three children, two daughters and a son, and they were another reason I wanted to spend more time at home.

"I asked God to show us if He wanted us to move to Detroit. I decided to put out a fleece like Gideon did in the Bible and ask God for confirmation. I told God that if I get the second position on a DC-10 aircraft, I will know we are to move. To get the second position of co-pilot was unheard of, given my limited seniority with the airline. Third position, yes, but not second. It takes ten to twelve years of seniority with a major airline before you are offered that job. Yet I knew God is a God of miracles, and He would arrange it if He wanted it to happen.

"Two months later God said, 'Here is the job you want.' I was awarded the last co-pilot opening at that time. The reason I got the job was because most pilots didn't want to give up their summer vacations to go to training. I was moved at how God had done the impossible for me.

"When our minister heard of our plans to relocate, he suggested Archbold, Ohio. A large Mennonite community existed there, and it was only an hour-and-a-half commute to Detroit. After Northwest Airlines told us they would pay all moving expenses, hotels and everything, we felt it was time to go. As we drove through Archbold on Route 66, we liked what we saw. The cleanliness, the trees, the surrounding farmland—both Susan and I sensed God's affirmation: *You are home.*

"I needed housing for my family and was looking for a place with some acreage to raise horses or beef cattle. Driving north out of Archbold, I spotted a 'House for Sale' sign. I glimpsed a small barn and a pond beside the house. A teenage boy was in the drive washing his truck. When he heard I was interested in buying the place, he

Destiny *by* Choice

took me through the house, although his parents were not at home. I liked what I saw and made an appointment to bring Susan back that evening when his parents were home.

"That evening we found out they, too, were Mennonites. Before we left, the owner and I shook hands on the deal, and thirty days later we moved in.

"We started attending a Mennonite church and found many differences from the one in Pennsylvania. Women were in the ministry. The head covering was nearly non-existent. Divorce and remarriage was freely accepted. Living beside our landlord and his family in Pennsylvania for ten years, we had learned Scriptural principles and doctrine in God's Word. I shared some of my questions about this new church with Tyler, one of the members.

"I asked how they can keep Sunday holy if they eat out. He replied indifferently that the restaurant staff would work anyway, but I was not satisfied with his answer. He knew I was not in agreement with the church, and one day he told me about a men's retreat held by the Dunkard Brethren in Michigan.

"That February I attended the retreat along with Tyler and two of his friends. One of his friends was a Dunkard from Archbold who invited me to revival meetings their church was holding the following week, and we as a family attended several evenings. We enjoyed those services, but were not ready to commit ourselves, so we church hopped. We visited a house church, a Baptist church, a Dunkard Brethren church, and a few others. Fall revival meetings were being held at the Dunkard Brethren church and we again attended. One evening I asked my young daughters what they thought of the sermons at the meetings. They told me that they loved them and that, unlike many of the sermons in other churches, they could understand them!

"This was news to me, and I pondered the sermon we had just heard. Though simple, it was somehow profound. One of the evangelist's questions had made an impression: 'Is your prayer closet used enough, or do you have cobwebs and spiders in your prayer closet?'

"We kept attending the Dunkard Brethren church and seeking God. In time, we knew this was where we were to be. Neither of our daughters was baptized as a believer, only sprinkled as a baby in the Methodist church. Because the Dunkard Brethren emphasized a specific form of baptism—dunking three times while facing forward—we joined our daughters in baptism.

"Joining with a Biblical church brought many changes in how my wife and daughters dressed. We knew about modest dress from living beside the Old Order Mennonites in Pennsylvania, but we had never developed a conviction to do so until now. The devil made it hard for Susan. She had short hair and didn't know how to put it up. Our daughters helped her, but it was a daily struggle.

"Our minister's wife encouraged Susan to put her covering on and then pray, asking God to help her comb her hair in the way that will bring honor to Him. Susan did that, and in time she learned to do her hair without our girls' help.

"Because their best friends from the previous ten years dressed simply and modestly, our daughters did not find the changes in our new church to be a hardship. But Susan struggled with the change, often crying out to God, 'Is there not an easier way? Is there not a right way somewhere in between?' "

Tears stung the back of Susan's eyes as she relived the chasm she had had to cross. She looked over the assembly of ladies listening intently to her husband share their journey. Did they have any idea of the differences between their upbringing and hers? The practices and teachings she accepted as normal were opposite from what they had been taught from childhood up.

Why would someone raised to know and love Jesus Christ adopt the world's practices such as wearing jewelry or discarding the head covering? It was hard for her to understand why some of her Mennonite acquaintances were doing just that.

She prayed that everyone in the audience would experience, as they had, the blessings of obedience to Jesus Christ. A tear escaped, and Susan took a deep breath as she wiped it away. *I pray each girl in this audience will live a pure, holy life without scars of sin. Will Mark tell the part I am so ashamed of?*

She and Mark had become parents six months after they were married. It was a shame she had only recently disclosed to her daughters. After sharing many tears and hugs, she had encouraged her daughters to keep themselves pure.

Susan focused her attention on her husband, who was speaking about how she gave up jewelry. "We had honeymooned in Hawaii, and you could get guaranteed genuine pearls from a large tank of oysters. I told them I wanted two pearls as earrings for my wife. They were some of Susan's favorite pieces of jewelry.

"One day before we joined the Dunkard Brethren church, and before Susan wore a head covering, she was out mowing and had to drive under a low tree branch. *Whoosh!* The branch ripped off one earring. She stopped and began hunting with one thought: *My earring from our honeymoon! I've never lost them before!* But she could not find it. Getting back on the mower, she started mowing around the tree from the other direction when, *Whoosh!* The branch snagged the other earring. Both earrings were gone. Susan felt God was telling her to get rid of all her jewelry, including her wedding ring, and let her beauty come from her spirit instead, as Peter's epistle teaches women to do.

"Susan's mother was upset when she found out we had taken off our wedding rings. My wife assured her our love was as strong as ever and that we were committed to each other without wearing the rings. Susan also told her about the peace we felt in the decision.

"Serving God with our whole heart has created conflict with our families, especially Susan's parents. Someone even accused us once of killing Christmas. No Christmas tree? No Santa Claus? These are supposed to be the center of the celebration.

"When we changed our clothing styles, Susan's parents thought we had joined a cult. They tolerated us, expecting us to return to being 'normal' people. After twelve years, they now believe we are sincere, and even my mother-in-law is slowly changing her thinking. They have heard us pray audibly before meals. They have seen us turn off their television when we come as a family. They know we do not watch it or have it in our home.

"Though my father continues to live an ungodly life, he also accepts our decision. One of the past Christmases we were in my home area. On Christmas Day, I arranged to meet Dad, but icy weather prevented it. Since that was the only day that had suited him, he called my sister and asked her if she could meet him at a bar where he would give her money to distribute among the family as presents.

"As a single lady, my sister was stunned by Dad's request. She asked him why I could not meet him at the bar instead. My father responded, 'Mark would not be caught dead in a bar.' Hanging up the phone, my sister turned to me and fumed, 'I'm a Christian too! Why does Dad think I can go into the bar but you can't?'

"I can say without feeling arrogant that their response was a testimony of God's work in my life. There is a difference between 'Christian' and 'Biblical believer.' Sadly, though Dad sees and respects the difference Christ has made in my life, it has not impacted him enough to accept Christ as his Lord and Savior. I have a deep burden for our families. Before God, nothing is hidden or covered. Each one of us is accountable for what we do or don't do."

Glued to his seat, Craig felt weak. Had he been asked to stand or move, he would have found it difficult. Nothing hidden. God knew all about him. He felt as if the audience saw his sins parading before them.

"We are thankful our families see Christ in our lives, and our prayer is that they, too, will personally know Jesus Christ as their Lord and Savior. We are nothing without the blood of Jesus. His words are the truth.

"Our family needs your prayers. Especially pray for our son. He is being tested and needs to make a choice. He is asking, 'Is this way the only right way? Do we have to give up all the world to follow Jesus?'

"Those are important questions—questions we need to ask ourselves. Do I run from the things of the flesh? Am I willing to give up all for an eternal home? In the Gospel of Luke, Jesus asks us what profit there is in gaining the whole world if we lose our soul in the effort.

"Brothers and sisters, youth—I wish I could stand before you and say I have always been victorious since I have followed Jesus Christ. But I can't. I have slipped. I thought I had reached it all when I became a Biblical believer. But I coasted, neglecting to pray and feast on God's Word. But praise God for His convicting Spirit!

"Praise God that His mercies are new every morning! We can never coast. We need to continue until our last breath. Never allow yourself to think differently. People are watching our lives and, most import- ant, God is watching.

"God may ask you to give up something you thought was important. I mentioned in the beginning of my talk that my goal was to become a commercial pilot with a major airline and fly overseas. I accomplished that goal. I would leave Detroit in the evening and fly to Amsterdam. From there I would go to India, where I would rest a day before return- ing to Amsterdam and either Washington D.C. or Miami, then on again to Amsterdam before returning home. Sometimes I was away from my family for twelve days. I would also miss attending church services for two Sundays in a row. Then God convicted me. Could I give up my dream? Was I willing to work in a lower position? It meant fewer hours and therefore lower pay, but I could have more time at home and Sundays off. I had to choose.

"Patiently God showed me the tradeoff: dollars or rest and worship, the American dream or peace and eternal riches. When I put it in that light, the answer became plain. I no longer fly overseas, and I am home on weekends. Over 9/11 there was another cutback, and since then I have stayed with the smaller aircraft. Was the decision easy? No. Is following Christ always easy? No, it isn't, but Jesus said that no one who puts his hand to the plow and looks back is fit for the kingdom of heaven. We must accept the cross along with the crown.

"Are you giving up the idols of this world for the riches of heaven? Remember, it is only by God's love, His mercy, His grace, and the precious blood of Jesus that I can share this testimony. 'Amazing grace! How sweet the sound that saved a wretch like me! I once was lost, but now I'm found; Was blind, but now I see.'

"This is my favorite song, and my prayer is that each one here will claim the same mercy and victory, and sing with joy the testimony of this song."

As Craig left the church house, he felt as if he stood at the crossroads. The wide, well-traveled road glittered with false dreams of fulfillment but ended in destruction. The narrow way of the cross led to an eternal, heavenly refuge. There were only two choices. He alone would have to choose.

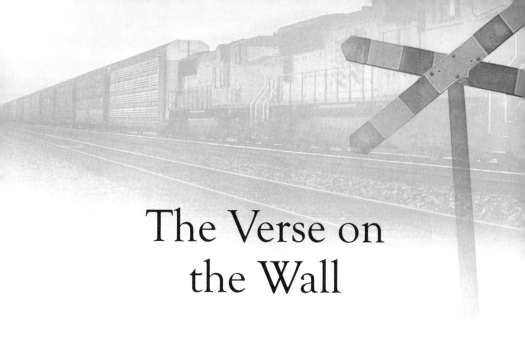

The Verse on the Wall

"Mom, I need to know this is what God wants for us. I need confirmation. I'm worn out!" Amy's voice broke as she talked to her mother on the phone.

Sara could offer little comfort other than to continue listening. The stress of moving, breaking ties with dear friends, the unknown future—all of it seemed like a steep, rugged mountain to her daughter and son-in-law, Don. Feeling God's call to move to another community, Don had advertised their property the first week of August. The next day an interested party came to look at it, but they had still not purchased it. School was set to begin in five days, and Don felt their four school-aged children should start their studies at home, using the curriculum from the community where they hoped to relocate.

"Our children love going to school, Mom." Amy's words drew her back to the present conversation. "What if we homeschool and end up not moving within the year? We don't have confirmed buyers for our place. We don't have another house waiting for us. Don doesn't even have a job there yet!"

Amy's fears were real. Her mother understood them, and her heart ached for the family. "Amy, I have no answer but prayer," Sara began.

"But Mom, I *have* been praying!" Tension edged her daughter's words as tears slipped down her cheeks. Hadn't she come in brokenness? Didn't God know her heart was inclined toward Him? It seemed He did not even hear her prayers. *Maybe He doesn't*, she thought dully. *Maybe my failures are standing in the way.*

"We need to pray without preconceived ideas," her mom's voice continued. "It is so easy to pray for God's leading when we already have a solution in mind."

"Mom! That's why I'm praying! I don't know what God wants for our family!"

"Hear me out," her mother stated kindly but firmly. "We must commit everything into God's merciful hand. Then we need to thank God for answering because He *will* answer."

God will answer. We need to thank God. Her mother's words pounded in Amy's ears.

"Amy, God knows you need to sell your place. He knows who is going to buy it. He has a place waiting for you. He also has a job for your husband. Keep packing, keep trusting and preparing, then when the day comes to move you will be ready. When worry and fear hit you, claim the promise of His care and trust Him. That is living our faith."

Silence hummed across the distance, and Sara thought the connection was broken. "Amy, are you still there?" she asked.

"Thanks, Mom. I had forgotten about thanking God before our needs were supplied. Our needs were consuming my thoughts. I thought I was giving all to God, but then I would find myself struggling with all these fears again and again."

Sara rejoiced to hear strength returning in her daughter's voice.

"Remember, I will be praying for you every time I think of you and the family, and that is almost all the time!"

Throughout the following days, mother and daughter prayed many prayers of thanksgiving and trust. Peace replaced Amy's fears. Two days before school began, Amy experienced a deep, settled peace about homeschooling their children. It did not matter anymore that she did not know when they would move. She knew with certainty that God was in control.

She and her girls packed in earnest. Two more weeks rolled by. Walls and closets were stripped. Cupboards were emptied and filled boxes piled up without a place to go. Many times Amy wanted to panic, tempted to worry about the "what ifs," but each time she clung to the promise—*God will answer prayer. With Him all things are possible.* She took her fears to God, thanking Him for supplying her family's needs.

Sometimes when the rest of the family slept, fear rose up, taunting her, but she turned the quiet nighttime into a time of praise. She praised God for health and strength to pack and for a husband who could work. She thanked Him for the job and house He was going to provide. In doing so, she found she could go back to sleep and awake refreshed.

The month of September began. Tuesday morning her husband Don entered the kitchen and told her, "I think I should make a trip today to look once more for a house as well as nail down a job. I know it is the first of the week, but I am caught up with my work here. I sense that I should go today."

Amy called home to ask for her mother's prayers. Finding a place suitable to rent for their family, selling their place, finding a new job—all these were responsibilities her husband and provider had to look after that day.

Amy kept busy with her home duties that day with a continual prayer of trust in her heart. Answering the phone mid-afternoon, she heard the caller ask, "Can we come out this Thursday evening to sign the papers for buying your place?" Amy sank into a nearby chair. They were giving a positive answer! *Thank you, Lord!*

Late that afternoon her husband called. "Guess what?" She instantly knew it had been a rewarding trip. *Thank you, Lord!* she cried before the words had left his mouth. "I found a four-bedroom house in the country to rent, but the owner wants you to see it before we sign papers. And, sweetheart, I have a job!"

Thank you, Lord, thank you! Amy thought her heart would burst with gratefulness; a four-bedroom house in a rural setting where it was supposed to be difficult to find a place. *Lord, you knew the needs of our family!*

Saturday afternoon found the family en route to see their new place. Tears of gratitude welled up in Amy's eyes as her husband pulled into the lane. She eyed the cows grazing in the pasture surrounding the buildings. A thick tree line crowded the pasture's edge with a creek flowing to the east. *Oh, Lord, so much more than I would have asked for. A paradise for our boys!*

As if in a dream, she entered the house. It felt like coming home. Somehow the place reminded her of her childhood home on the farm. *Thank you, Lord, thank you,* her heart throbbed in praise. She did not see the dirty floor but noticed the smooth hardwood beneath. She did not think about the grimy walls, only of the adequate, spacious rooms for their family.

"What do you think?" her husband asked anxiously as he took in the cleaning that would need to be done before it was livable. "I didn't tell you how bad it looked. I wanted you to see it first. The owner said he had such a bad experience with his previous renters that he wasn't going to rent it out again. But if we are willing to clean it up and do minor repairs, he will let us rent it. I know it will take a lot of cleaning, but it is a sound house," he finished lamely, as he saw the dirty house through the eyes of his wife.

"Oh, Don, I'm thanking God for this place! I feel as though I already love it. I have prayed for confirmation in our move and God has answered with much more than I ever dreamed," she assured her husband with a smile that kept getting bigger and bigger.

"Look, Mom! Look what I found on the wall!" One of her daughters pointed to a wall-cling. *With God all things are possible*, was written on it in elegant black script.

I think you put it there for me, Lord, Amy thought as she hugged her daughter. "That is definitely going to stay," she answered with a smile. Her mind went to another verse she had just read in Proverbs 29:25. *The fear of man bringeth a snare, but whoso putteth his trust in the Lord shall be safe.*

The verse did stay. It was waiting for them as they moved into the house the third week of October. Thanks to her husband's foresight, the children found it easy to slip into the routine of the new school as they were familiar with the curriculum now.

Trust. Faith. Obedience. All were necessary to find true peace in whatever circumstance a person faced. *Thank you, Lord*, Amy prayed in humble gratitude.

Lesson From the Mango Seed

Paul Young laid his head against his jeep steering wheel and wept with loneliness, uncertainty, and despair. "Oh, God," his lips whispered in brokenness, "why did you bring us to New Guinea? Did I misunderstand your leading? Why does every door seem to shut in our face? Don't you want everyone to be saved?

"Oh, God, I don't understand. Your leading seemed so clear to my dear Angela and me. And now that we have come . . ." His pleading prayer gave way to sobs as he thought of Angela, alone in Port Moresby. Three days ago he had sent her back on the little plane to the island's capital.

One week had gone by since they landed in this low, swampy area in the northeastern tip of New Guinea. Anguish filled Paul at their failure. With great anticipation—too great perhaps—they had come to this land where approximately 70,000 people still lived in spiritual darkness. Were their hopes going to be dashed?

Paul's tormented thoughts turned to the people in Carmenta, the village where he was sitting in the dark of night. He felt as if its 6,000 inhabitants were holding him hostage in his jeep.

He wondered how his wife was doing. Angela had loved the country even before they landed on the lone airstrip between swamps of mangroves and tall sago palms. Nothing had prepared them for the exquisite blue-green waters of the Coral Sea bordering the south edge of Carmenta and the lush green mountain ridges that lay to the north. His wife's acceptance and enthusiasm had quieted his fears of bringing her to this remote jungle country.

The first four days he and Angela had looked for housing in this village, but none was available. The people of Carmenta were hostile, turning their backs on them when they asked for help. They refused a handshake and ignored them whenever they passed on the village streets. It was as if the villagers hated them, and were not even planning to give the missionaries a chance to prove they had come to be friends.

"You will have to return to Port Moresby," he had told his wife, voicing the inevitable decision. "I can live in the jeep but I can't have you doing so."

For three days he had been alone in this hostile village, and he knew he couldn't stay any longer. As night grew blacker, he wept into the darkness, pouring his soul out to God. "Lord God in heaven," he prayed in exhaustion. "Forgive me for being so faithless. I do believe you opened the door for us to minister to your people here in Papua. Right now I feel as though we are inside a locked room, yet if this is where you want us, Lord, give me peace.

"Forgive me if I have run ahead of you. I never meant to pursue this mission undertaking without your blessing. I am claiming the promise of Hebrews 13:5, 'I will never leave thee nor forsake thee.' I also claim the precious encouragement, 'Cast thy burden upon the Lord, and he shall sustain thee' (Psalm 55:22). I claim these and believe you will provide."

Destiny *by* Choice

Oppressive, ominous blackness surrounded Paul as he lay in the front seat of his jeep, weeping and crying out to God. Distant drumbeats punctuated the night. He opened his eyes and they strayed to the open sunroof where bright stars dotted the otherwise dark sky.

I'm here, God seemed to be telling him in the stars. *You are not alone.* He fell into a restful sleep, like a child wrapped in the arms of his father.

Morning sunlight stole over the tropical village, bathing the dew on the sun-bleached, thatched homes with sparkling freshness. High tide surged inland, swirling around the stilts of the nearest homes before washing back to meet the next gentle wave.

Paul awoke hours after the sun had completed its majestic ascent to the mountain tops. The tide had ebbed out, leaving a wide berth of washed sand. Relishing the beauty, he took his morning swim in the warm water. Refreshed in both body and spirit, he chose a shady spot at the edge of the sand and breakfasted on bananas and mangoes before opening his Bible.

"God, show me your will." Time stood still as he met with God and read the words of eternal life with an open, seeking heart. So intent was he in his discourse with his heavenly Father that he was oblivious to the curious villagers spying on him from behind the trees.

Paul closed his Bible. Holding it reverently in his hands, he knelt in the sand, bowed his head, and praised God for His protection and guidance. A village man living close to the water had been watching Paul perform this daily ritual on the shore. Each morning he sat on his top step outside his thatched house to observe the white foreigner, noting that on this particular morning the foreigner was late in arriving and late in staying. His curiosity piqued, he sat motionless for the next hour, watching the man no one wanted in their village.

Who was this man who would not leave? What God did he worship? Why was he so persistent in staying when no one wanted him to? The villager continued to sit immobile, his heart warming slightly.

When Paul rose and turned his face toward Carmenta, the Papuan's dark eyes followed the white foreigner as he walked nearer and nearer to his house on stilts.

"Hello!" Paul called out in English, the official language of this country. *"Daba namona!"* he added—"Good morning" in the Papuans' common Creole tongue. A smile lighting his face, Paul climbed the ladder and held out his hand in friendship. The villager, surprising himself, found his own hand reaching out, and he touched the white man's hand.

The villager did not know the joy and encouragement Paul experienced at this breakthrough. He could not hear the missionary's heart crying out, *Praise God! I've touched one of the people from the village!*

That evening Paul was granted permission to rent an abandoned church building. The roof needed to be thatched and the walls had gaps where poles were missing, but to Paul it was a priceless gift. He spent the next week repairing one end to make an apartment for himself and Angela before flying back to Port Moresby to get his wife and their belongings.

Most of their week in Port Moresby was spent purchasing supplies. Once finished, Paul went to the docks to secure passage for shipping their cargo, only to be met with disheartening news. "All cargo ships are banned from Port Samarai!" Samarai was the only port near Carmenta.

"Why?" Angela sputtered, unable to believe this was happening.

"They won't say!" Frustration tinged each of Paul's words. "They only tell me, no shipping to that port."

"Won't it be terribly expensive to fly everything in? Can we even afford it?" His wife expressed the questions he had been struggling with.

"I guess I had better go see." He left their apartment and Angela viewed the crates surrounding her. *Do we dare leave any of this behind? Every crate holds bare necessities!* She sighed. Medical supplies took up

Destiny *by* Choice

over half the space but were the most important cargo. Mosquitoes thrived in the low, wet swamps of Carmenta. She and Paul wanted to reach the people by administering medical help and supplies. They hoped people would trust them as they recovered and spread the word, "Go to the missionaries! They will help you!"

Hadn't this been her vivid dream since planning to come here? Wasn't it what Jesus had done when He walked on earth? They couldn't leave the medical supplies! It was their only way to reach the people.

When her husband returned, she could tell by the droop of his shoulders that the news was not good. Tears welled up. *Why isn't God blessing our efforts?* She brushed away her tears and went to meet her husband, determined to act encouraging. Alas, his words revealed another closed door. "Angela, the airstrip to Carmenta is closed! No one knows why or for how long!" Her tears did fall then, and she did not try to stop them.

In helplessness both husband and wife knelt, submitting themselves to God until their troubled hearts were still.

Sometime later Paul burst into their apartment. "Angela!" he called. A smile wreathed his face and buoyancy marked his step. "I was walking back and forth under the palms asking God to show me what we should do, and I heard Him tell me to go to the docks! I'm going! Pray, Angela. I'll be back as soon as I can."

Paul did not return until late afternoon. "We leave tomorrow morning at low tide. That is—" he hesitated. "That is, if you consent to travel by canoe."

"Canoe?" she whispered. A shudder ran though her as she pictured the frail craft bobbing up and down in the vast Coral Sea with no land in sight.

"My dear, it is a large canoe," Paul consoled. "I promise. In fact, there are three large canoes. These canoes sail to Port Samarai all the time. We have no reason to worry." Seeing her doubt, he hastened to assure her further. "We are not even near hurricane season! Besides, we will be keeping near to shore and these canoes are more like flat-bottomed boats with motors."

Angela took a deep breath. Hadn't she prayed for a way to go? She swallowed and answered in a small voice, "If you think it is safe, I am willing." She found herself wrapped in her husband's arms and felt rewarded when he whispered, "Thank you, thank you!"

Low tide didn't come until eleven o'clock the next morning, but they needed those hours to haul the crates down to the dock and secure everything. Angela's courage almost failed when she saw the log canoes tied together with what looked suspiciously like strips of bark. They were large if you compared them with American canoes, but they looked like tiny specks of wood in the water. "I won't look!" she declared under her breath. "I'll keep my eyes closed until we reach Port Samarai!"

Gingerly she seated herself in the middle of the raft canoe, making sure she was surrounded by crates tied tightly to the flat bottom. The motor sprang to life, and their flimsy canoe surged forward. Riding with the rise and fall of the water's swell, she soon admitted she may as well open her eyes. It would not be any safer to keep them closed. *Increase my faith! Increase my faith!* Her heart's cry and the throb of the engine became as one until several hours later when they finally docked.

It was exhausting work. They had to unload the crates from the canoes, reload them into the jeep, drive to Carmenta to unload them, and then return to begin the process all over again. The last trip was made in darkness. Finally, the exhausted pair crawled into the back of the jeep for the night.

"Thank you, Lord, for keeping us safe," Angela murmured as she pulled a pillow under her head. "Yes, Lord," her husband mumbled beside her. "And thank God the cargo ships were running when we sent the jeep over!"

Day after day, week after week, month after month, the couple continued to face stony hatred. They repaired the church, but no one attended. They went visiting, but doors shut in their faces. Obed, the man who lived by the water and the first man to extend his hand to Paul, was the only one who would acknowledge them. When they smiled and tried talking to the people, they were answered with scowls or threats. What more could they be doing to win these people's acceptance?

Paul and Angela knew the people of Carmenta were deeply superstitious, holding rigidly to customs passed down from previous generations. What they did not know was how much the people resented change. Danger lurked in the oppressive darkness of Carmenta, a darkness that seemed to cling to their frail apartment walls. Nightly voodoo chants were targeted at them as the villagers tried to get rid of the unwanted missionaries. The nightly dangers and the villagers' lack of acceptance were wearing them down.

They wept, prayed, and fasted, but nothing seemed to penetrate the shell of the Carmenta people. Two years passed. When the third year was well underway, the people finally tolerated them—if they refrained from talking of Jesus Christ.

"I can't take this any longer," Paul told his wife. "I'm going to ask the mission board to send someone to take our place here." Pausing, he reflected on his canoe trip up north, from which he had just returned.

"Angela, the mountain people of O'Power welcomed me! They begged me to return! Why can't the people of Carmenta have the same interest? We have accomplished nothing in almost three years. Nothing!

"But the reception at O'Power?" He glowed with exhilaration, remembering the mountain village and his promise to return next Tuesday to hold a series of meetings for three days. His wife's sadness at their change in focus smote him, but he pressed on with his plans.

"I'm sorry it hasn't worked out here in Carmenta. Maybe someone else can bridge the gap better," he consoled. Paul knew his wife loved these unfriendly people and longed for them to meet Jesus.

But, Paul, Angela wanted to beg. *What about Obed who always shakes your hand? He has never stopped doing so. I believe the door to the people's hearts are beginning to crack. I feel friendship wanting to take root, but something holds them back. What will happen if we leave?* She knew her energetic, ambitious husband had experienced frequent frustration at the periods of inactivity the past three years had brought.

But she did not feel that she should tell her husband what she was thinking. Wordlessly she nodded, her heart too full to speak. *Why Lord?* her soul cried. *Why did you send us here if you want us to leave?* Uneasiness pervaded her sadness. Was Paul following God's leading?

Several weeks later Paul received word that Stanley, a former student he had taught at a Bible institute in Texas, would come and take over the work at Carmenta. "Maybe Stanley will be the one to reach the people," Paul said excitedly. Angela quietly received the news and committed their future to God.

Though Paul held Bible classes for several days at a time in the north, he and his wife still lived in the church apartment. With Stanley coming, they found another house to rent in Carmenta until they could build one in O'Power. "The mountain people are hungering for truth. They always beg me to return," he said, as if convincing his wife of his decision.

Over the next year, Carmenta saw less and less of Paul and Angela. Taking up the work they had started, Stanley soon felt their discouragement. Only one or two villagers came to the church services, and he heard how twenty or more villagers were attending services where Paul was preaching. Bitterness took root in Stanley's heart when he heard that souls in the northern villages were accepting Jesus Christ while none were responding to his teaching. *Why does Paul get all the glory? Why couldn't the people of Carmenta accept me? Did Paul bring me here just to experience defeat?*

His jealousy and bitterness spread to the village people. The Youngs soon felt it too. Every time Paul and Angela took the canoe back to O'Power, they took more supplies to the house they had purchased there. "We need to cut all ties with Carmenta," Paul decided with finality, but his peace fled. He continued to move their things, but a heaviness now weighed on him.

One day, Paul made a solo trip to O'Power with a load of plywood for their new house. As the canoe's engine hummed along the waterway, Paul's unrest grew. He felt alone and forsaken, and the closer he came to O'Power, the heavier his burden became. Finally he shut off the engine, knelt in his canoe and wept.

"Oh, Father, my heavenly Father, where are you? Why have you left me? I can't go on like this any longer. Am I taking my own way by moving to O'Power? Should I stay in Carmenta?"

In the stillness, the Spirit of God reminded him, "For as the heavens are higher than the earth, so are my ways higher than your ways, and my thoughts than your thoughts. So shall my word be that goeth forth out of my mouth: it shall not return unto me void, but it shall accomplish that which I please, and it shall prosper in the thing whereto I sent it" (Isaiah 55:10-11). The command to stay in Carmenta became crystal clear in Paul's heart.

"But I have stayed in Carmenta four years. They won't listen to me," he argued. It was so hard to lay aside his new plans. "Stanley acts as if he hates me! My heart is broken. Stanley is like a son. I taught him in Bible college and yet he ignores me. I've asked forgiveness, but nothing has mended our relationship. I can't take this anymore."

I want you to stay in Carmenta. The still small voice of God did not change direction.

"Why, Lord, why? It hasn't done any good!" Paul felt like a beaten man as he sat in his drifting canoe. His eyes lighted on a mango seed left in the canoe from a previous trip. He picked it up, turning the ugly, scarred seed in his hand.

You are like this seed, God spoke to him. *You are of no use unless you change.* Paul held the seed reverently, light dawning in his soul.

"Can the scars I see on this seed be likened to my scars of suffering wrongfully?" he asked. Suddenly, the verse in 1 Peter 2:19 came to his mind. "For this is thankworthy, if a man for conscience toward God endure grief, suffering wrongfully." He felt his courage return. "How could I have forgotten so quickly?" he chided himself as he looked again at the seed in his hand.

"If I plant this seed," he marveled, "in several years it will produce unblemished fruit!" He studied the seed, realizing he needed to change. He had been running ahead of God. He wanted results. He wanted people to like him and flock to his church. Instead, he needed to be content where God placed him. He needed to serve faithfully and love even in opposition. He needed to let God show him how to reach the people. The people of Carmenta did not need Paul Young; they needed Jesus Christ.

"Forgive me, Lord. I have sinned in taking my own way," he prayed in repentance. Restarting his boat motor, he turned the canoe around and headed back to Carmenta.

The following week, Stanley was stricken with malaria and returned to the mainland. Once again Paul and Angela were the only missionaries living in the village. Paul fasted and prayed, pleading with God to show him how to reach the people. One name kept coming to his mind: Isle. Eighty-two-year-old Isle seemed to hate him more than any other man in the village. Every time Paul had tried to visit him, the old man would curse and throw whatever was within reach. He would scream at him to leave his property.

"Get out! I don't need you here; I don't need your Bible or your God! Don't come back!"

Paul knew the old man owned most of the land around the village and that he was an important figure. But how would God use Isle to reach the village? He shook his head. It made no sense.

He kept seeing him in his mind. Every time he prayed, Isle was there.

He even dreamed of Isle. "Lord," Paul said in surrender, "if I can reach the people through Isle, you will need to show me. He won't listen to me. He won't even let me into his house!"

For days Paul wrestled with his problem. Every day he tried to visit Isle. Every day the old man cursed before Paul could set foot in his house. Isle was watching for him, it seemed, waiting to drive him off.

Gingerly, Paul touched his swollen ankle, the ankle Isle had hit that morning with a pan. He had barely stepped into the yard when Isle hurled the cooking pan at him, demanding he leave.

"Show me, Lord, how to reach him," he pleaded as he reached for his Bible to find comfort. "My little children, of whom I travail in birth again until Christ be formed in you." Paul read the verse in Galatians 4:19. He read the verse a second time. *Travail.* The word grabbed his attention. He studied the meaning: painful effort or exertion. He reworded the verse, "My little children, of whom I labor in painful exertion until Christ be formed in you."

The words gripped him. *Have I travailed? Have I labored in painful exertion for Isle's soul?* Paul's heart smote him as he heard the still, small voice of God convicting him. *That is what I want you to do, Paul. Travail for Isle that he may experience new birth.* There was no doubt in Paul's mind what he needed to do.

In the days following, Paul learned what God meant by *travail* as he agonized for Isle's salvation. Though Angela knew his burden, he could not describe it with words. She only knew her husband could not sleep or eat. Instead he prayed and fasted—and wept.

"Dear wife," he cried out. "This burden is almost more than I can bear. Its pain is tearing me apart." He grew old. His life felt unnatural, and he wondered if he would be able to carry on until Isle found redemption. Every hour of each day and night was consumed in anguish for Isle to be delivered.

For two months he travailed. He pleaded. He sought to talk to Isle but to no avail. One evening Paul went to bed in great weakness and

Lesson From the Mango Seed   233

wept in failure. "I can't do this anymore, Father!" he cried. "Where are you? You will have to do this work for me; I can't go on."

When Paul woke up the next morning, he pinched himself. He felt normal. God seemed close and he sensed today was the day God would answer his prayers for Isle to be delivered.

"Angela, I have not seen Isle for a few days," said Paul. "I think he might be sick. Could you make him some soup? I want to take it to him and feed him." He drew his wife tenderly to himself. "Dear wife," he said, "today something will happen. I slept and awoke with the knowledge that today is the appointed day. Come, let's praise God."

Paul carried the hot soup over to Isle's house. He climbed the ladder and knocked on the closed door.

"Come in," Isle called feebly from his bed.

Paul entered the house as if in a dream. Quietly he walked over to the bed and told Isle, "I have brought you some soup and I am going to feed you." Obediently Isle ate the soup. Love welled up in Paul as he fed the old man spoonful after spoonful of soup. He gazed tenderly at the sunken, dull eyes within the old man's deeply lined face. How sad to be engulfed with hatred for so long.

When Isle had eaten all the soup, Paul opened his Bible. "Isle, today is the last time I am going to tell you how you can be saved from your sins. I am going to read to you. May I show you the way to peace through Jesus Christ?" He waited for Isle to begin cursing, but the room remained quiet as the frail, suffering man lay on his bed.

"Yes," came the slow whispered reply.

Wonder and joy surged through Paul as he reverently turned to the third chapter in the Gospel of John and read aloud. Isle lay still, listening, drinking in Jesus' words. After reading the account of Nicodemus, Paul turned to Romans 10:9 and said, "Isle, this is what God is asking of you. 'If thou wilt confess with thy mouth the Lord Jesus, and shalt believe in thine heart that God hath raised him from the dead, thou shalt be saved.'

"Do you believe these words of Jesus Christ?" he asked pleadingly. "Do you want to accept Jesus as your Savior?"

"Yes, I do," the old man said, the three sweetest words Paul had heard for years.

"If God can forgive me, great sinner that I am . . ." Tears rolled down his withered cheeks. "If He has any grace for me, I would like a little bit of it." He held up both hands and wept.

"Isle, my friend, God has grace enough," Paul assured him.

Isle's thatched-roof house became a hallowed sanctuary as he experienced new birth in Christ Jesus and felt the shackles of sin fall away. As Paul watched the transformation, he thought of the mango seed. He knew God had not been able to use him until he himself had changed. He had to suffer, to bear scars, before he could assist in bringing forth new life—Isle's birth. Paul marveled and rejoiced at God's patience.

"My son," Isle said as he took the hand of his new friend. "I can see your heart yearns for all of Carmenta. But the people will not accept you. It won't do you any good to keep befriending them because no one will listen to you. You are an outsider. You don't belong." Isle's words were a blow to Paul's heart, but before he could answer, Isle continued.

"I will help you. We have an old custom that hasn't been used for years. I think . . . I think now is the time to use it again.

"Paul, I want to adopt you as my son."

The implication of the offer left Paul dumbfounded. At Isle's death, he would inherit land. Isle was a respected elder and as his adopted son, Paul would no longer be an outsider.

God's purposes were finally becoming clear. Paul's heart rang with praise at the meaning of Isle's words. With great rejoicing he clasped Isle's outstretched hand. "I would be honored to be your son and a part of your family!"

Isle called his sons and daughters. Neighbors heard and came to witness this ancient custom that had almost been forgotten among them.

The respected elder was carried outside, and the ceremony began. "Before my family and my friends, I adopt you, Paul Young, as my son." Isle's voice was steady despite his age. "When I die my land will be equally divided among my sons." His glowing eyes circled around his family and the village people as they all nodded in agreement.

"This is a great honor, Father Isle," Paul assured him. "I praise God you now call me son, just as Jesus Christ calls you His son."

"Paul, your name is no longer Paul Young, but Paul Isle." The people cheered and Paul bent down to embrace his new father. After the people quieted down, Isle continued.

"Now we will do still more. You are now one of us, but we also must be one of you. There has to be an exchange." The people all beamed and nodded while Paul and Angela looked at each other in confusion. *What does he mean by an exchange?*

They didn't have to wonder long. "Paul Isle, I now give you LaEva, one of my granddaughters. She will make you a part of us."

Stunned at what they were hearing, the missionary couple watched as one of Isle's daughters brought her baby to her father. Isle took the child in his arms and beckoned to Angela. Tears streamed down Angela's face as the village elder placed the child in her arms and she clasped the gift to her heart. Walking over to the baby's mother, Angela put her arms around her, hugging her while she held their child between them.

"Your daughter is the most precious gift. I already love her dearly," she said through her tears. The baby's mother smiled and slipped back into the crowd.

Though it was devastating for them to think of the mother's loss that day, Paul and Angela sensed it would be unacceptable to refuse. Paul knew Angela's arms had yearned to care for a baby of their own. Now God was giving them a child of their own—one that made them a part of the village family. The people cheered. Children danced around them. Paul and his wife knew the people of Carmenta accepted them.

They now belonged.

Each breath Paul drew filled him with awe. Already his mind drew parallels between what had just happened and what takes place when people choose to enter God's family. He prayed aloud as he and Angela walked home with the baby. "Father, you have always been with us here in Carmenta, but it was I who had left your side to walk in discouragement. Thank you for drawing me back. Help me to teach my adopted people that it is only when they give themselves to you that you will give new life to them."

"Amen," said Angela at his side, and together they walked the path back to their house, the mango trees swaying in the afternoon breeze.

About the Author

*L*ily Bear and her husband live in northwestern Ohio where she has been a homemaker forty-six years. God has blessed them with five children and eighteen grandchildren.

She shares, "This book of short stories has been brewing for a long time. Reading is my relaxation. I love being able to read a whole story in one sitting, but never dreamed that writing short stories would be harder than writing a book-length story! May you be as blessed in reading as I was in writing!"

Lily has written numerous books, including *Shepherd of the Highlands, Report for Duty, Weeping for Abigail, Amish by Adoption,* and *Daddy, Are You Sad?* all available from Christian Aid Ministries.

If you wish to contact Lily, you may write to her in care of Christian Aid Ministries, P.O. Box 360, Berlin, Ohio 44610.

About Christian Aid Ministries

*C*hristian Aid Ministries was founded in 1981 as a nonprofit, tax-exempt 501(c)(3) organization. Its primary purpose is to provide a trustworthy and efficient channel for Amish, Mennonite, and other conservative Anabaptist groups and individuals to minister to physical and spiritual needs around the world. This is in response to the command to ". . . do good unto all men, especially unto them who are of the household of faith" (Galatians 6:10).

Each year, CAM supporters provide 15–20 million pounds of food, clothing, medicines, seeds, Bibles, Bible story books, and other Christian literature for needy people. Most of the aid goes to orphans and Christian families. Supporters' funds also help to clean up and rebuild for natural disaster victims, put up Gospel billboards in the U.S., support several church-planting efforts, operate two medical clinics, and provide resources for needy families to make their own living. CAM's main purposes for providing aid are to help and encourage God's people and bring the Gospel to a lost and dying world.

CAM has staff, warehouses, and distribution networks in Romania, Moldova, Ukraine, Haiti, Nicaragua, Liberia, Israel, and Kenya. Aside from management, supervisory personnel, and bookkeeping operations, volunteers do most of the work at CAM locations. Each year, volunteers at our warehouses, field bases, Disaster Response Services projects, and other locations donate over 200,000 hours of work.

CAM's ultimate purpose is to glorify God and help enlarge His kingdom. ". . . whatsoever ye do, do all to the glory of God" (1 Corinthians 10:31).

The Way to God and Peace

*W*e live in a world contaminated by sin. Sin is anything that goes against God's holy standards. When we do not follow the guidelines that God our Creator gave us, we are guilty of sin. Sin separates us from God, the source of life.

Since the time when the first man and woman, Adam and Eve, sinned in the Garden of Eden, sin has been universal. The Bible says that we all have "sinned and come short of the glory of God" (Romans 3:23). It also says that the natural consequence for that sin is eternal death, or punishment in an eternal hell: "Then when lust hath conceived, it bringeth forth sin: and sin, when it is finished, bringeth forth death" (James 1:15).

But we do not have to suffer eternal death in hell. God provided forgiveness for our sins through the death of His only Son, Jesus Christ. Because Jesus was perfect and without sin, He could die in our place.

"For God so loved the world that he gave his only begotten Son, that whosoever believeth in him should not perish, but have everlasting life" (John 3:16).

A sacrifice is something given to benefit someone else. It costs the giver greatly. Jesus was God's sacrifice. Jesus' death takes away the penalty of sin for all those who accept this sacrifice and truly repent of their sins. To repent of sins means to be truly sorry for and turn away from the things we have done that have violated God's standards (Acts 2:38; 3:19).

Jesus died, but He did not remain dead. After three days, God's Spirit miraculously raised Him to life again. God's Spirit does something similar in us. When we receive Jesus as our sacrifice and repent of our sins, our hearts are changed. We become spiritually alive! We develop new desires and attitudes (2 Corinthians 5:17). We begin to make choices that please God (1 John 3:9). If we do fail and commit sins, we can ask God for forgiveness. "If we confess our sins, he is faithful and just to forgive us our sins, and to cleanse us from all unrighteousness" (1 John 1:9).

Once our hearts have been changed, we want to continue growing spiritually. We will be happy to let Jesus be the Master of our lives and will want to become more like Him. To do this, we must meditate on God's Word and commune with God in prayer. We will testify to others of this change by being baptized and sharing the good news of God's victory over sin and death. Fellowship with a faithful group of believers will strengthen our walk with God (1 John 1:7).